D0174887

NANCY DREW®

girl detective

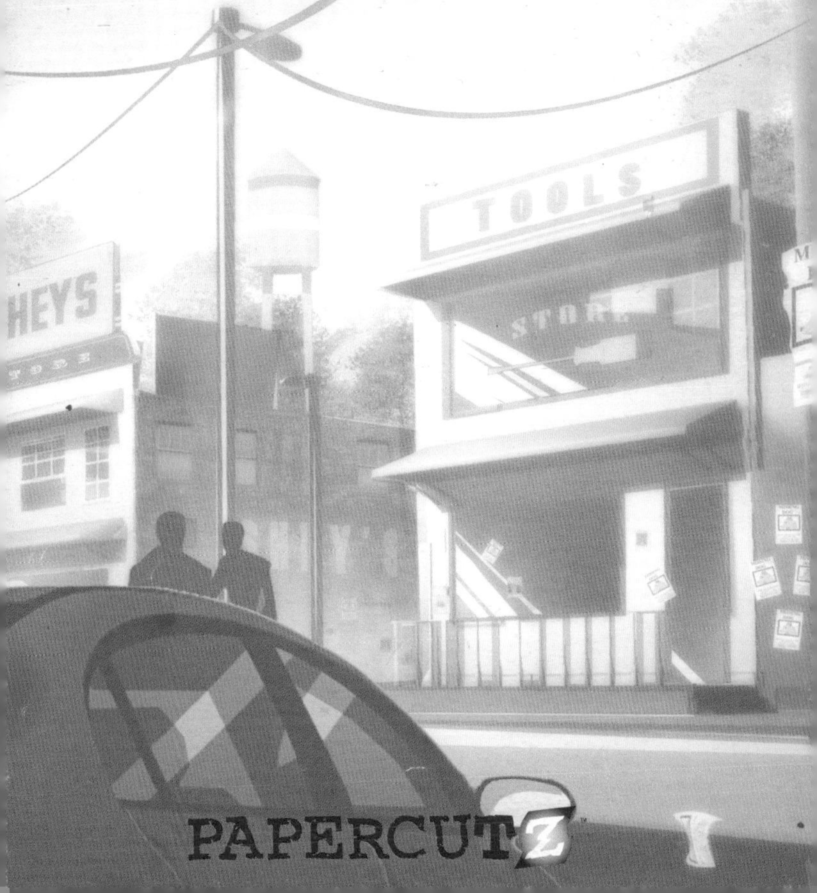

PAPERCUTZ

NANCY DREW GRAPHIC NOVELS AVAILABLE FROM PAPERCUT

NEW STORY! FULL-COLOR GRAPHIC NOVEL
NANCY DREW
#1
BASED ON THE SERIES BY CAROLYN KEENE

#1 "The Demon of River Heights"

NEW STORY! FULL-COLOR GRAPHIC NOVEL
NANCY DREW
#2
BASED ON THE SERIES BY CAROLYN KEENE

#2 "Writ In Stone"

NEW STORY! FULL-COLOR GRAPHIC NOVEL
NANCY DREW
#3
BASED ON THE SERIES BY CAROLYN KEENE

#3 "The Haunted Dollhouse"

NANCY DREW
#4

#4 "The Girl W Wasn't There'

NEW STORY! FULL-COLOR GRAPHIC NOVEL
NANCY DREW
#5
BASED ON THE SERIES BY CAROLYN KEENE

#5 "The Fake Heir"

NEW STORY! FULL-COLOR GRAPHIC NOVEL
NANCY DREW
#6
BASED ON THE SERIES BY CAROLYN KEENE

#6 "Mr. Cheeters Is Missing"

NEW STORY! FULL-COLOR GRAPHIC NOVEL
NANCY DREW
#7
BASED ON THE SERIES BY CAROLYN KEENE

#7 "The Charmed Bracelet"

NANCY DREW
#8

#8 "Global Warning"

NEW STORY! FULL-COLOR GRAPHIC NOVEL
NANCY DREW
#9
BASED ON THE SERIES BY CAROLYN KEENE

#9"Ghost In The Machinery"

NEW STORY! FULL-COLOR GRAPHIC NOVEL
NANCY DREW
#10
BASED ON THE SERIES BY CAROLYN KEENE

#10 "The Disoriented Express"

NEW STORY! FULL-COLOR GRAPHIC NOVEL
NANCY DREW
#11
BASED ON THE SERIES BY CAROLYN KEENE

#11"Monkey Wrench Blues"

NANCY DREW
#12
BASED ON THE SERIES BY CAROLYN KEENE

#12 "Dress Reversal"

NEW STORY! FULL-COLOR GRAPHIC NOVEL
NANCY DREW

#13 "Doggone Town"

NEW STORY! FULL-COLOR GRAPHIC NOVEL
NANCY DREW
#14

Coming August '08
#14 "Sleight of Dan"

$7.95 each in paperback,
$12.95 each in hardcover.
Please add $3.00 for postage and handlin for the first book, add $1.00 for each add tional book. Please make check payable t NBM Publishing. Send to:

Papercutz, 40 Exchange Place,
Suite 1308 New York, NY 10005
www.papercutz.com

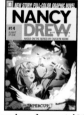

NANCY DREW

DREW
girl detective ®

#13

Doggone Town

STEFAN PETRUCHA & SARAH KINNEY • Writers
SHO MURASE • Artist
with 3D CG elements and color by CARLOS JOSE GUZMAN
Based on the series by
CAROLYN KEENE

New York

Doggone Town
STEFAN PETRUCHA & SARAH KINNEY – Writers
SHO MURASE – Artist
with 3D CG elements and color by CARLOS JOSE GUZMAN
BRYAN SENKA – Letterer
JOHN McCARTHY – Production
JIM SALICRUP
Editor-in-Chief

ISBN 10: 1-59707-098-X paperback edition
ISBN 13: 978-1-59707-098-0 paperback edition
ISBN 10: 1-59707-099-8 hardcover edition
ISBN 13: 978-1-59707-099-7 hardcover edition

Printed in China.
Distributed by Macmillan.

10   9   8   7   6   5   4   3   2   1

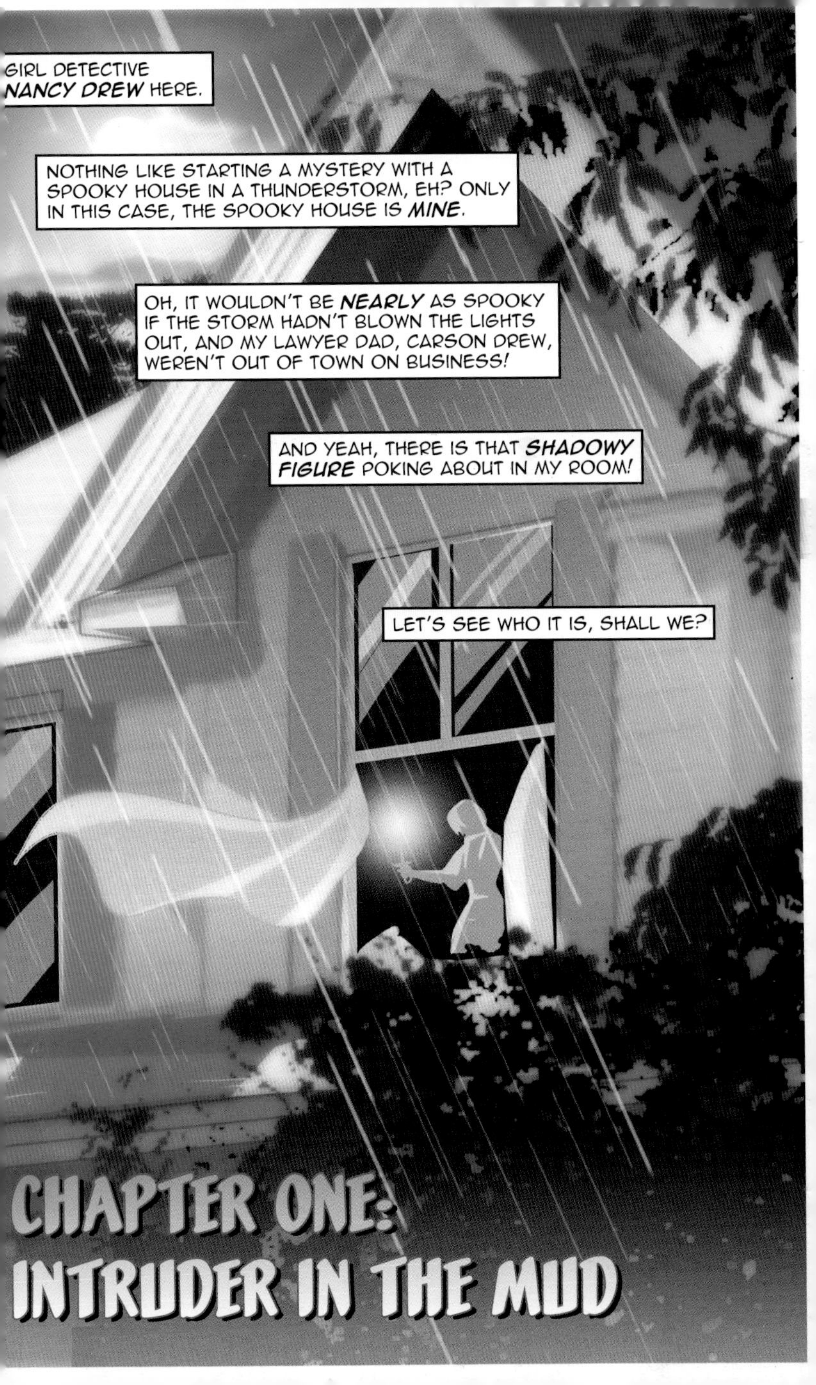
GIRL DETECTIVE NANCY DREW HERE.
NOTHING LIKE STARTING A MYSTERY WITH A SPOOKY HOUSE IN A THUNDERSTORM, EH? ONLY IN THIS CASE, THE SPOOKY HOUSE IS MINE.
OH, IT WOULDN'T BE NEARLY AS SPOOKY IF THE STORM HADN'T BLOWN THE LIGHTS OUT, AND MY LAWYER DAD, CARSON DREW, WEREN'T OUT OF TOWN ON BUSINESS!
AND YEAH, THERE IS THAT SHADOWY FIGURE POKING ABOUT IN MY ROOM!
LET'S SEE WHO IT IS, SHALL WE?
CHAPTER ONE:
INTRUDER IN THE MUD

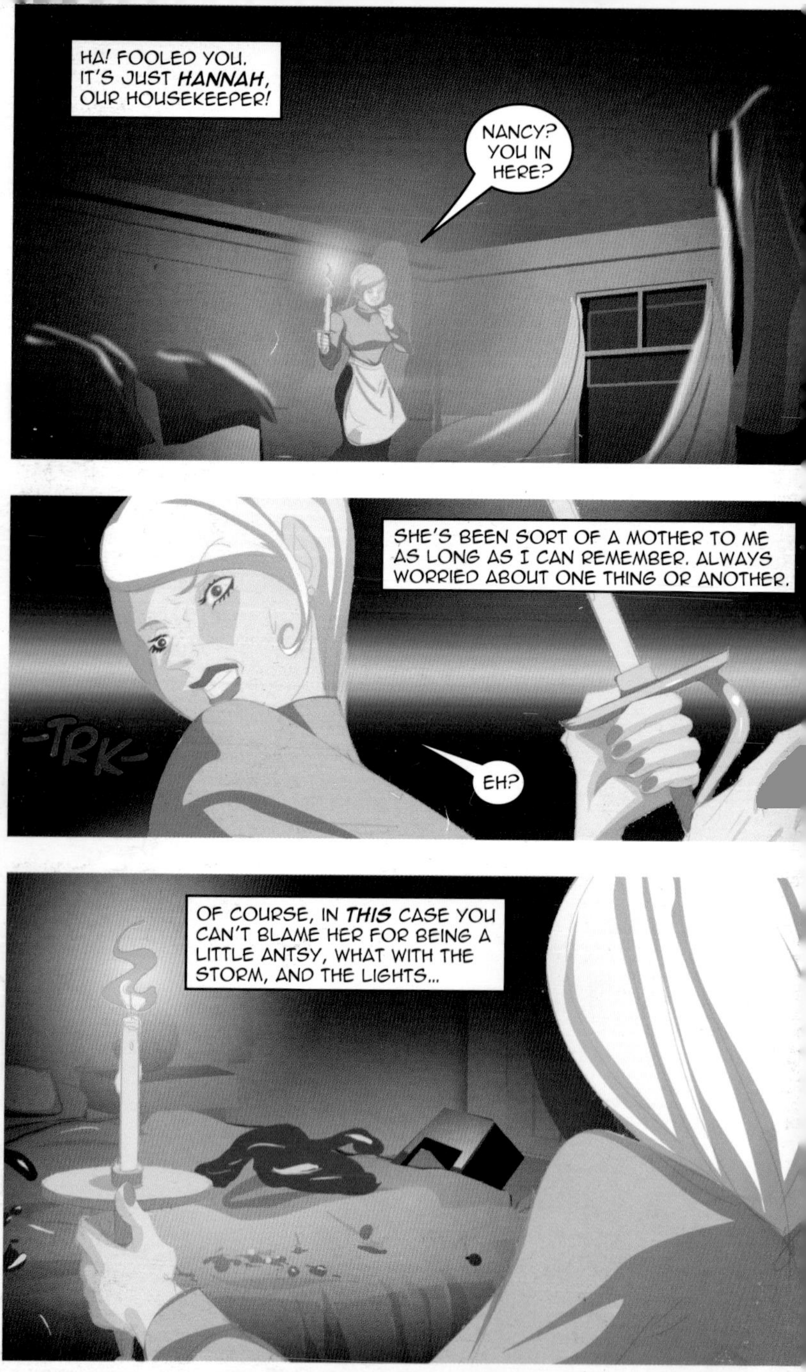
HA! FOOLED YOU. IT'S JUST *HANNAH*, OUR HOUSEKEEPER!
NANCY? YOU IN HERE?
SHE'S BEEN SORT OF A MOTHER TO ME AS LONG AS I CAN REMEMBER. ALWAYS WORRIED ABOUT ONE THING OR ANOTHER.
-TRK-
EH?
OF COURSE, IN *THIS* CASE YOU CAN'T BLAME HER FOR BEING A LITTLE ANTSY, WHAT WITH THE STORM, AND THE LIGHTS...

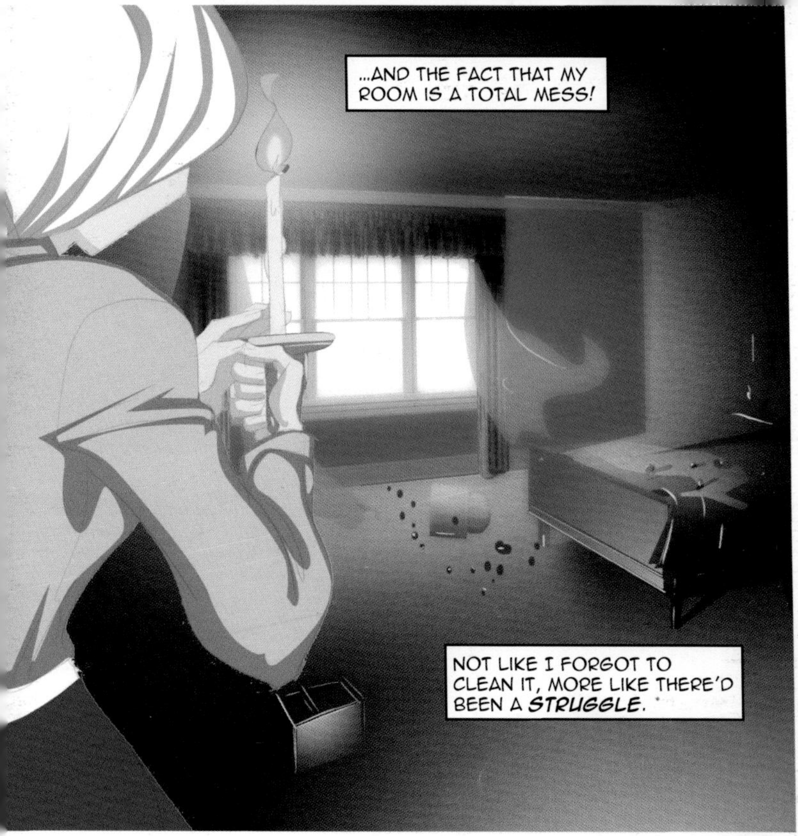
...AND THE FACT THAT MY ROOM IS A TOTAL MESS!
NOT LIKE I FORGOT TO CLEAN IT, MORE LIKE THERE'D BEEN A STRUGGLE.

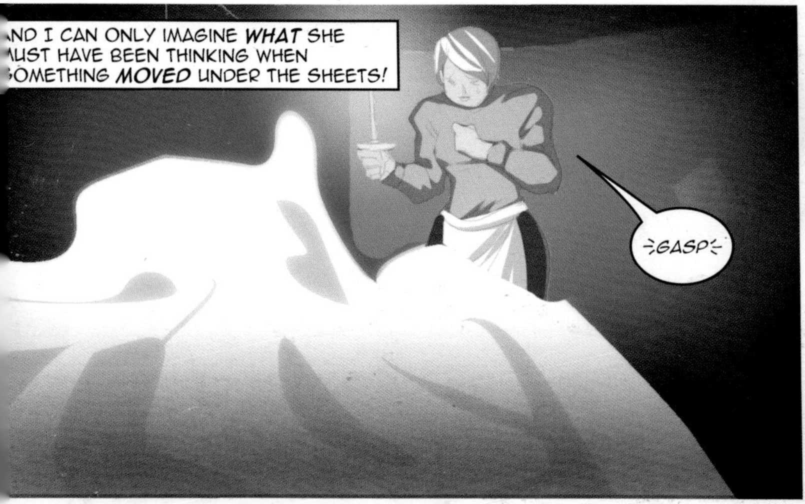
ND I CAN ONLY IMAGINE WHAT SHE
MUST HAVE BEEN THINKING WHEN
OMETHING MOVED UNDER THE SHEETS!
GASP

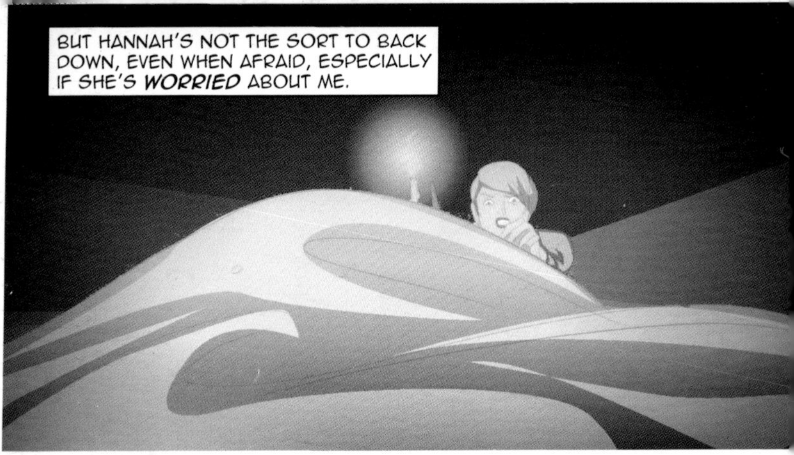
BUT HANNAH'S NOT THE SORT TO BACK DOWN, EVEN WHEN AFRAID, ESPECIALLY IF SHE'S WORRIED ABOUT ME.

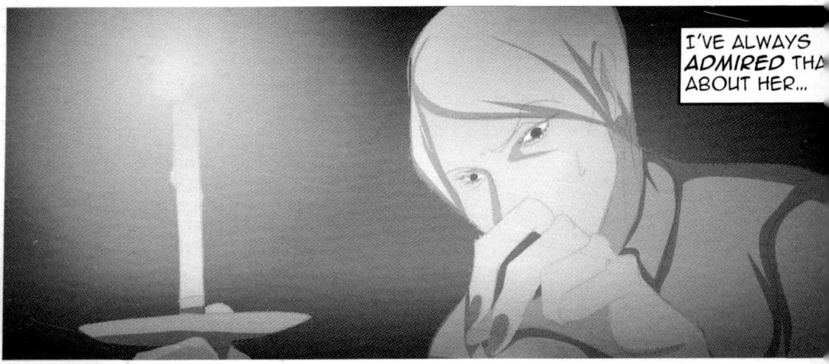
I'VE ALWAYS ADMIRED THA ABOUT HER...

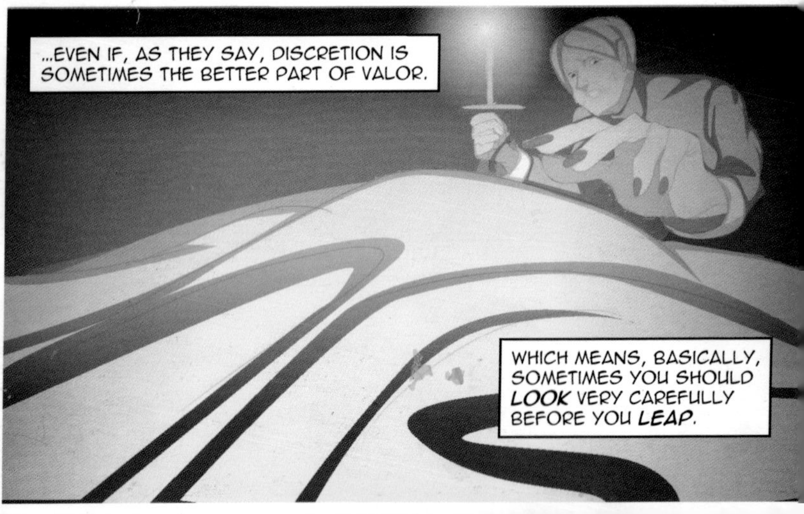
...EVEN IF, AS THEY SAY, DISCRETION IS SOMETIMES THE BETTER PART OF VALOR.
WHICH MEANS, BASICALLY, SOMETIMES YOU SHOULD LOOK VERY CAREFULLY BEFORE YOU LEAP.

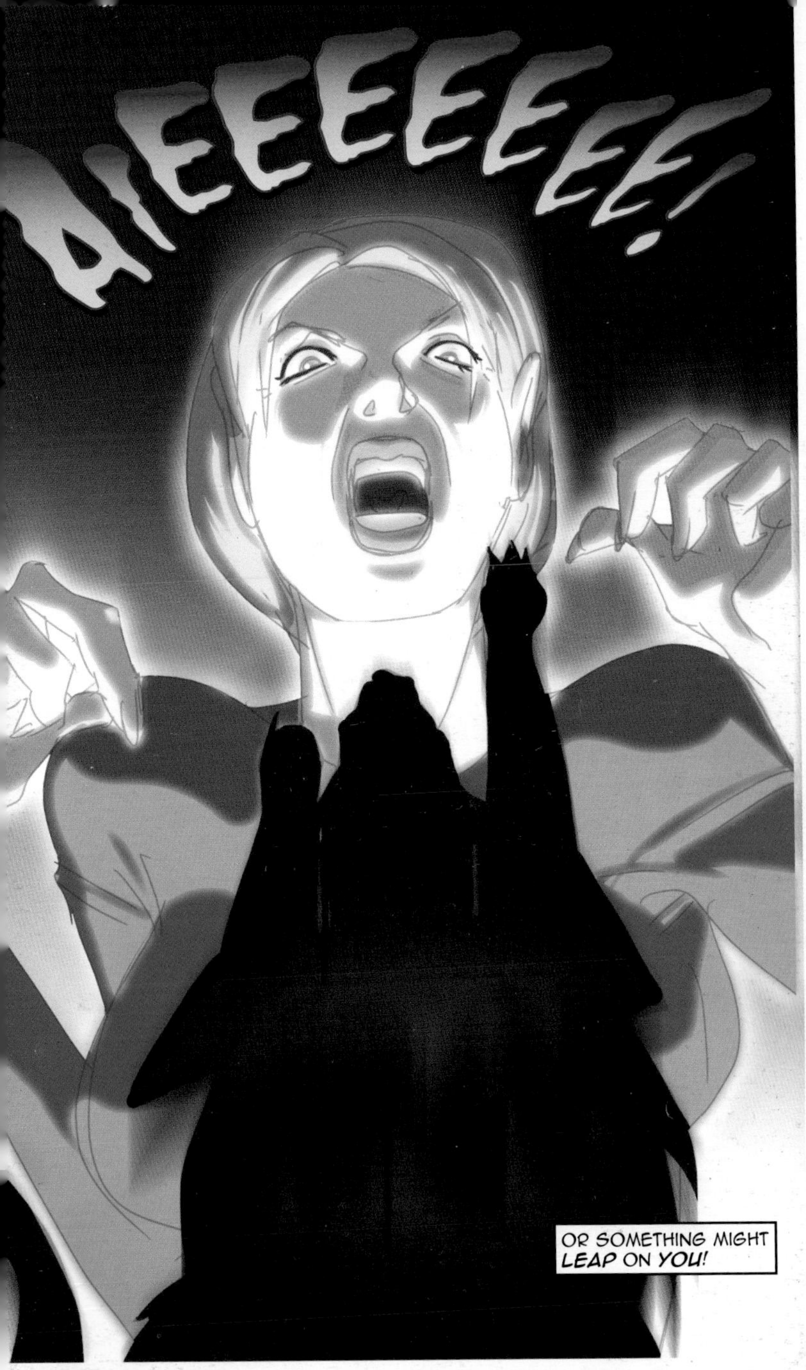
AIEEEEEEEE!
OR SOMETHING MIGHT LEAP ON YOU!

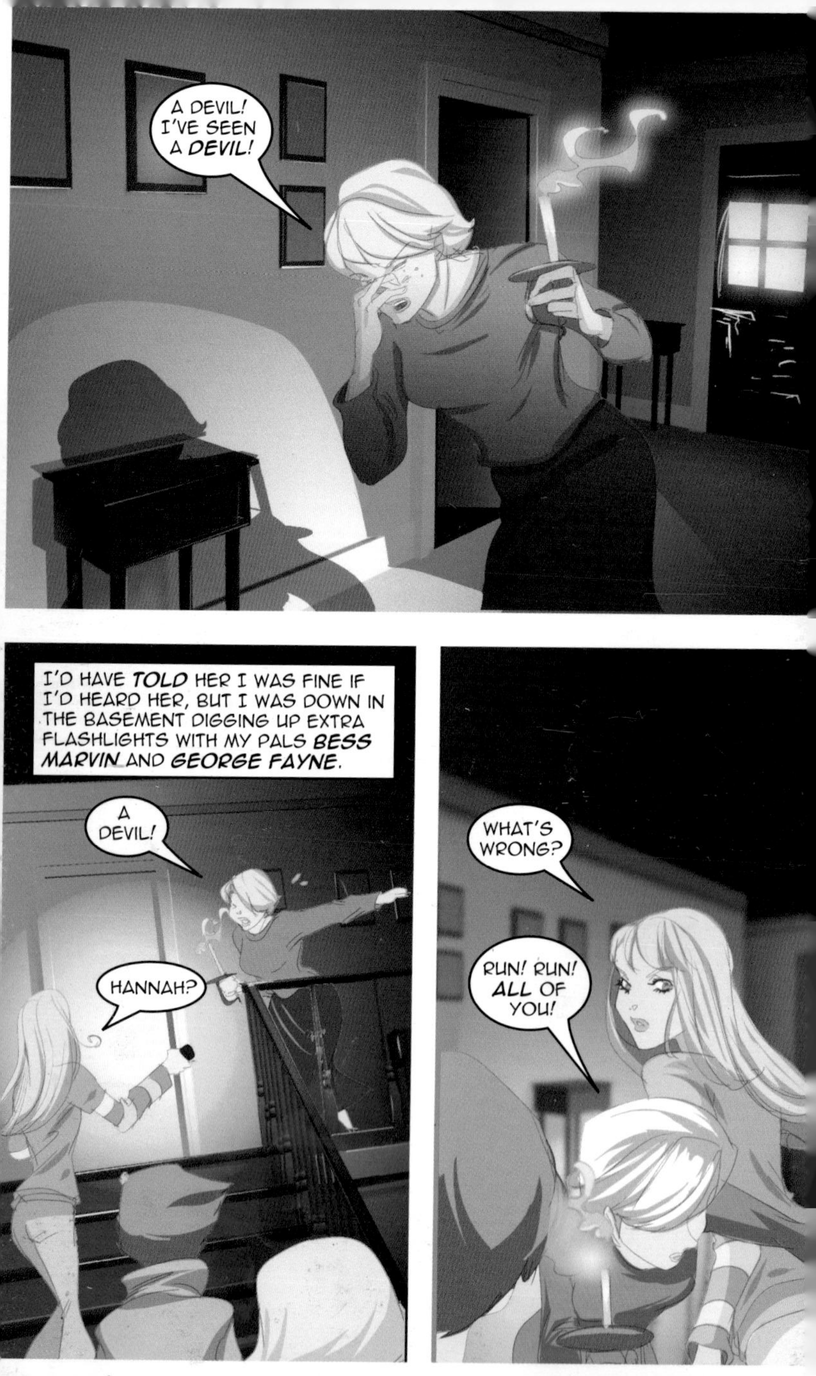
A DEVIL! I'VE SEEN A DEVIL!
I'D HAVE TOLD HER I WAS FINE IF I'D HEARD HER, BUT I WAS DOWN IN THE BASEMENT DIGGING UP EXTRA FLASHLIGHTS WITH MY PALS BESS MARVIN AND GEORGE FAYNE.
A DEVIL!
HANNAH?
WHAT'S WRONG?
RUN! RUN! ALL OF YOU!

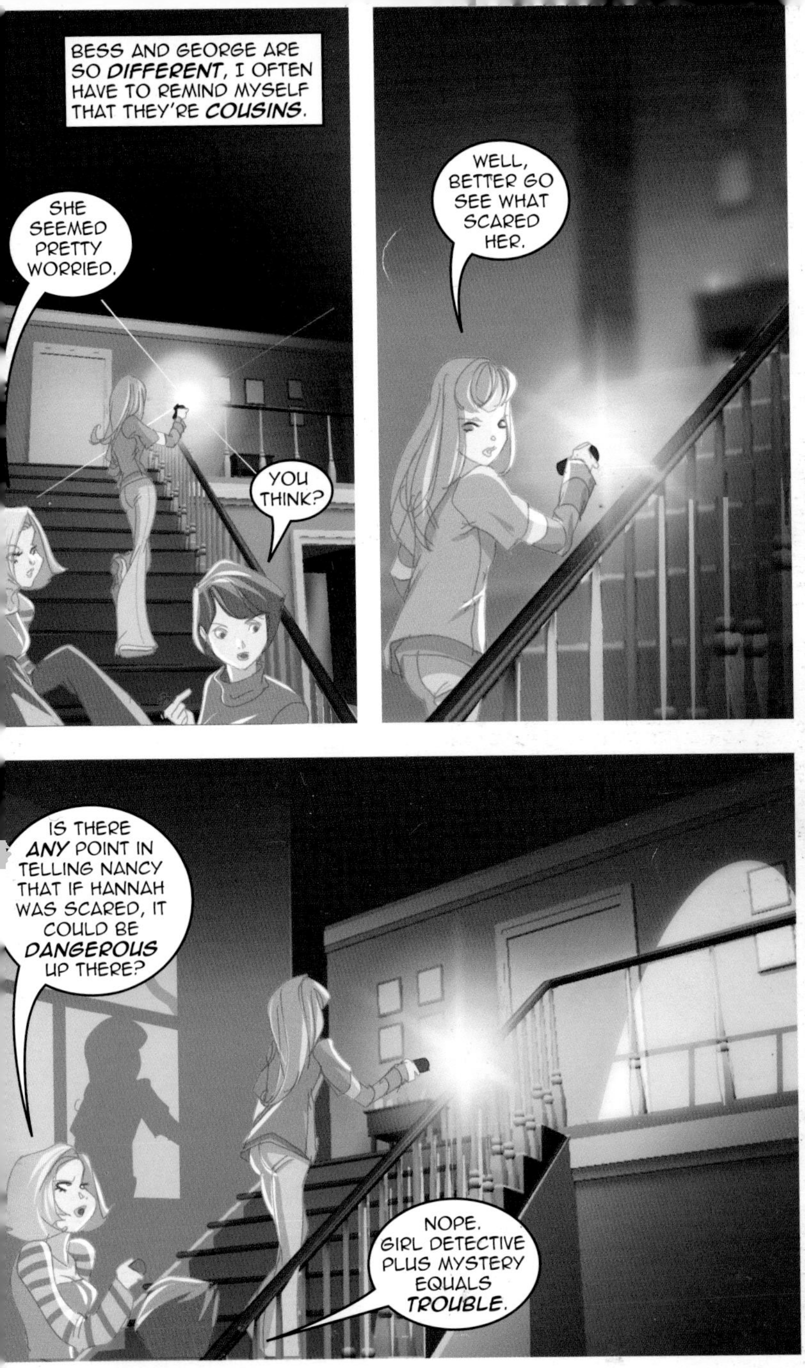
BESS AND GEORGE ARE SO *DIFFERENT*, I OFTEN HAVE TO REMIND MYSELF THAT THEY'RE *COUSINS*.
SHE SEEMED PRETTY WORRIED.
YOU THINK?
WELL, BETTER GO SEE WHAT SCARED HER.
IS THERE *ANY* POINT IN TELLING NANCY THAT IF HANNAH WAS SCARED, IT COULD BE *DANGEROUS* UP THERE?
NOPE. GIRL DETECTIVE PLUS MYSTERY EQUALS *TROUBLE*.

WHAT'S THAT LIGHT? A UFO?

NO. LIGHTNING. THERE'S A *STORM*, REMEMBER?

GEORGE IS RIGHT. I AM ALWA GETTING MYSELF INTO TROUB BUT HOW ELSE CAN YOU SOL A MYSTERY IF YOU'RE NOT WILLING TO TAKE SOME RISKS

AND MY PALS, BLESS 'EM, ARE ALWAYS BEHIND ME. SOMETIMES A FEW *FEET* BEHIND ME, BUT BEHIND ME.

IT'S OKAY, GUYS. I THINK WHATEVER IT WAS IS *GONE*.

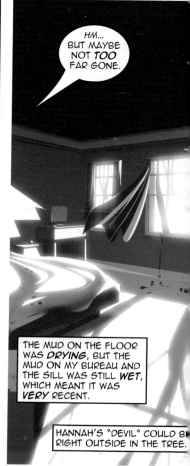

HM... BUT MAYBE NOT *TOO* FAR GONE.

THE MUD ON THE FLOOR WAS *DRYING*, BUT THE MUD ON MY BUREAU AND THE SILL WAS STILL *WET*, WHICH MEANT IT WAS *VERY* RECENT.

HANNAH'S "DEVIL" COULD B RIGHT OUTSIDE IN THE TREE.

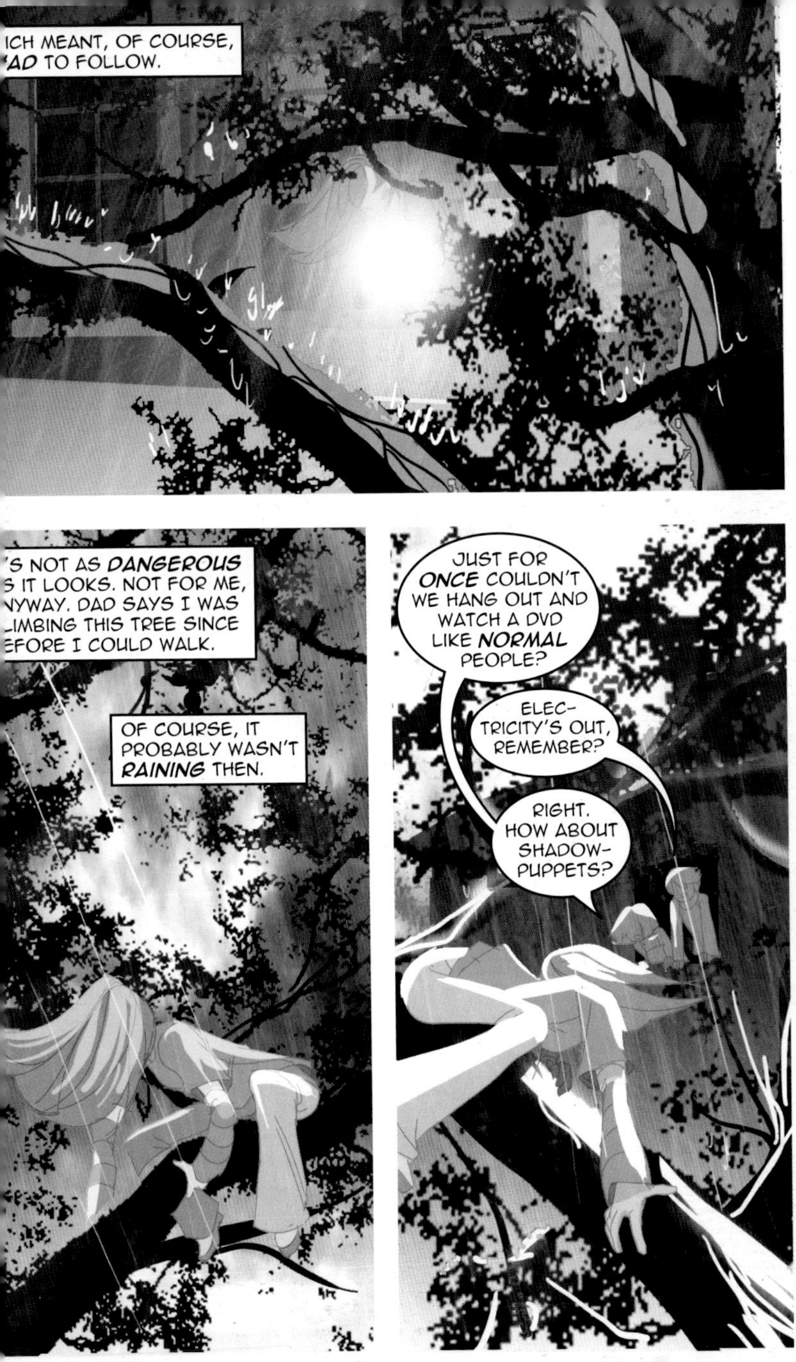
ICH MEANT, OF COURSE,
'AD TO FOLLOW.
'S NOT AS DANGEROUS
S IT LOOKS. NOT FOR ME,
NYWAY. DAD SAYS I WAS
LIMBING THIS TREE SINCE
EFORE I COULD WALK.
OF COURSE, IT PROBABLY WASN'T RAINING THEN.
JUST FOR ONCE COULDN'T WE HANG OUT AND WATCH A DVD LIKE NORMAL PEOPLE?
ELEC-TRICITY'S OUT, REMEMBER?
RIGHT. HOW ABOUT SHADOW-PUPPETS?

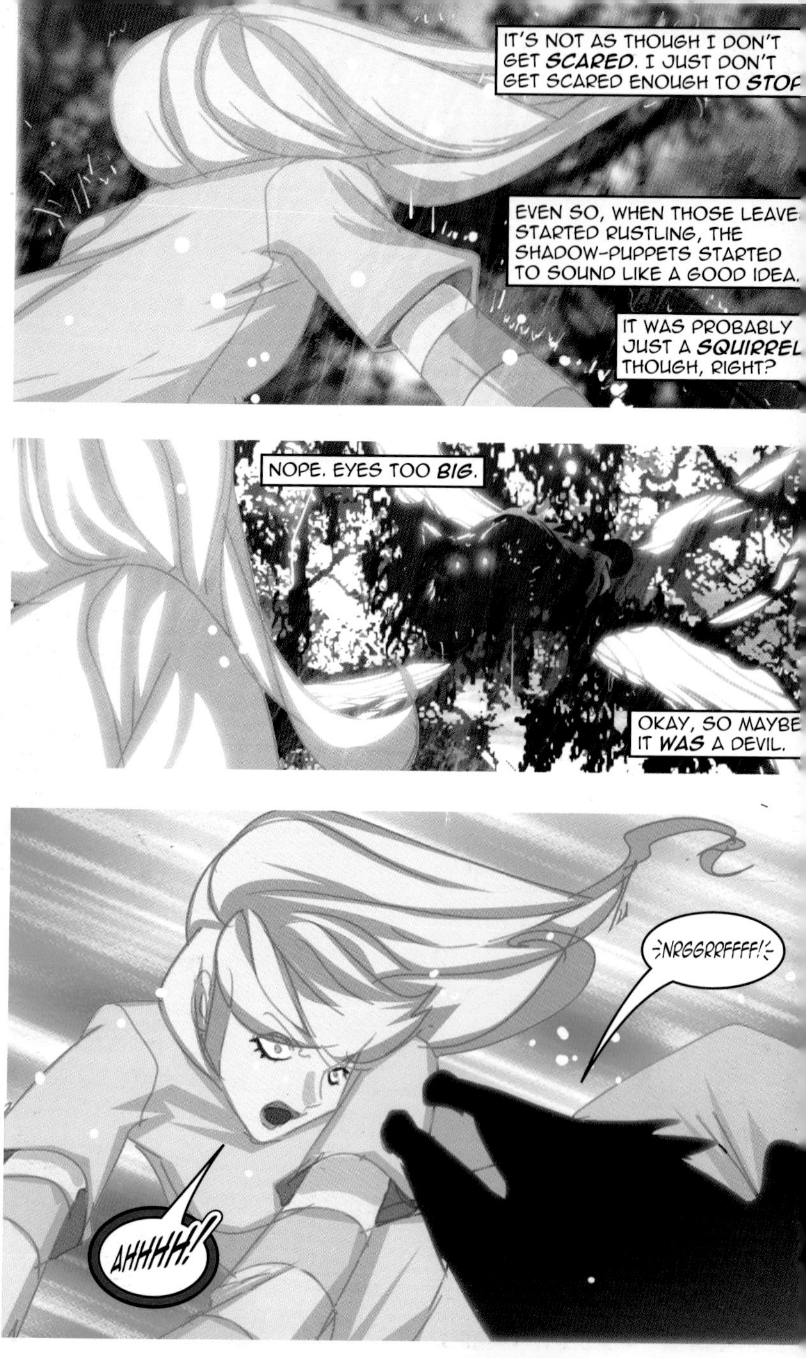
IT'S NOT AS THOUGH I DON'T GET SCARED. I JUST DON'T GET SCARED ENOUGH TO STOP
EVEN SO, WHEN THOSE LEAVES STARTED RUSTLING, THE SHADOW-PUPPETS STARTED TO SOUND LIKE A GOOD IDEA.
IT WAS PROBABLY JUST A SQUIRREL THOUGH, RIGHT?
NOPE. EYES TOO BIG.
OKAY, SO MAYBE IT WAS A DEVIL.
NRGGRRFFFF!
AHHHH!

WHATEVER IT WAS, UP IN A TALL TREE, THEN IT LATCHED ONTO MY FACE, WAS DEFINITELY NOT THE BEST PLACE TO BE.

≥GLERP≥

I PROBABLY WOULDN'T *DIE* FROM THE FALL, UNLESS I LANDED FUNNY, BUT A FEW BROKEN BONES WAS A GOOD BET!

≥AHHHH≥

IT WAS EXACTLY TWENTY-THREE FEET, SEVEN INCHES TO THE GROUND. I KNOW BECAUSE I'D MEASURED.

THEN THERE WAS THE QUESTION OF WHAT THE *THING-ON-MY-FACE* HAD PLANNED FOR ME...

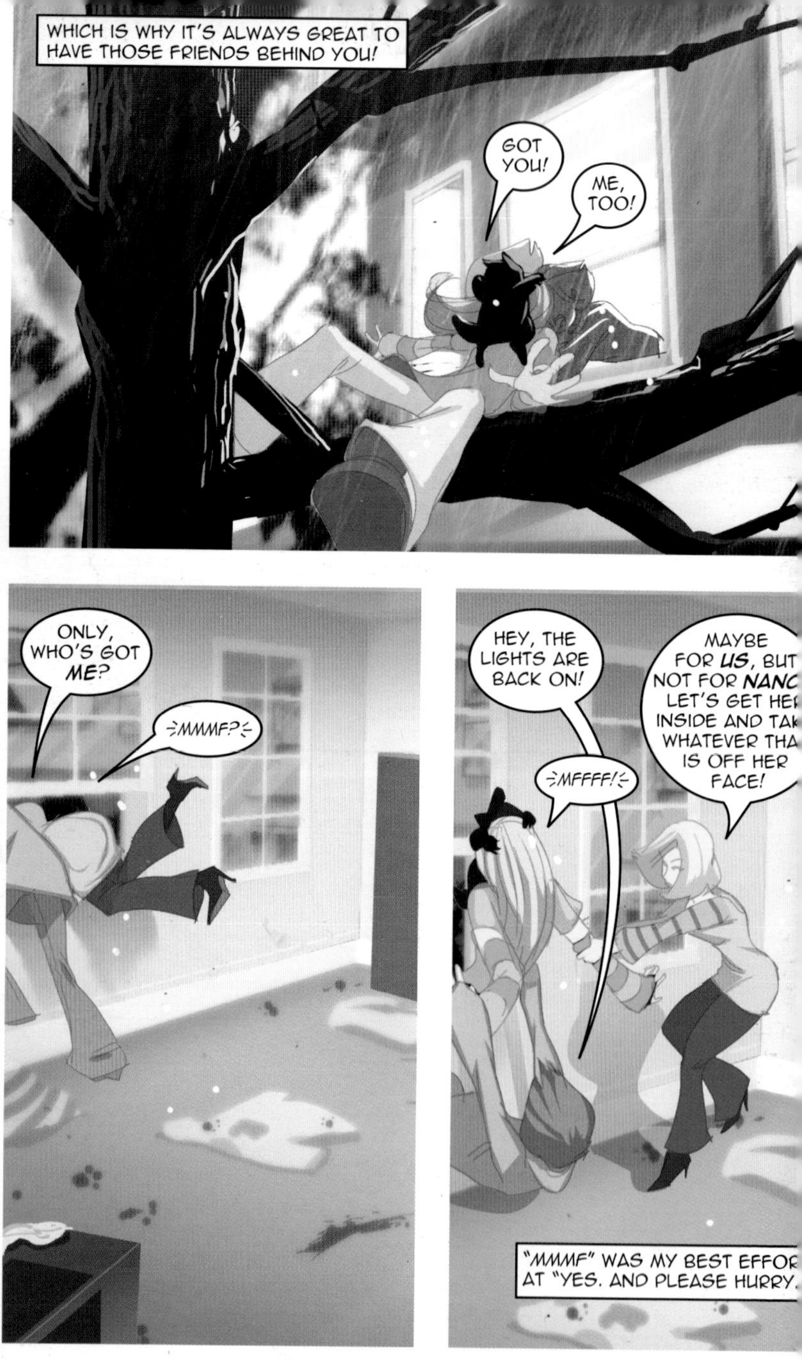
WHICH IS WHY IT'S ALWAYS GREAT TO HAVE THOSE FRIENDS BEHIND YOU!
GOT YOU!
ME, TOO!
ONLY, WHO'S GOT *ME*?
MMMF?
HEY, THE LIGHTS ARE BACK ON!
MAYBE FOR *US*, BUT NOT FOR *NANC* LET'S GET HE INSIDE AND TA WHATEVER THA IS OFF HER FACE!
MFFFF!
"MMMF" WAS MY BEST EFFOR AT "YES. AND PLEASE HURRY.

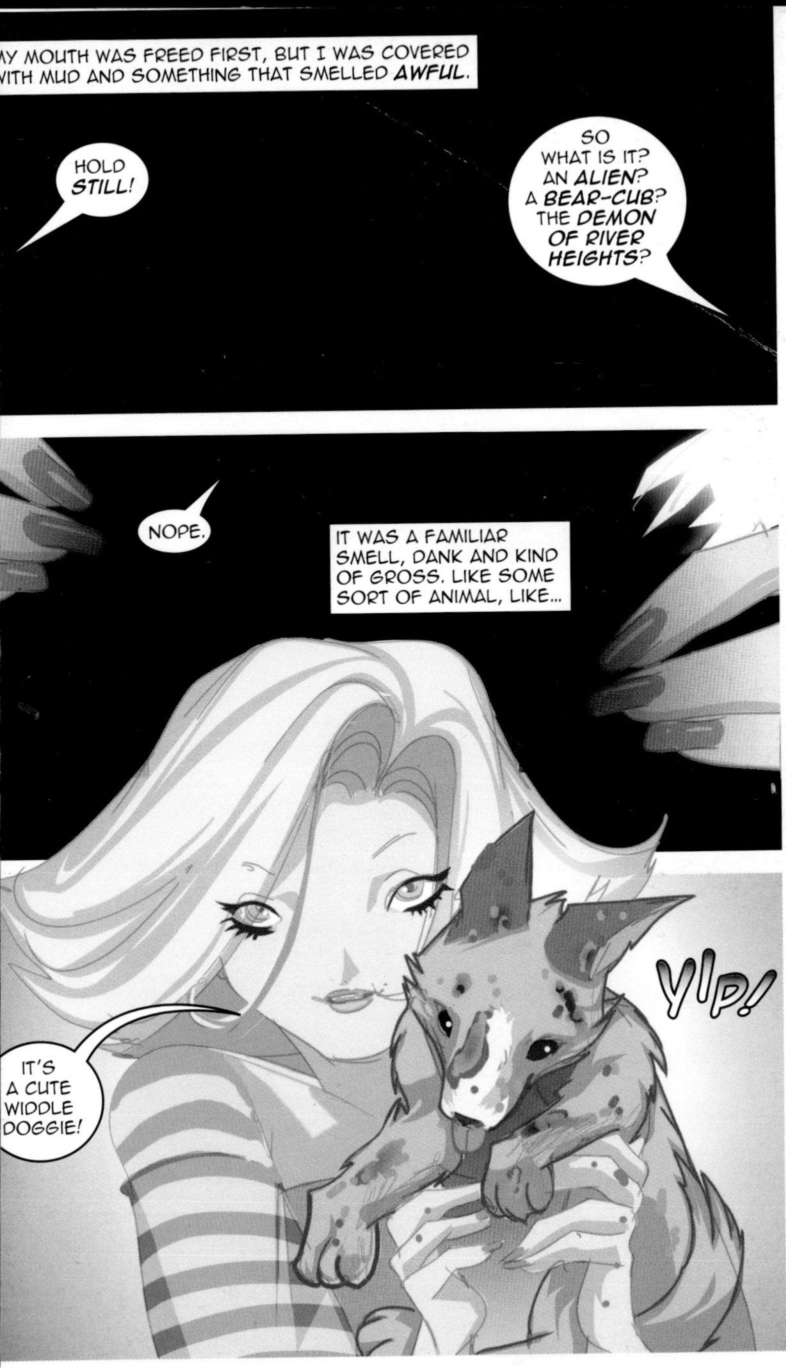
MY MOUTH WAS FREED FIRST, BUT I WAS COVERED WITH MUD AND SOMETHING THAT SMELLED AWFUL.
HOLD STILL!
SO WHAT IS IT? AN ALIEN? A BEAR-CUB? THE DEMON OF RIVER HEIGHTS?
NOPE.
IT WAS A FAMILIAR SMELL, DANK AND KIND OF GROSS. LIKE SOME SORT OF ANIMAL, LIKE...
IT'S A CUTE WIDDLE DOGGIE!
YIP!

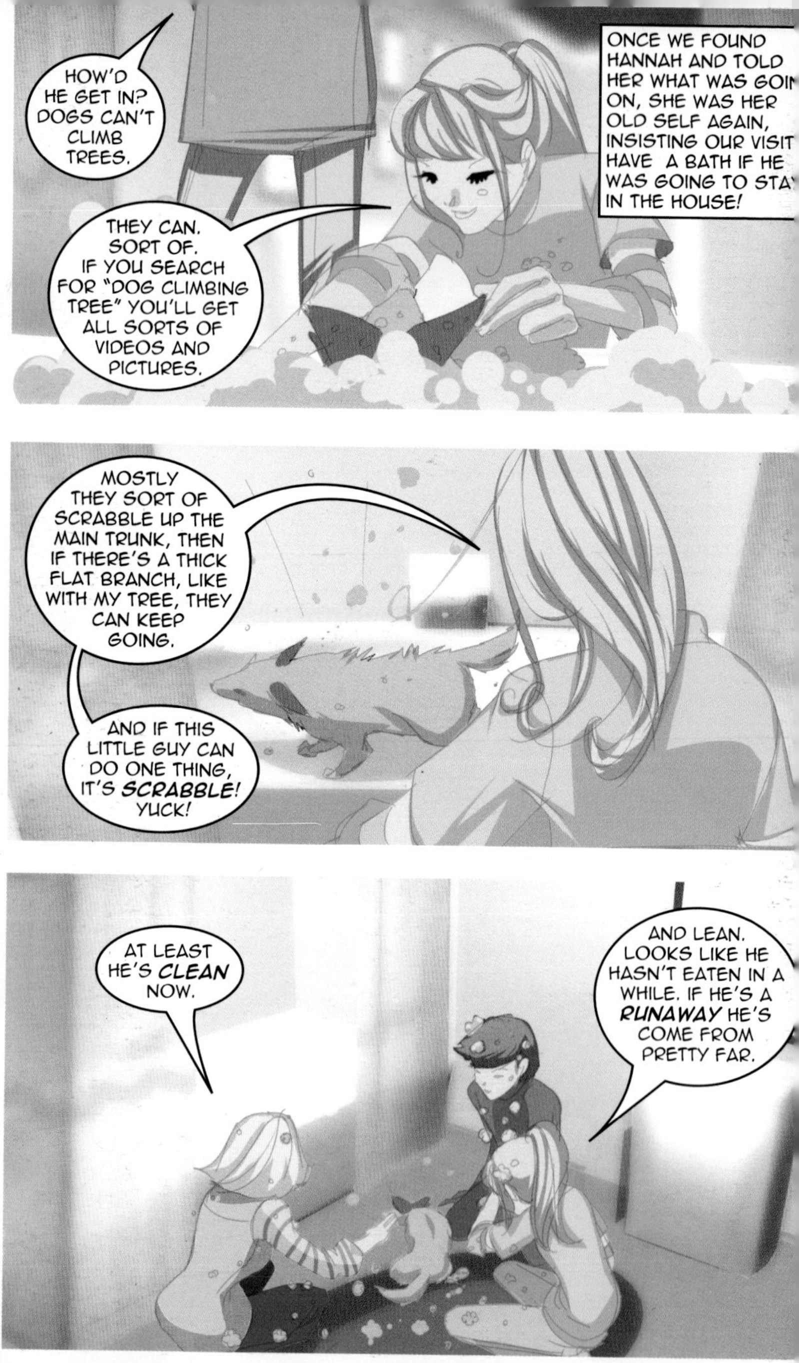
HOW'D HE GET IN? DOGS CAN'T CLIMB TREES.
ONCE WE FOUND HANNAH AND TOLD HER WHAT WAS GOIN ON, SHE WAS HER OLD SELF AGAIN, INSISTING OUR VISIT HAVE A BATH IF HE WAS GOING TO STA IN THE HOUSE!
THEY CAN. SORT OF. IF YOU SEARCH FOR "DOG CLIMBING TREE" YOU'LL GET ALL SORTS OF VIDEOS AND PICTURES.
MOSTLY THEY SORT OF SCRABBLE UP THE MAIN TRUNK, THEN IF THERE'S A THICK FLAT BRANCH, LIKE WITH MY TREE, THEY CAN KEEP GOING.
AND IF THIS LITTLE GUY CAN DO ONE THING, IT'S *SCRABBLE*! YUCK!
AT LEAST HE'S *CLEAN* NOW.
AND LEAN. LOOKS LIKE HE HASN'T EATEN IN A WHILE. IF HE'S A *RUNAWAY* HE'S COME FROM PRETTY FAR.

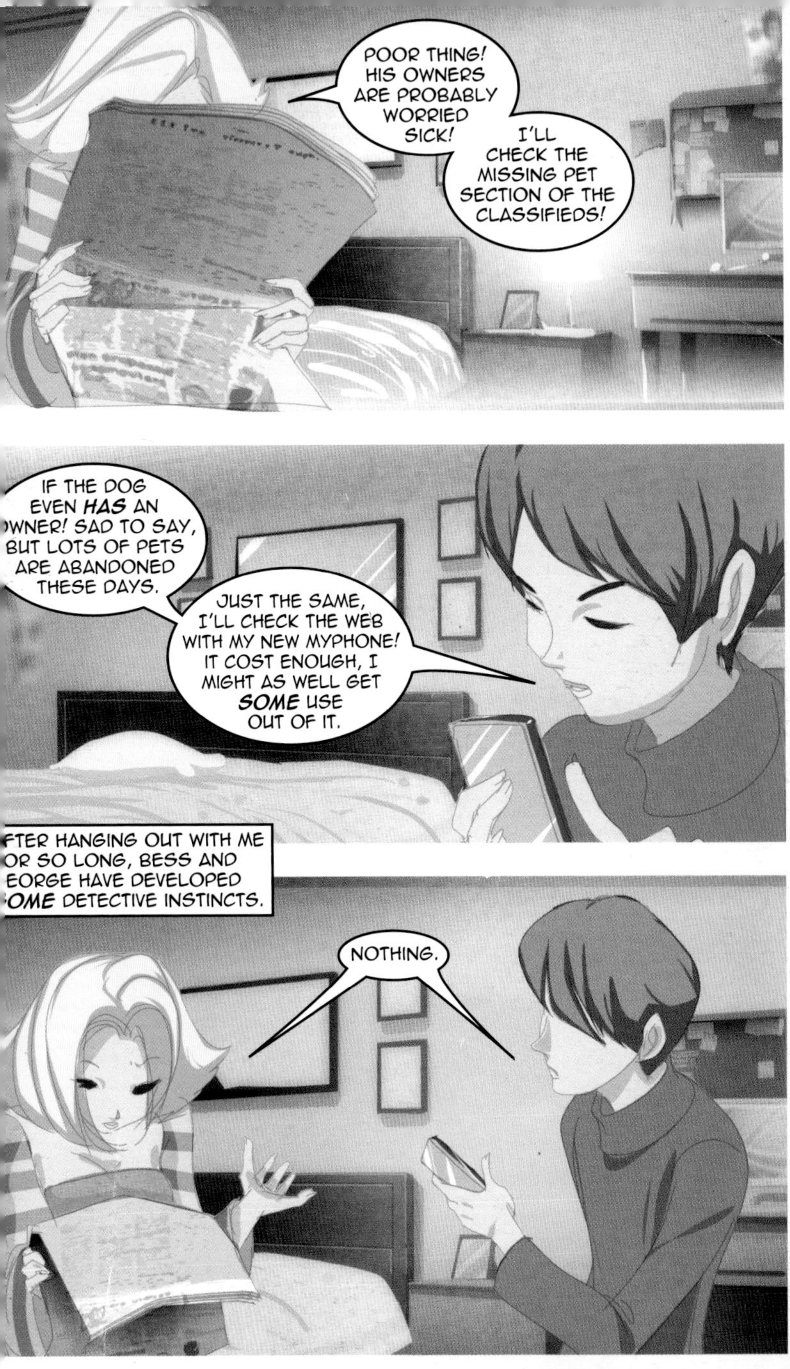
POOR THING! HIS OWNERS ARE PROBABLY WORRIED SICK!
I'LL CHECK THE MISSING PET SECTION OF THE CLASSIFIEDS!
IF THE DOG EVEN **HAS** AN WNER! SAD TO SAY, BUT LOTS OF PETS ARE ABANDONED THESE DAYS.
JUST THE SAME, I'LL CHECK THE WEB WITH MY NEW MYPHONE! IT COST ENOUGH, I MIGHT AS WELL GET **SOME** USE OUT OF IT.
FTER HANGING OUT WITH ME OR SO LONG, BESS AND EORGE HAVE DEVELOPED OME DETECTIVE INSTINCTS.
NOTHING.

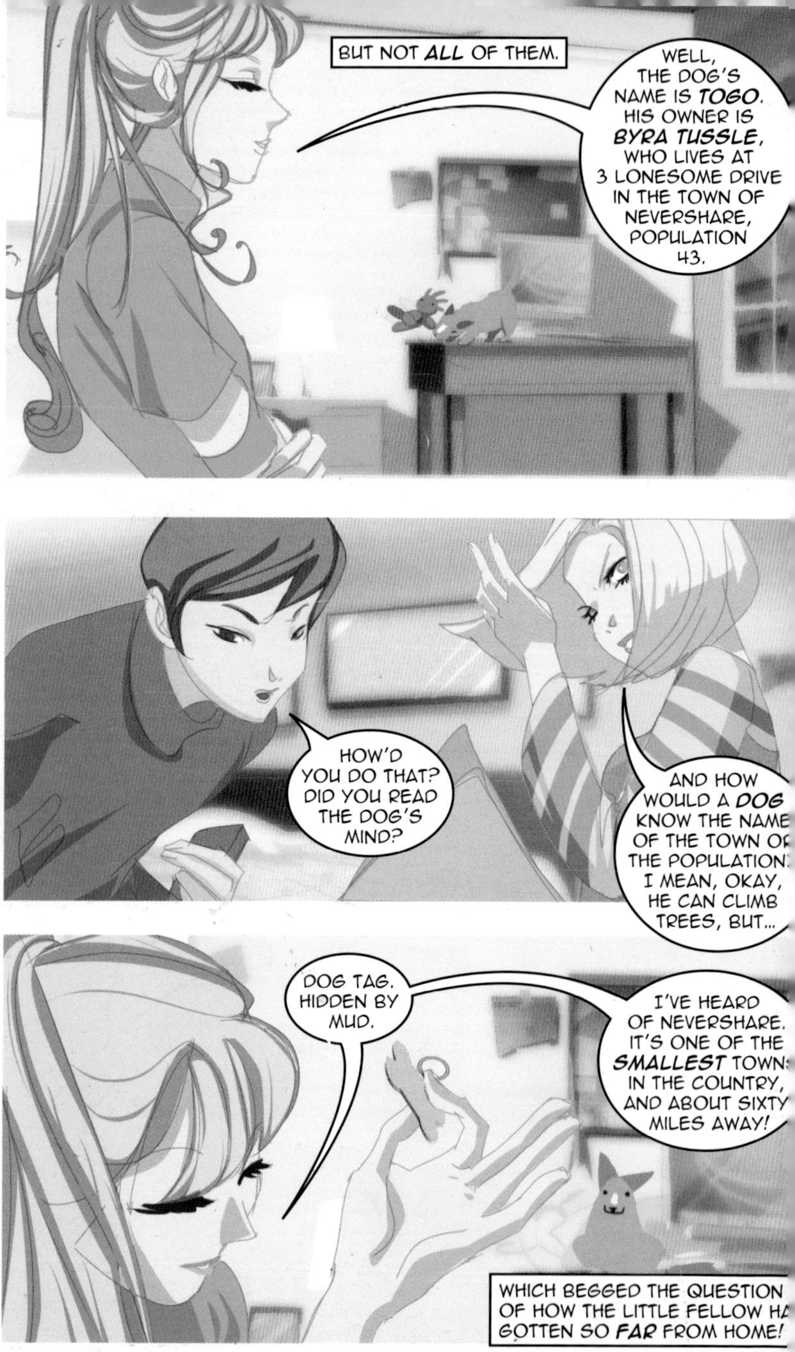
BUT NOT ALL OF THEM.
WELL, THE DOG'S NAME IS TOGO. HIS OWNER IS BYRA TUSSLE, WHO LIVES AT 3 LONESOME DRIVE IN THE TOWN OF NEVERSHARE, POPULATION 43.
HOW'D YOU DO THAT? DID YOU READ THE DOG'S MIND?
AND HOW WOULD A DOG KNOW THE NAME OF THE TOWN OR THE POPULATION? I MEAN, OKAY, HE CAN CLIMB TREES, BUT...
DOG TAG. HIDDEN BY MUD.
I'VE HEARD OF NEVERSHARE. IT'S ONE OF THE SMALLEST TOWNS IN THE COUNTRY, AND ABOUT SIXTY MILES AWAY!
WHICH BEGGED THE QUESTION OF HOW THE LITTLE FELLOW HA GOTTEN SO FAR FROM HOME!

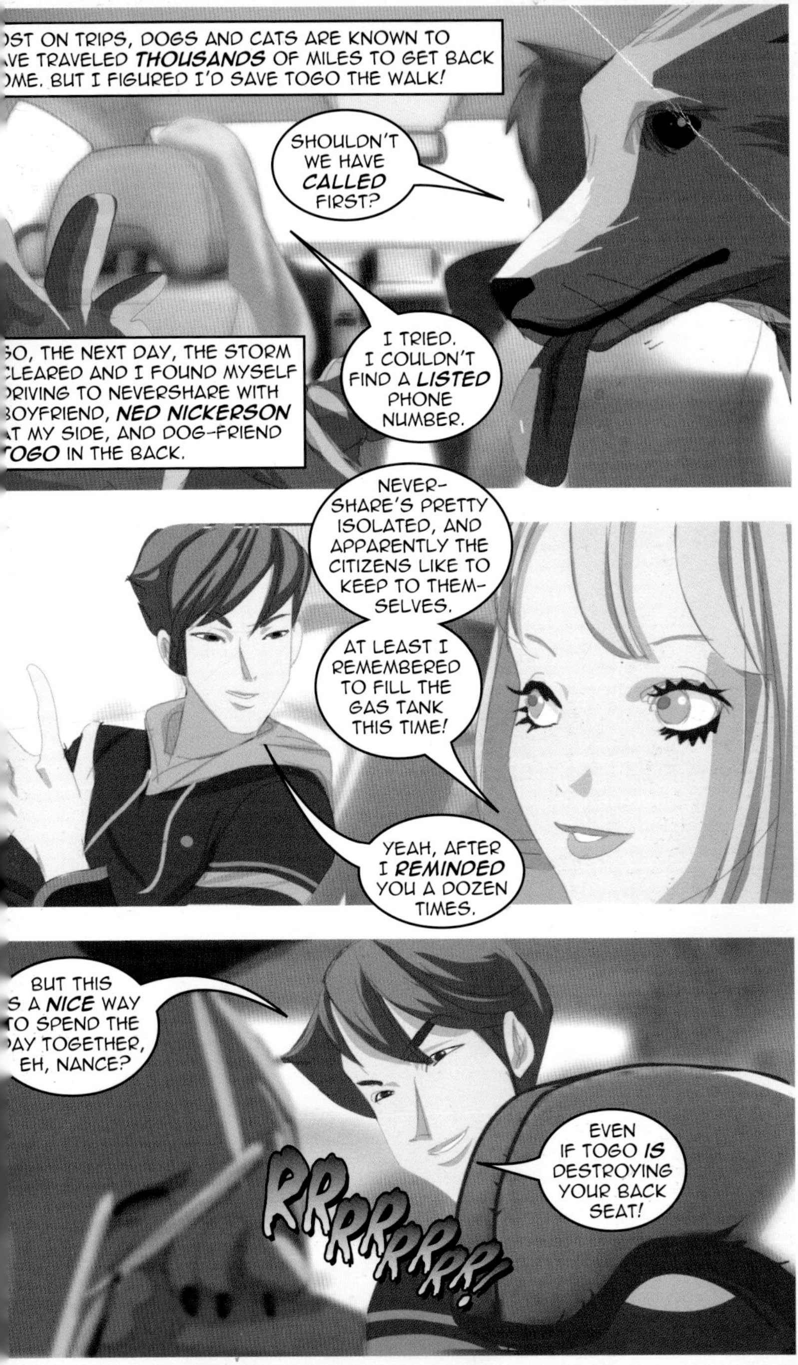

OST ON TRIPS, DOGS AND CATS ARE KNOWN TO
VE TRAVELED THOUSANDS OF MILES TO GET BACK
OME. BUT I FIGURED I'D SAVE TOGO THE WALK!
SHOULDN'T WE HAVE CALLED FIRST?
I TRIED. I COULDN'T FIND A LISTED PHONE NUMBER.
O, THE NEXT DAY, THE STORM
LEARED AND I FOUND MYSELF
RIVING TO NEVERSHARE WITH
OYFRIEND, NED NICKERSON
T MY SIDE, AND DOG-FRIEND
OGO IN THE BACK.
NEVER-SHARE'S PRETTY ISOLATED, AND APPARENTLY THE CITIZENS LIKE TO KEEP TO THEM-SELVES.
AT LEAST I REMEMBERED TO FILL THE GAS TANK THIS TIME!
YEAH, AFTER I REMINDED YOU A DOZEN TIMES.
BUT THIS S A NICE WAY TO SPEND THE AY TOGETHER, EH, NANCE?
EVEN IF TOGO IS DESTROYING YOUR BACK SEAT!
RRRRRRRR!

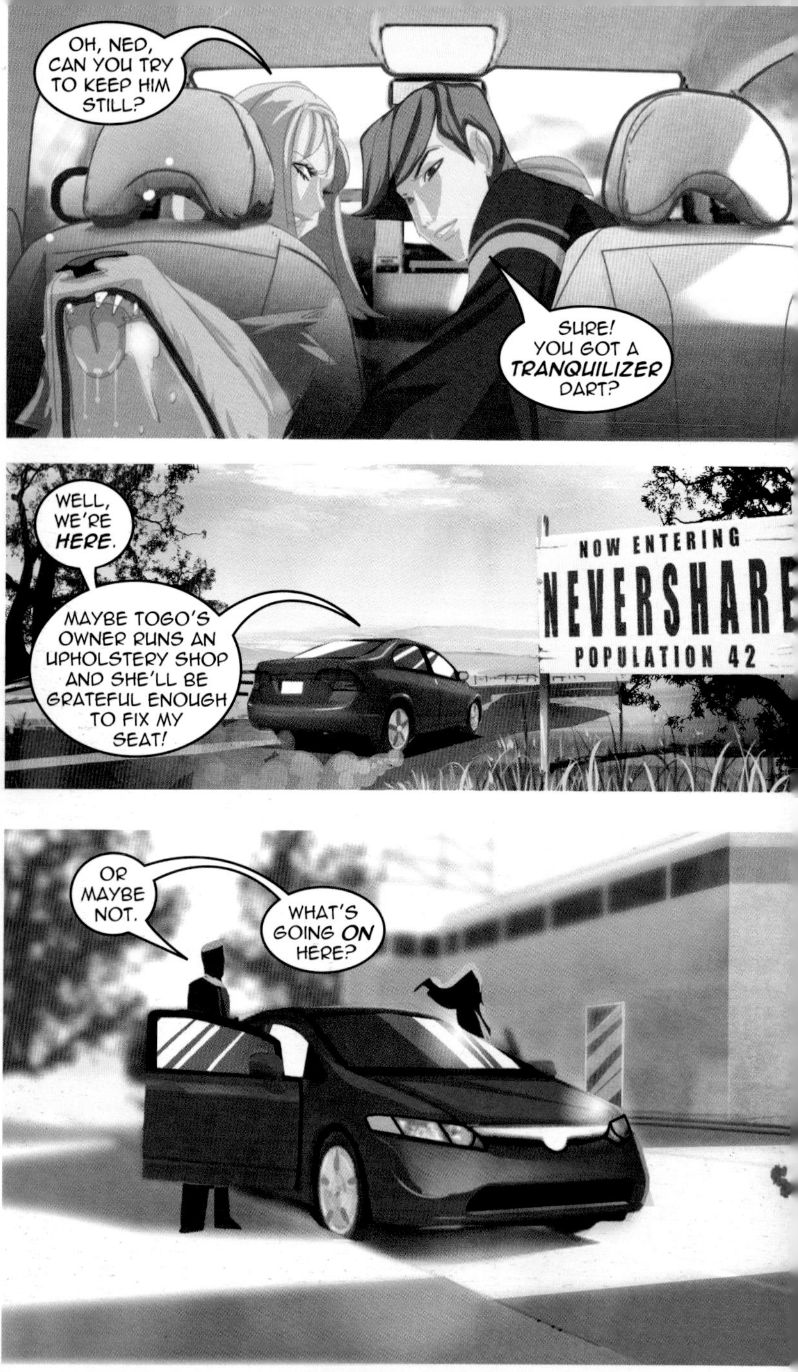
OH, NED, CAN YOU TRY TO KEEP HIM STILL?
SURE! YOU GOT A *TRANQUILIZER* DART?
WELL, WE'RE *HERE*.
MAYBE TOGO'S OWNER RUNS AN UPHOLSTERY SHOP AND SHE'LL BE GRATEFUL ENOUGH TO FIX MY SEAT!
NOW ENTERING
NEVERSHARE
POPULATION 42
OR MAYBE NOT.
WHAT'S GOING *ON* HERE?

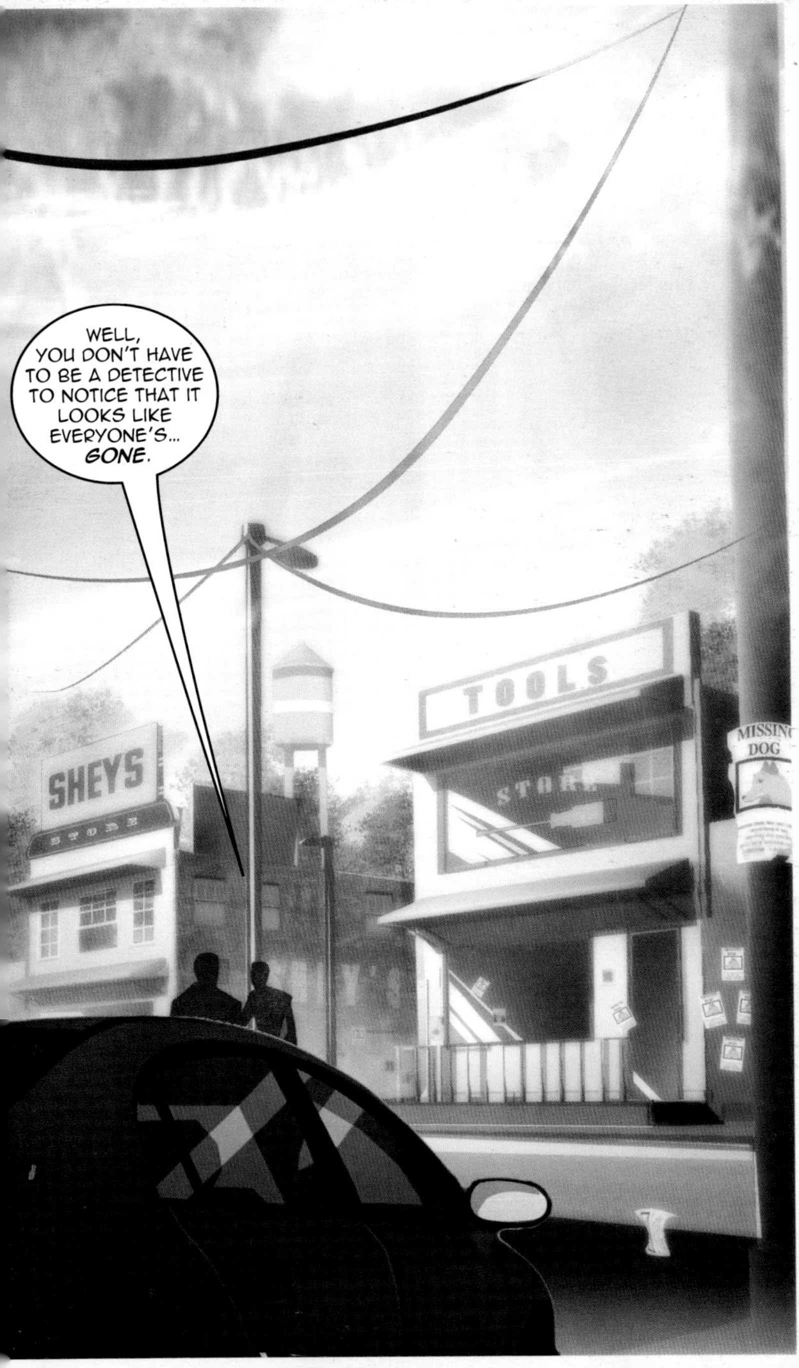
WELL, YOU DON'T HAVE TO BE A DETECTIVE TO NOTICE THAT IT LOOKS LIKE EVERYONE'S... *GONE*.
TOOLS
SHEYS
MISSING DOG

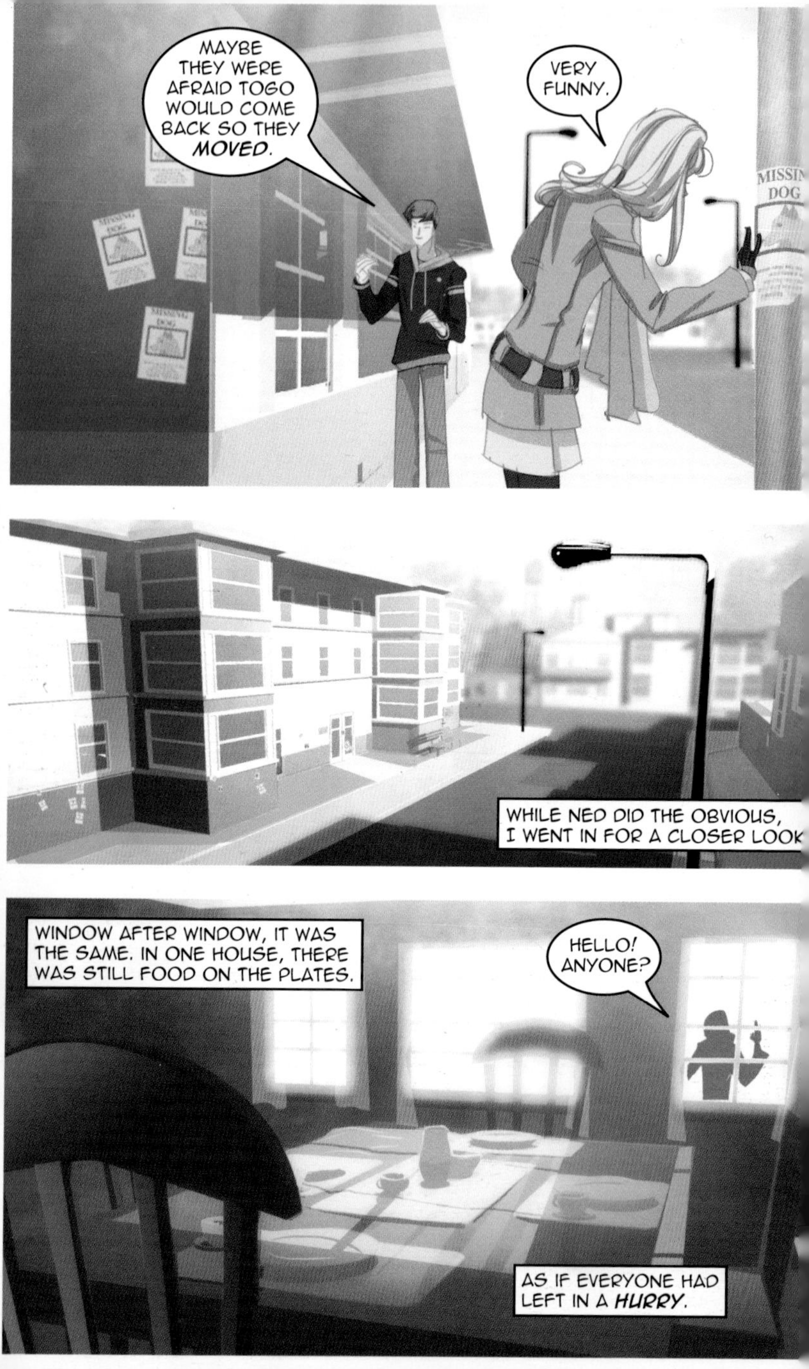
MAYBE THEY WERE AFRAID TOGO WOULD COME BACK SO THEY *MOVED*.
VERY FUNNY.
MISSING DOG
WHILE NED DID THE OBVIOUS, I WENT IN FOR A CLOSER LOOK
WINDOW AFTER WINDOW, IT WAS THE SAME. IN ONE HOUSE, THERE WAS STILL FOOD ON THE PLATES.
HELLO! ANYONE?
AS IF EVERYONE HAD LEFT IN A *HURRY*.

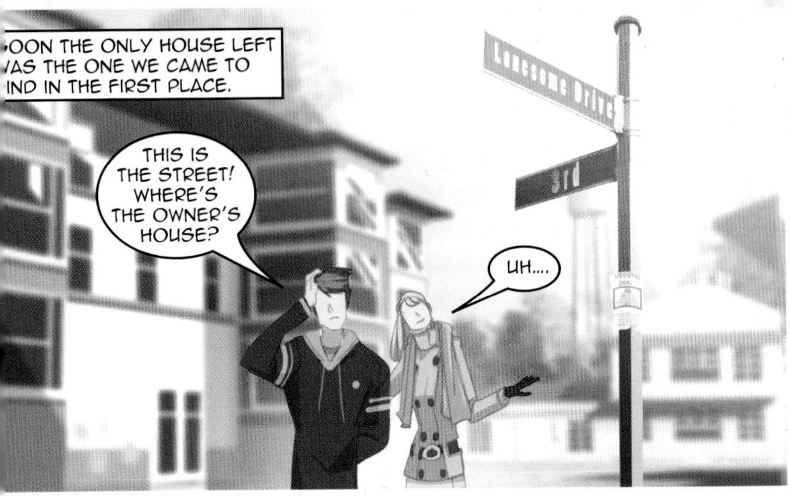

OON THE ONLY HOUSE LEFT
AS THE ONE WE CAME TO
IND IN THE FIRST PLACE.
Lonesome Drive
3rd
THIS IS THE STREET! WHERE'S THE OWNER'S HOUSE?
UH....
MISSING DOG

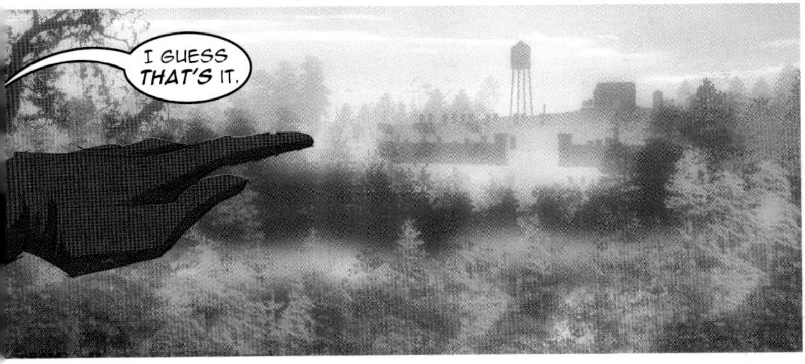

I GUESS *THAT'S* IT.

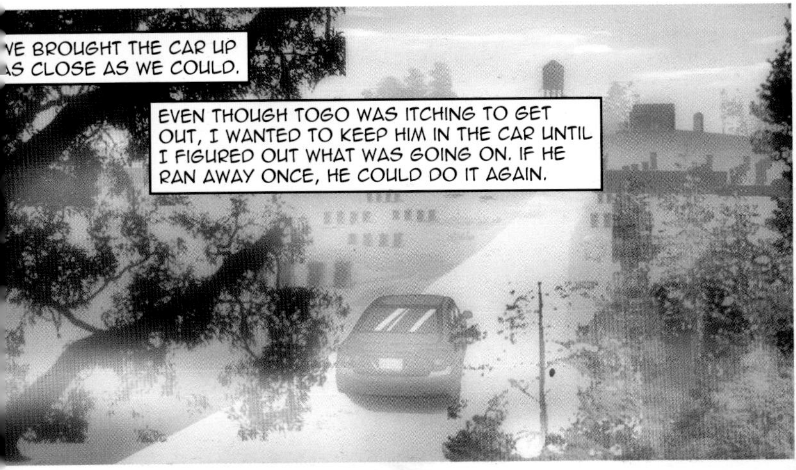

E BROUGHT THE CAR UP
S CLOSE AS WE COULD.
EVEN THOUGH TOGO WAS ITCHING TO GET OUT, I WANTED TO KEEP HIM IN THE CAR UNTIL I FIGURED OUT WHAT WAS GOING ON. IF HE RAN AWAY ONCE, HE COULD DO IT AGAIN.

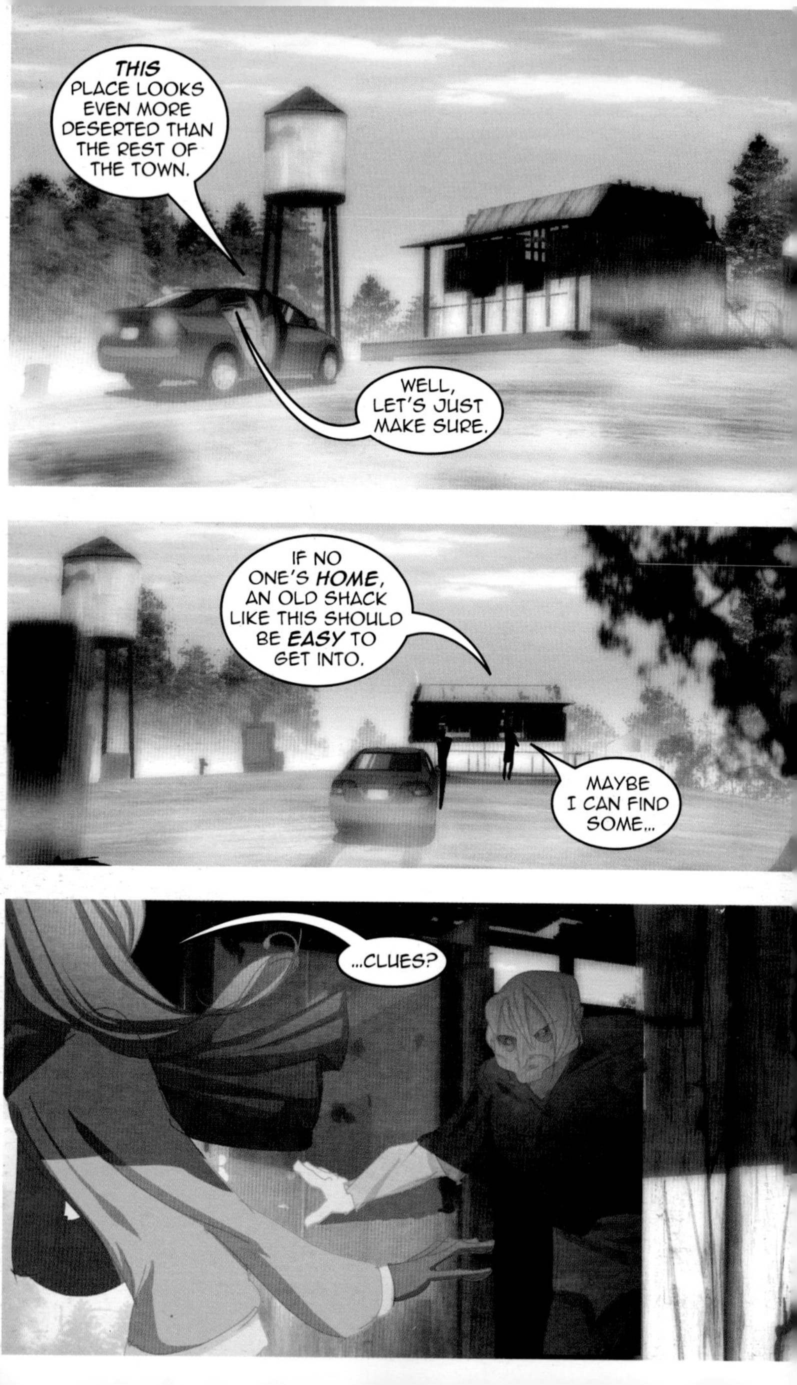
THIS PLACE LOOKS EVEN MORE DESERTED THAN THE REST OF THE TOWN.
WELL, LET'S JUST MAKE SURE.
IF NO ONE'S HOME, AN OLD SHACK LIKE THIS SHOULD BE EASY TO GET INTO.
MAYBE I CAN FIND SOME...
...CLUES?

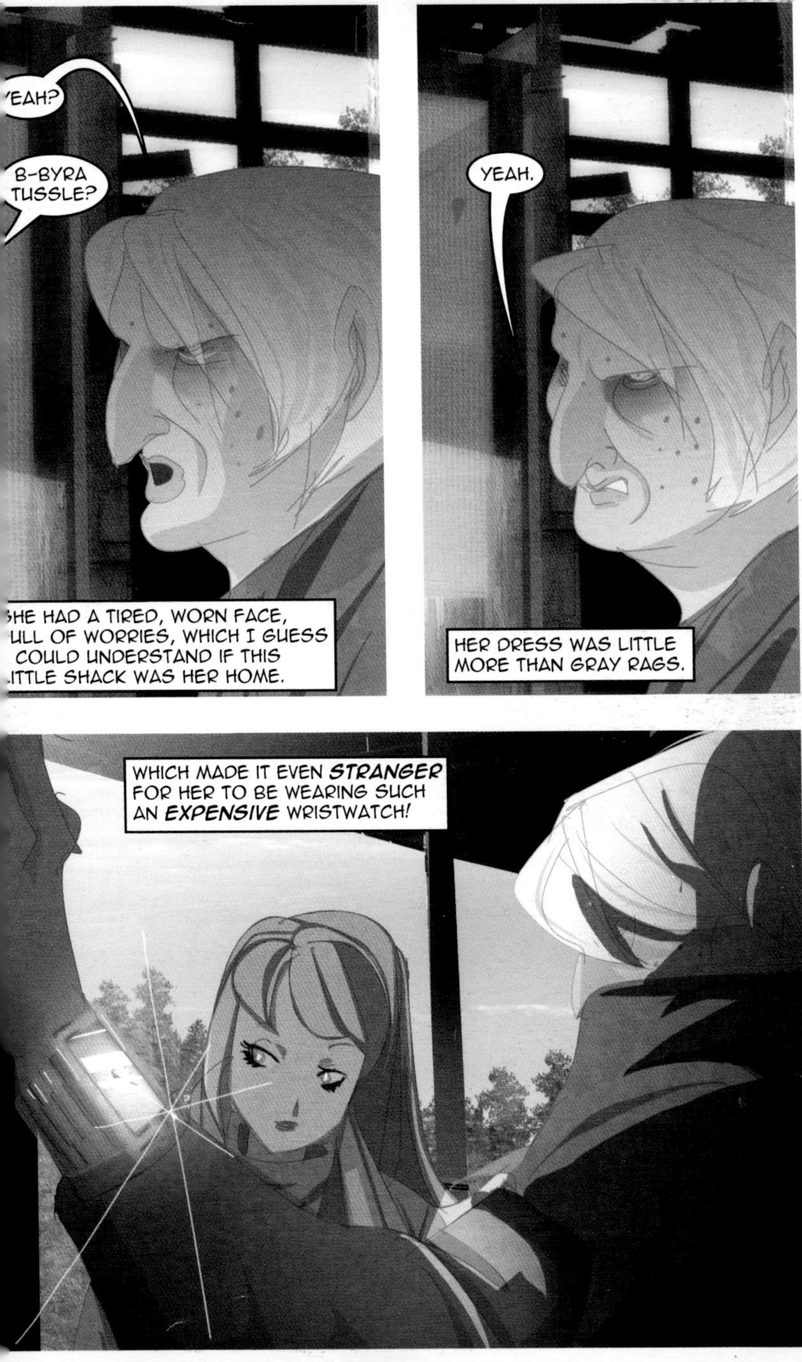

YEAH?
B-BYRA TUSSLE?
HE HAD A TIRED, WORN FACE, ULL OF WORRIES, WHICH I GUESS COULD UNDERSTAND IF THIS ITTLE SHACK WAS HER HOME.
YEAH.
HER DRESS WAS LITTLE MORE THAN GRAY RAGS.
WHICH MADE IT EVEN *STRANGER* FOR HER TO BE WEARING SUCH AN *EXPENSIVE* WRISTWATCH!

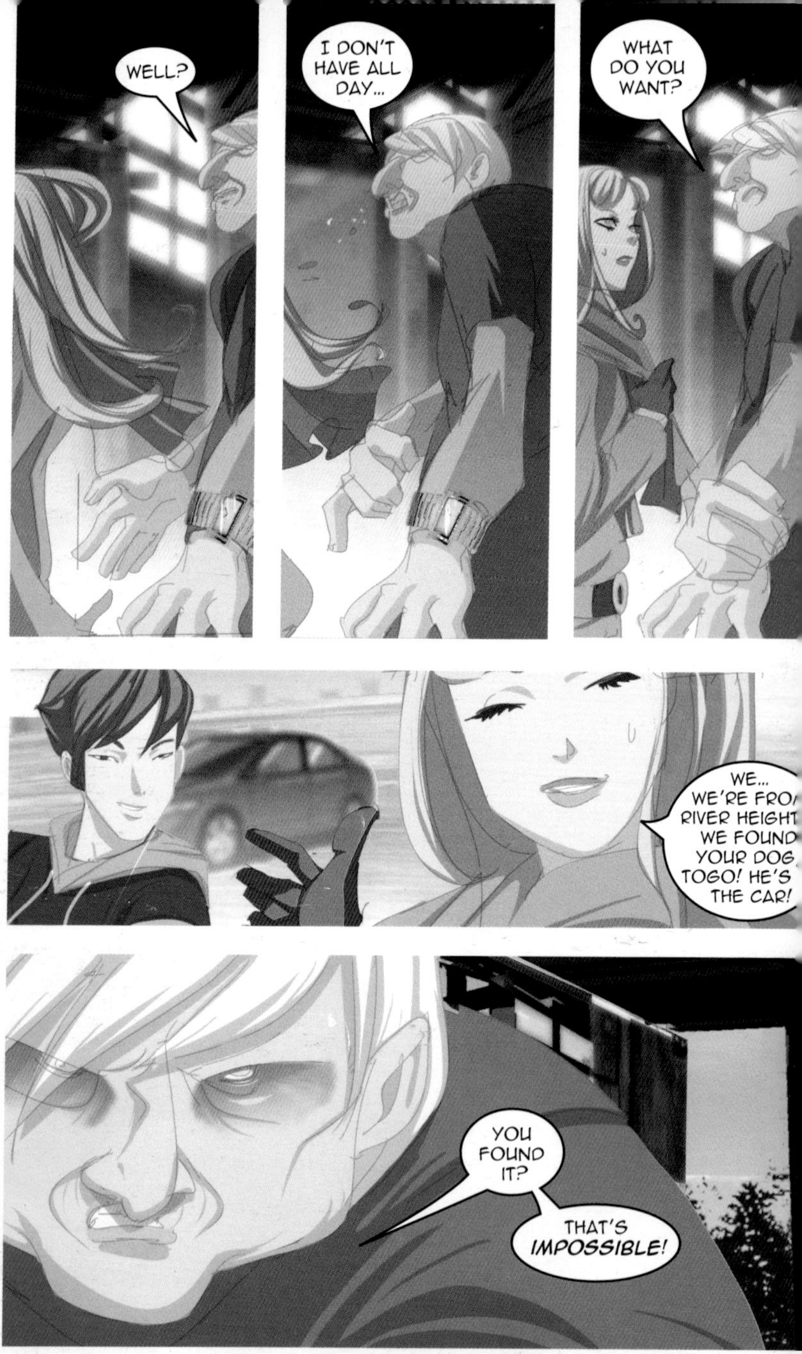
WELL?
I DON'T HAVE ALL DAY...
WHAT DO YOU WANT?
WE... WE'RE FRO
RIVER HEIGHT
WE FOUND
YOUR DOG
TOGO! HE'S
THE CAR!
YOU FOUND IT?
THAT'S *IMPOSSIBLE!*

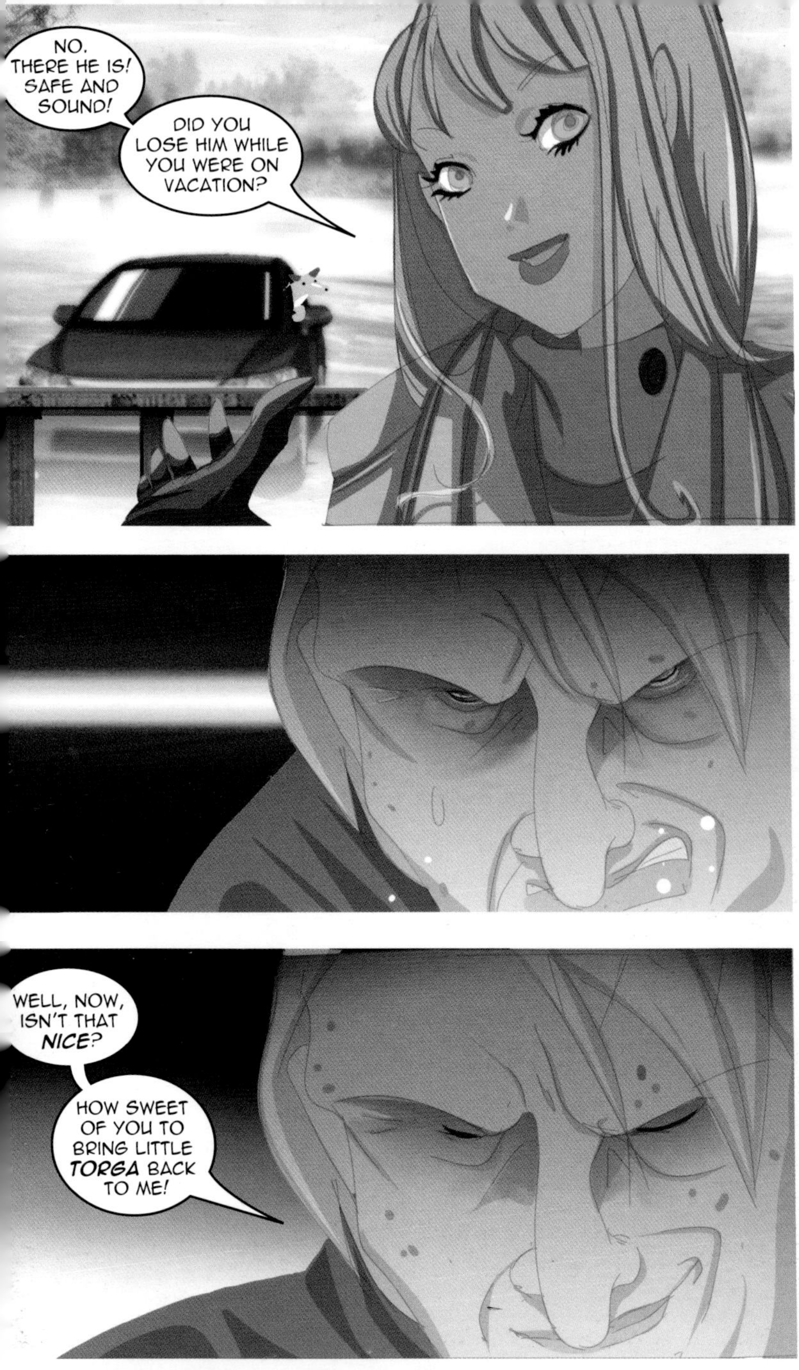
NO. THERE HE IS! SAFE AND SOUND!
DID YOU LOSE HIM WHILE YOU WERE ON VACATION?
WELL, NOW, ISN'T THAT *NICE*?
HOW SWEET OF YOU TO BRING LITTLE *TORGA* BACK TO ME!

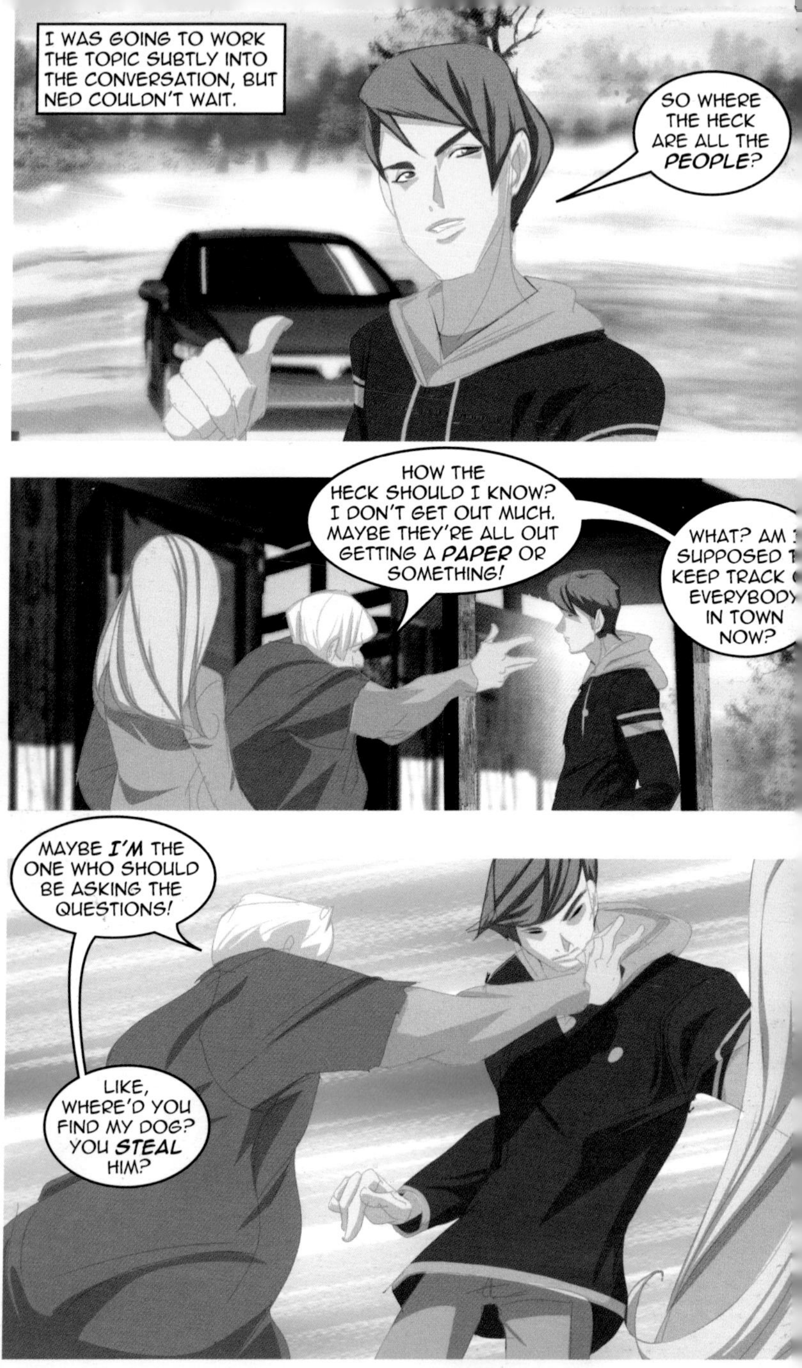
I WAS GOING TO WORK THE TOPIC SUBTLY INTO THE CONVERSATION, BUT NED COULDN'T WAIT.
SO WHERE THE HECK ARE ALL THE *PEOPLE*?
HOW THE HECK SHOULD I KNOW? I DON'T GET OUT MUCH. MAYBE THEY'RE ALL OUT GETTING A *PAPER* OR SOMETHING!
MAYBE *I'M* THE ONE WHO SHOULD BE ASKING THE QUESTIONS!
LIKE, WHERE'D YOU FIND MY DOG? YOU *STEAL* HIM?

'M NOT USED TO HAVING A
)G AROUND, SO I FORGOT
NE OF THE BASIC RULES.

NEVER LEAVE YOUR PET ALONE IN A CAR.

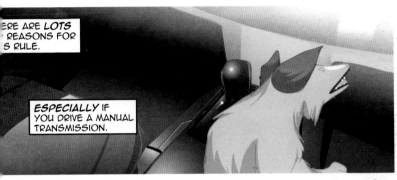

ERE ARE **LOTS**
REASONS FOR
S RULE.

ESPECIALLY IF YOU DRIVE A MANUAL TRANSMISSION.

FOR ONE THING, THE PET MIGHT ACCIDENTALLY HIT THE **STICK SHIFT** AND PUT THE CAR IN **NEUTRAL**.

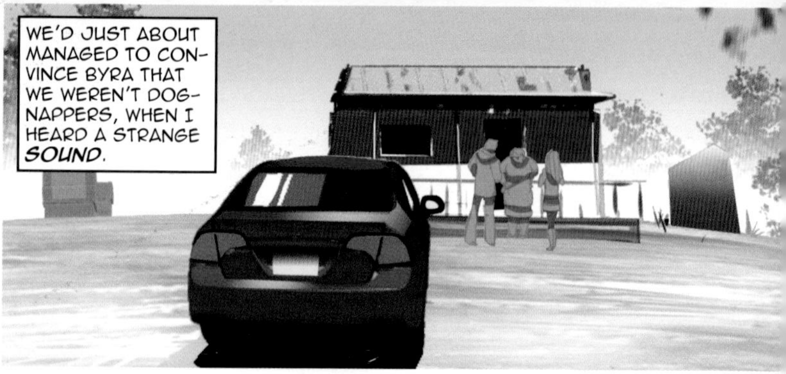
WE'D JUST ABOUT MANAGED TO CON-VINCE BYRA THAT WE WEREN'T DOG-NAPPERS, WHEN I HEARD A STRANGE *SOUND*.

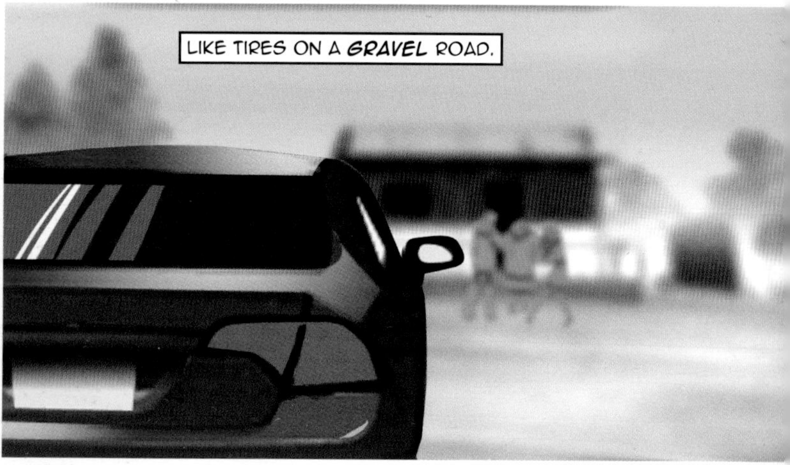
LIKE TIRES ON A *GRAVEL* ROAD.

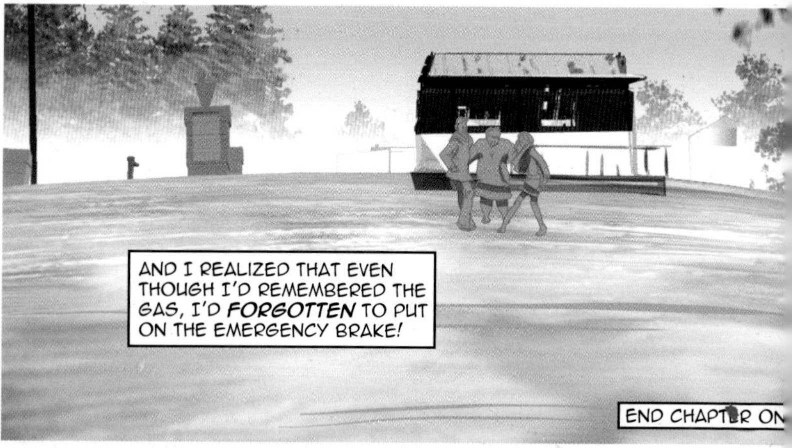
AND I REALIZED THAT EVEN THOUGH I'D REMEMBERED THE GAS, I'D *FORGOTTEN* TO PUT ON THE EMERGENCY BRAKE!
END CHAPTER ON

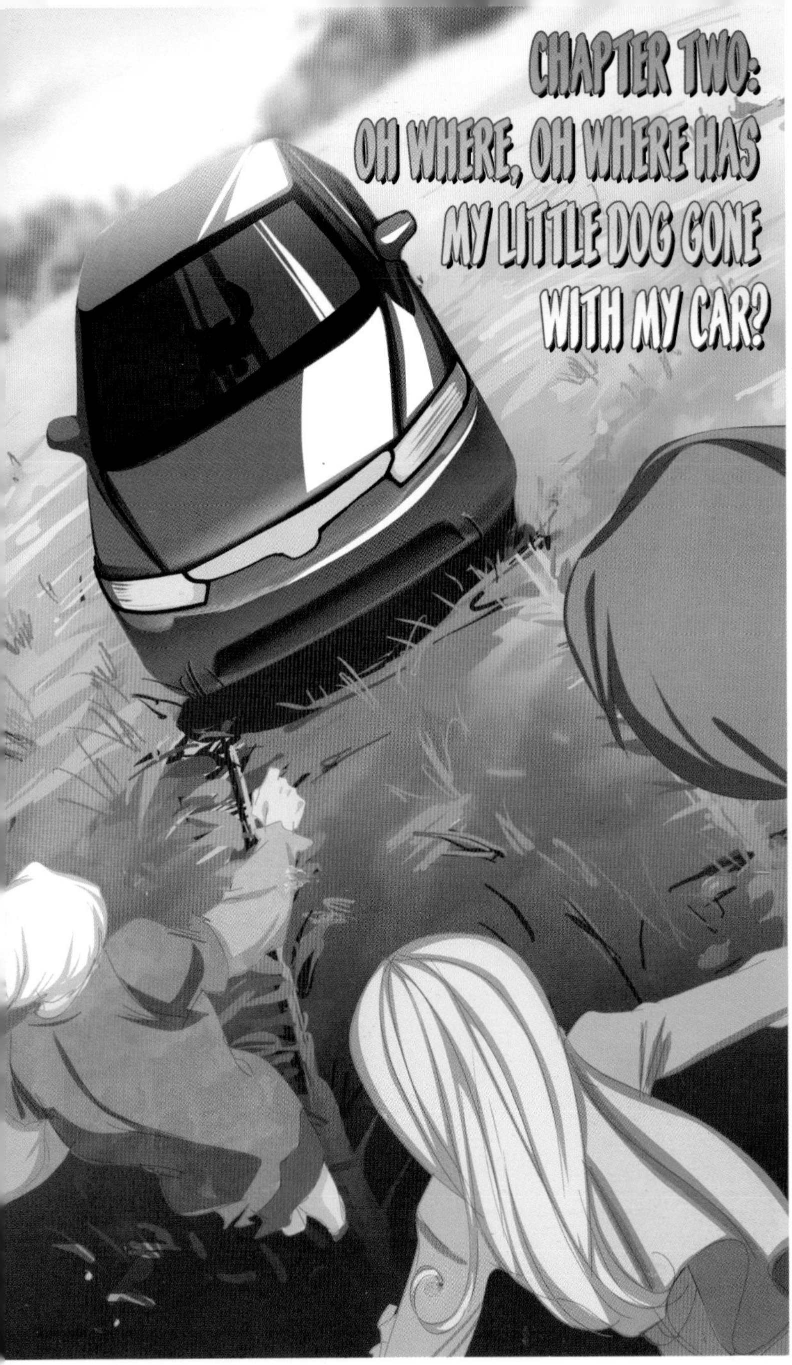
CHAPTER TWO:
OH WHERE, OH WHERE HAS
MY LITTLE DOG GONE
WITH MY CAR?

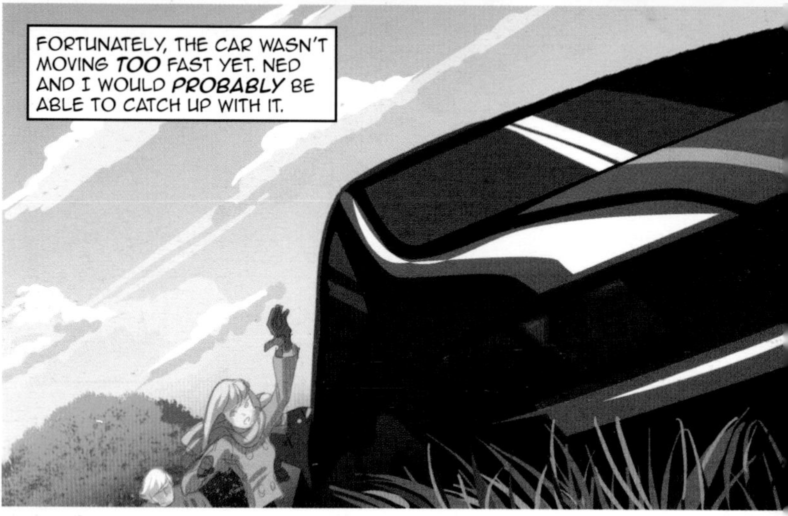
FORTUNATELY, THE CAR WASN'T MOVING TOO FAST YET. NED AND I WOULD PROBABLY BE ABLE TO CATCH UP WITH IT.

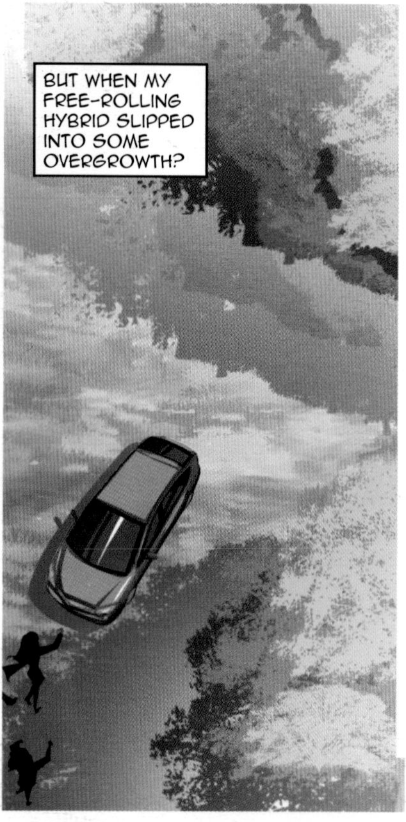
BUT WHEN MY FREE-ROLLING HYBRID SLIPPED INTO SOME OVERGROWTH?

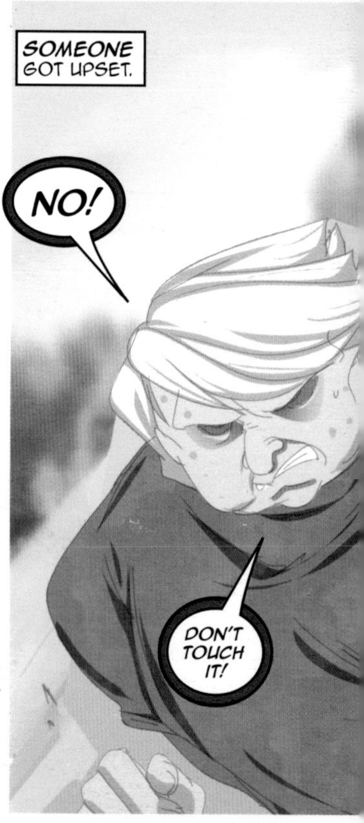
SOMEONE GOT UPSET.
NO!
DON'T TOUCH IT!

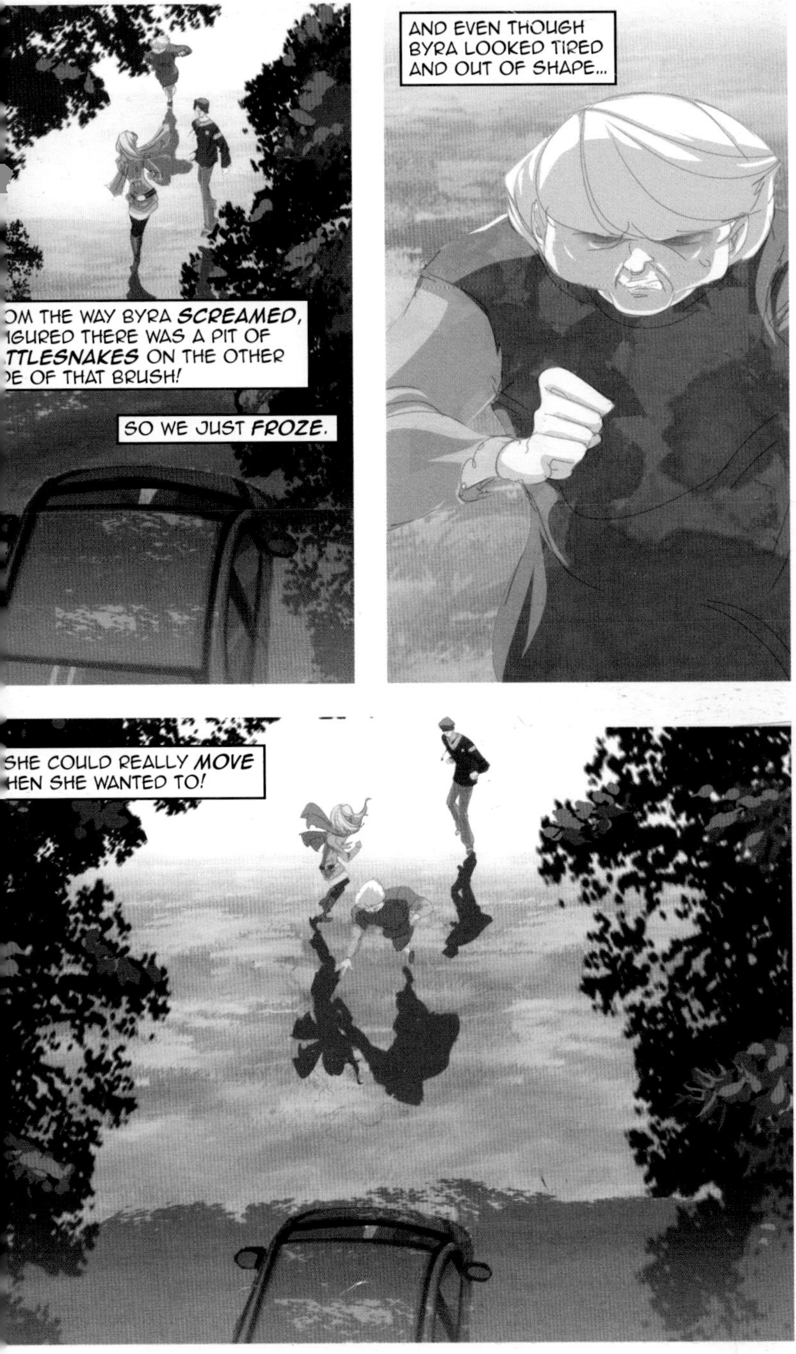
OM THE WAY BYRA SCREAMED, IGURED THERE WAS A PIT OF TTLESNAKES ON THE OTHER DE OF THAT BRUSH!
SO WE JUST FROZE.
AND EVEN THOUGH BYRA LOOKED TIRED AND OUT OF SHAPE...
SHE COULD REALLY MOVE HEN SHE WANTED TO!

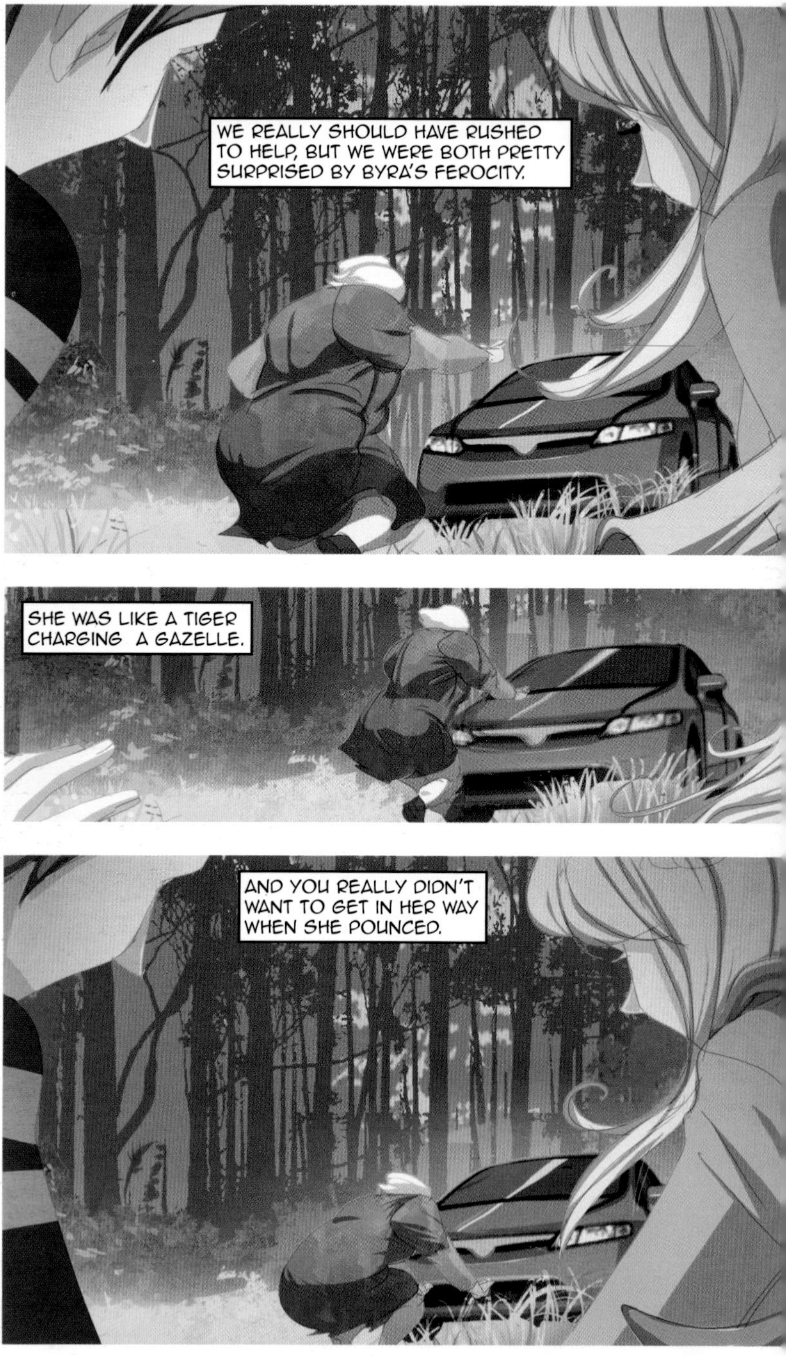
WE REALLY SHOULD HAVE RUSHED TO HELP, BUT WE WERE BOTH PRETTY SURPRISED BY BYRA'S FEROCITY.
SHE WAS LIKE A TIGER CHARGING A GAZELLE.
AND YOU REALLY DIDN'T WANT TO GET IN HER WAY WHEN SHE POUNCED.

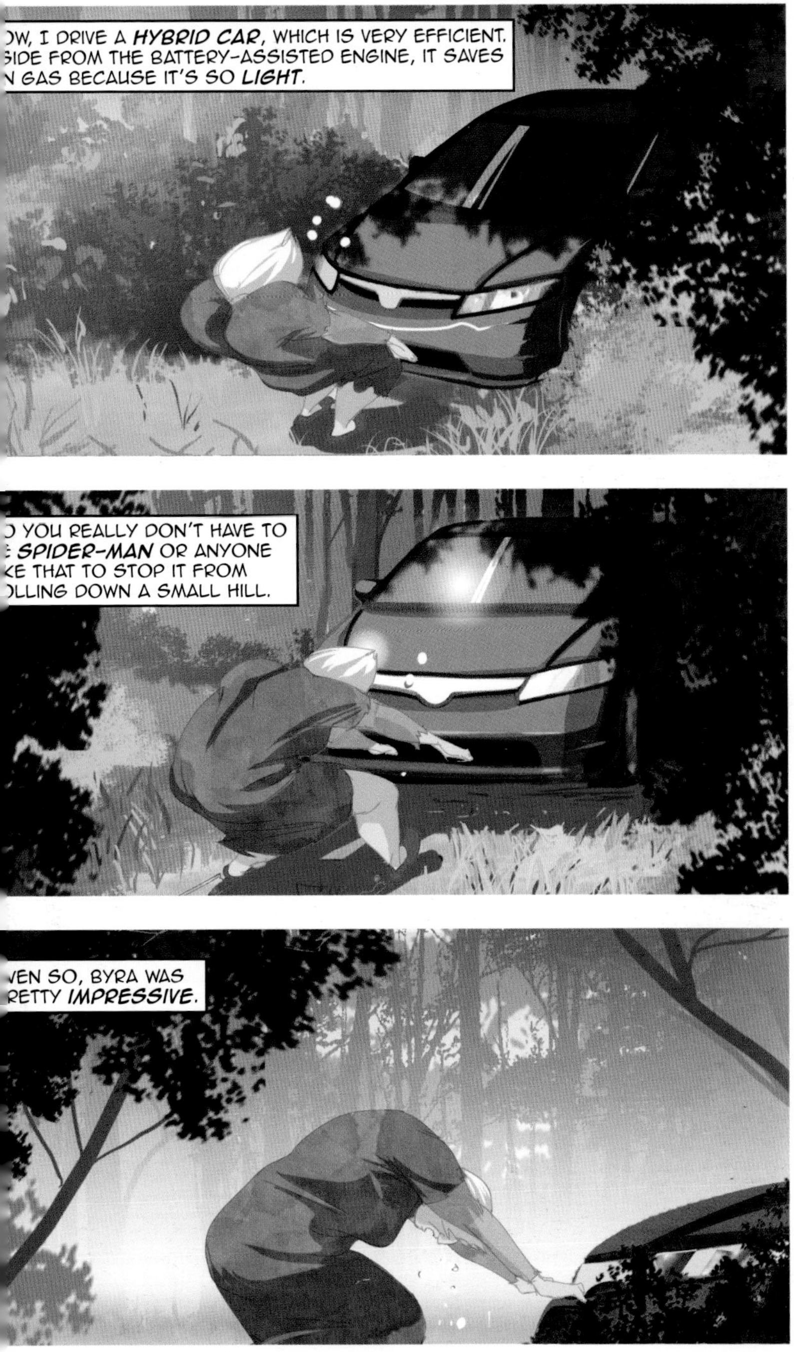

OW, I DRIVE A HYBRID CAR, WHICH IS VERY EFFICIENT.
SIDE FROM THE BATTERY-ASSISTED ENGINE, IT SAVES
N GAS BECAUSE IT'S SO LIGHT.
O YOU REALLY DON'T HAVE TO
E SPIDER-MAN OR ANYONE
KE THAT TO STOP IT FROM
OLLING DOWN A SMALL HILL.
VEN SO, BYRA WAS
RETTY IMPRESSIVE.

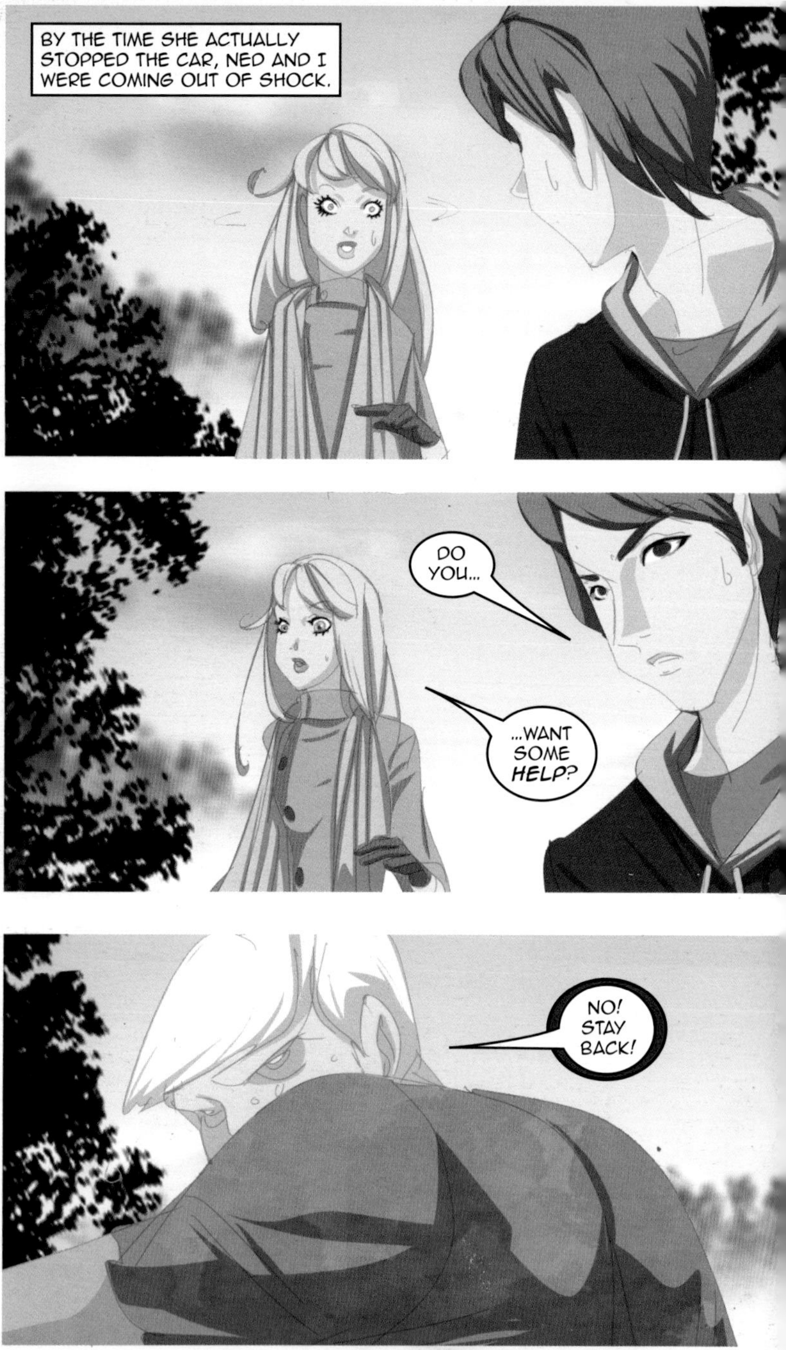
BY THE TIME SHE ACTUALLY STOPPED THE CAR, NED AND I WERE COMING OUT OF SHOCK.
DO YOU...
...WANT SOME HELP?
NO! STAY BACK!

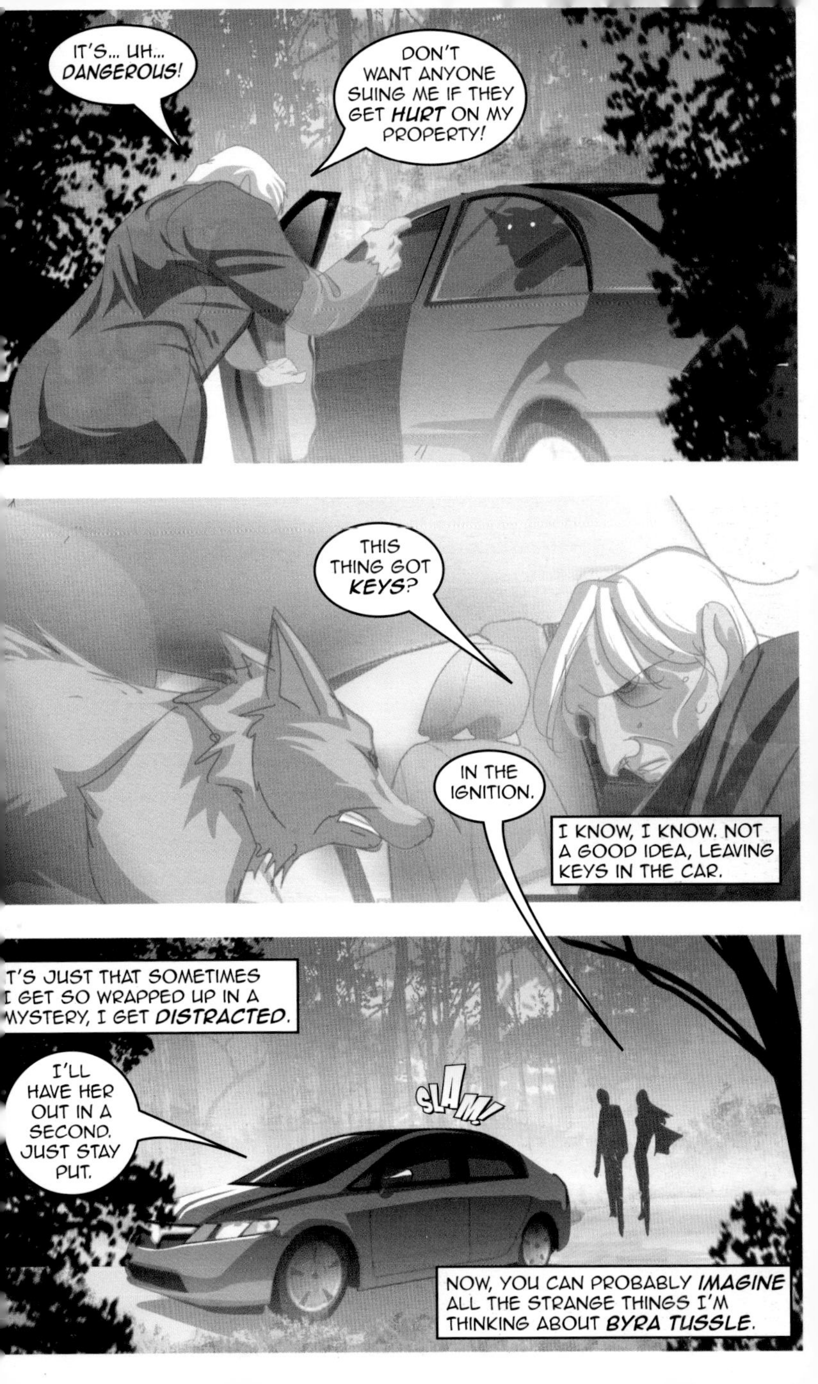
IT'S... UH... DANGEROUS!
DON'T WANT ANYONE SUING ME IF THEY GET HURT ON MY PROPERTY!
THIS THING GOT KEYS?
IN THE IGNITION.
I KNOW, I KNOW. NOT A GOOD IDEA, LEAVING KEYS IN THE CAR.
T'S JUST THAT SOMETIMES I GET SO WRAPPED UP IN A MYSTERY, I GET DISTRACTED.
I'LL HAVE HER OUT IN A SECOND. JUST STAY PUT.
SLAM!
NOW, YOU CAN PROBABLY IMAGINE ALL THE STRANGE THINGS I'M THINKING ABOUT BYRA TUSSLE.

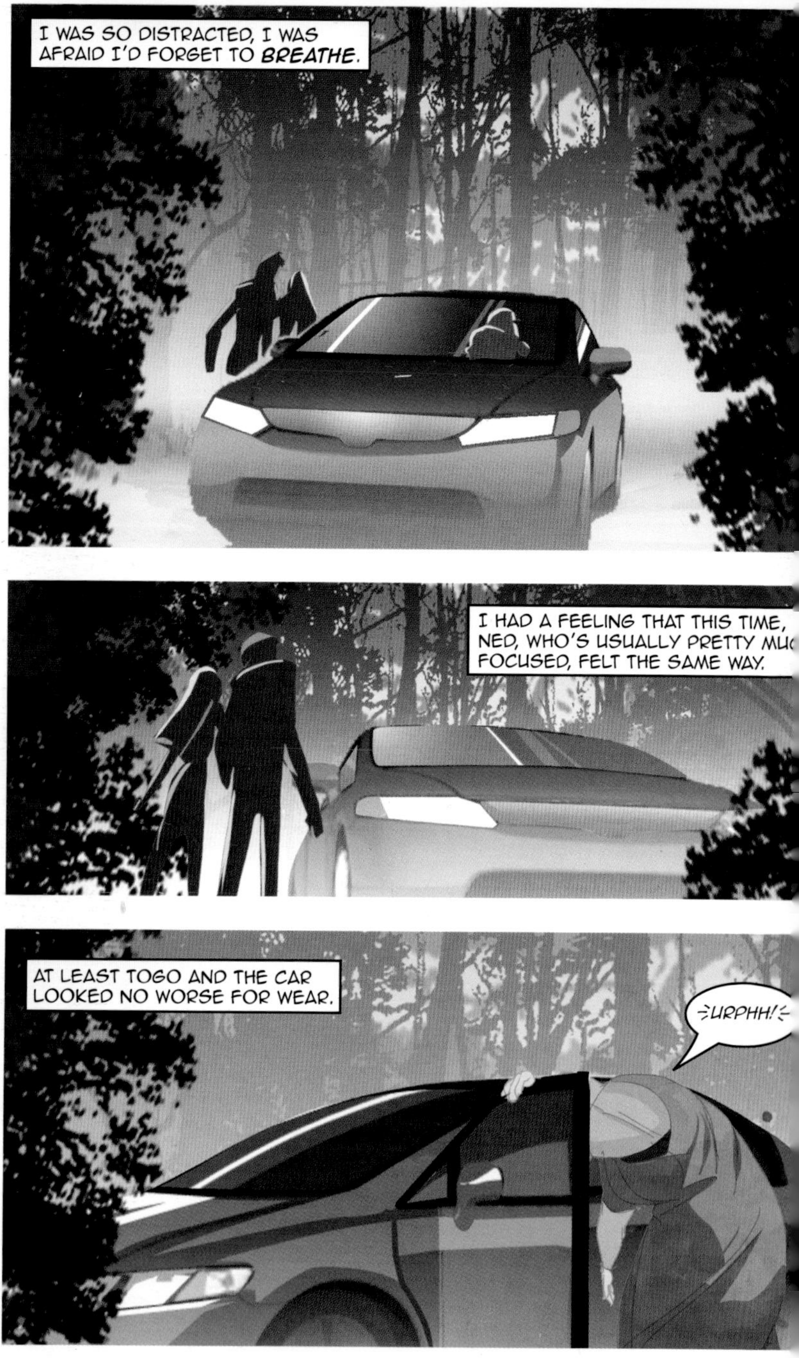
I WAS SO DISTRACTED, I WAS AFRAID I'D FORGET TO *BREATHE*.
I HAD A FEELING THAT THIS TIME, NED, WHO'S USUALLY PRETTY MU
FOCUSED, FELT THE SAME WAY.
AT LEAST TOGO AND THE CAR LOOKED NO WORSE FOR WEAR.
URPHH!

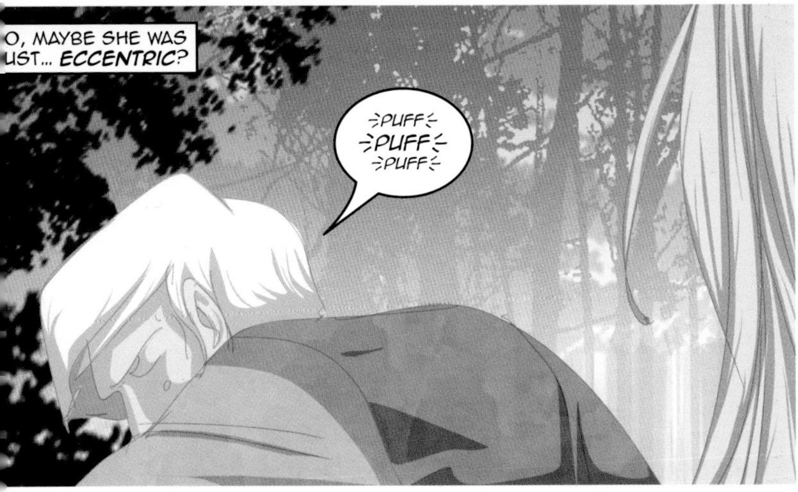
O, MAYBE SHE WAS
UST... ECCENTRIC?
PUFF PUFF PUFF

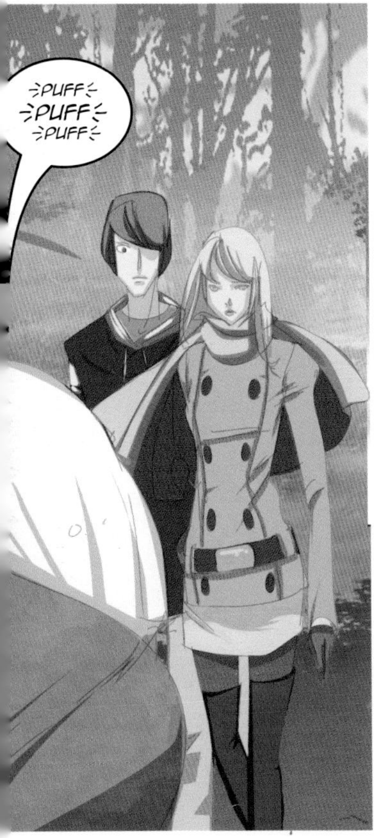
PUFF PUFF PUFF

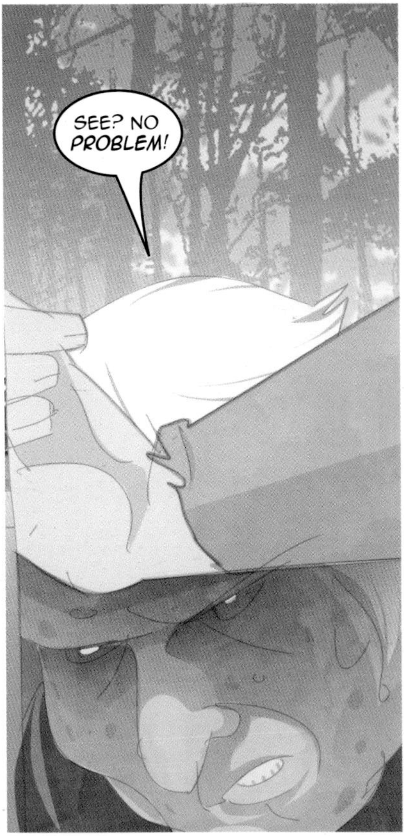
SEE? NO PROBLEM!

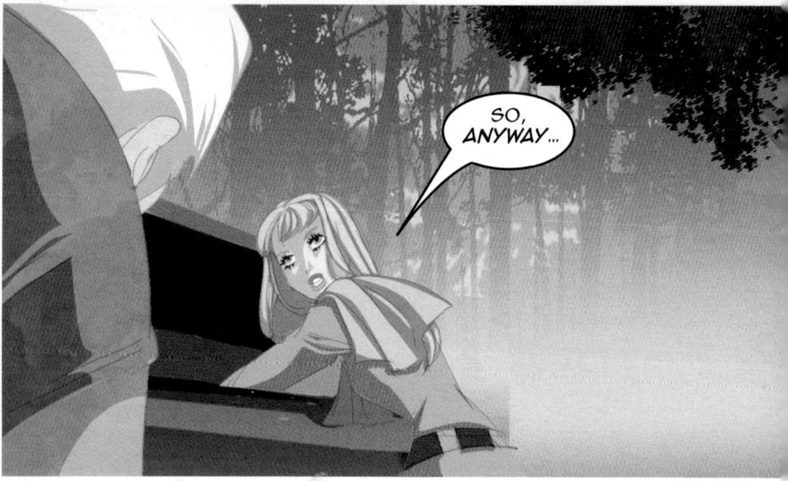
SO, ANYWAY...

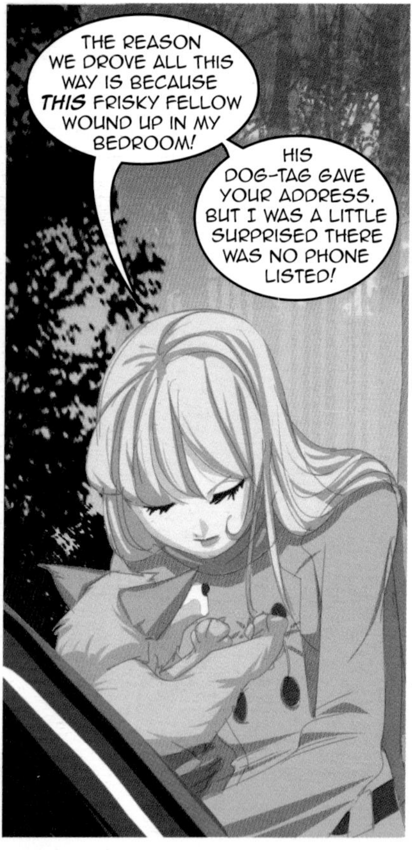
THE REASON WE DROVE ALL THIS WAY IS BECAUSE THIS FRISKY FELLOW WOUND UP IN MY BEDROOM!
HIS DOG-TAG GAVE YOUR ADDRESS. BUT I WAS A LITTLE SURPRISED THERE WAS NO PHONE LISTED!

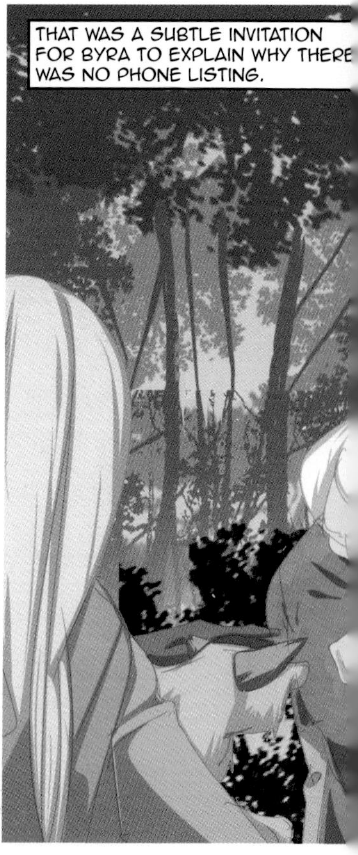
THAT WAS A SUBTLE INVITATION FOR BYRA TO EXPLAIN WHY THERE WAS NO PHONE LISTING.

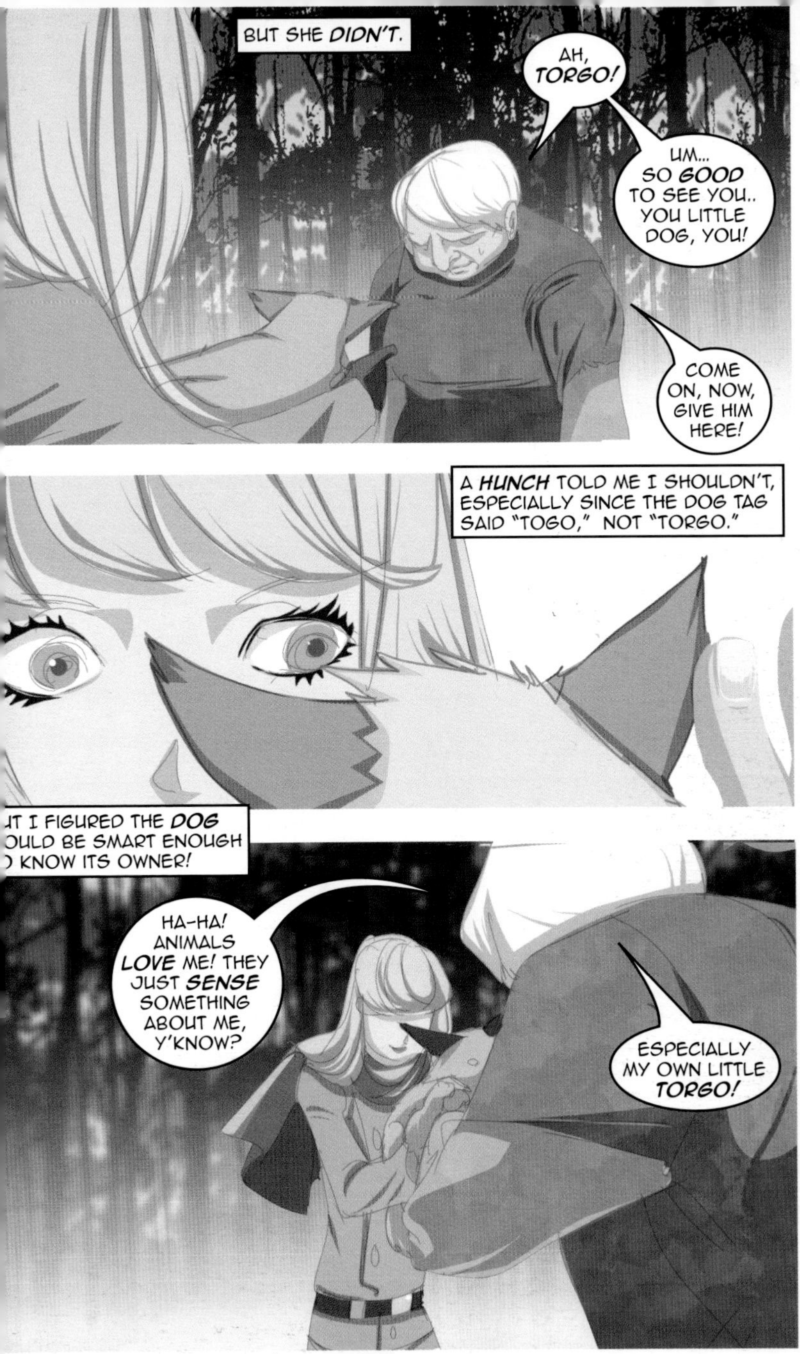
BUT SHE DIDN'T.
AH, TORGO!
UM... SO GOOD TO SEE YOU.. YOU LITTLE DOG, YOU!
COME ON, NOW, GIVE HIM HERE!
A HUNCH TOLD ME I SHOULDN'T, ESPECIALLY SINCE THE DOG TAG SAID "TOGO," NOT "TORGO."
T I FIGURED THE DOG OULD BE SMART ENOUGH O KNOW ITS OWNER!
HA-HA! ANIMALS LOVE ME! THEY JUST SENSE SOMETHING ABOUT ME, Y'KNOW?
ESPECIALLY MY OWN LITTLE TORGO!

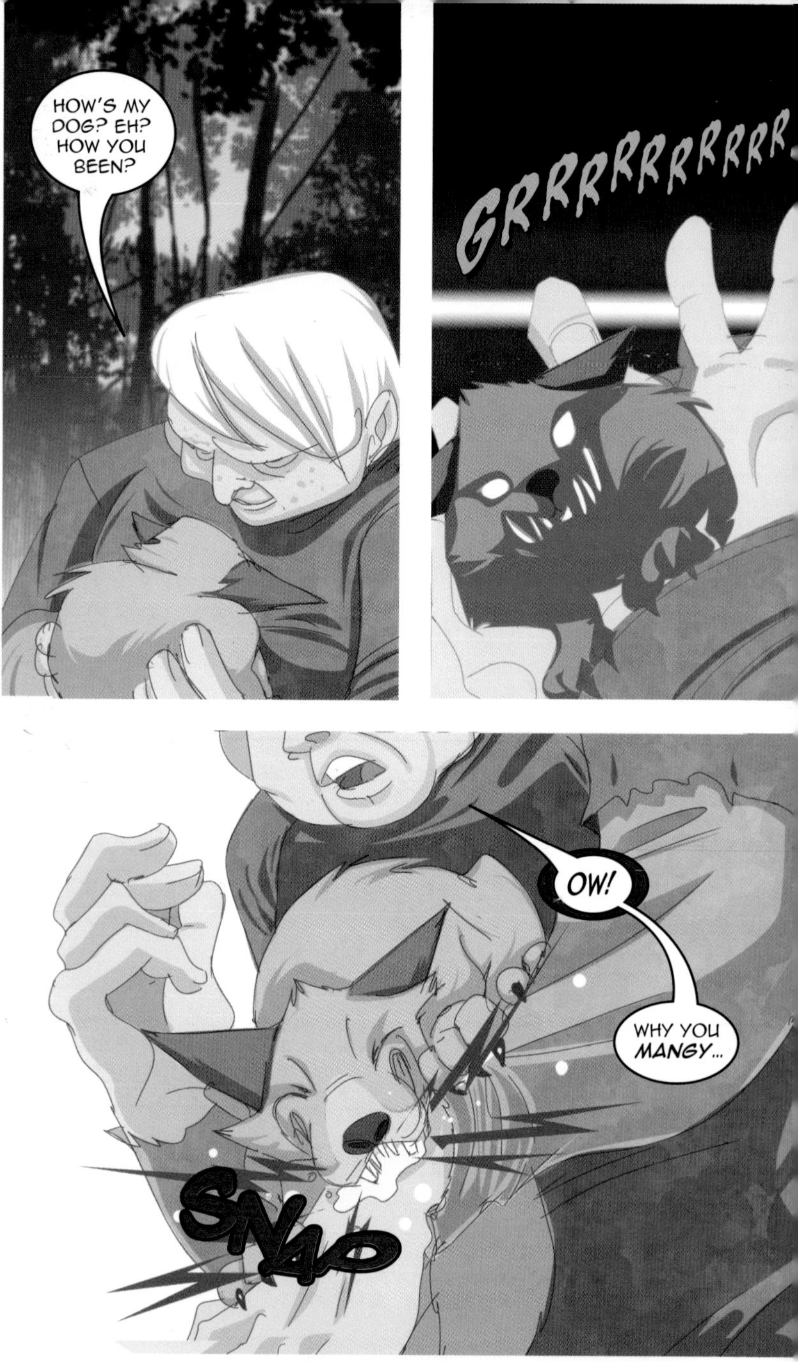
HOW'S MY DOG? EH? HOW YOU BEEN?
GRRRRRRRRRR
OW!
WHY YOU MANGY...
SNAP

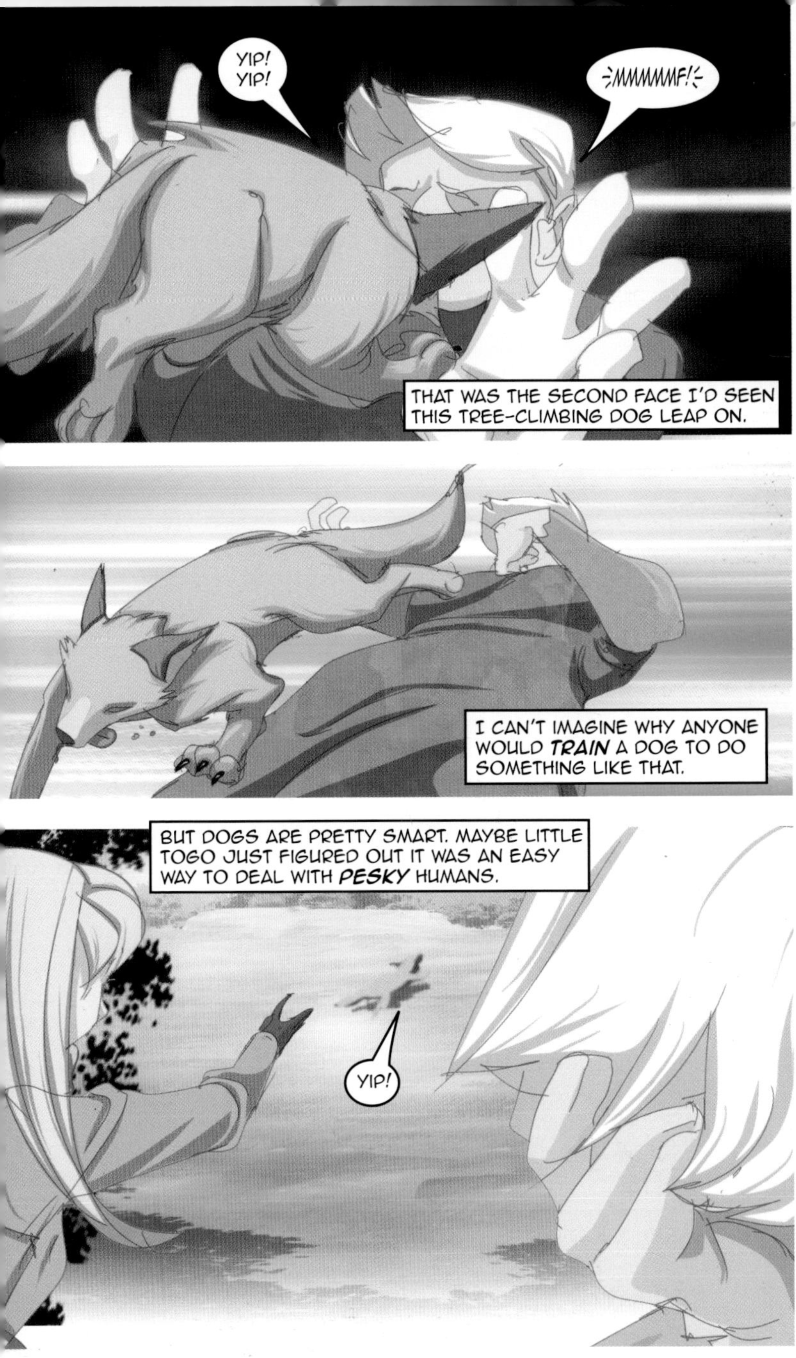
YIP! YIP!
MMMMMMF!
THAT WAS THE SECOND FACE I'D SEEN THIS TREE-CLIMBING DOG LEAP ON.
I CAN'T IMAGINE WHY ANYONE WOULD *TRAIN* A DOG TO DO SOMETHING LIKE THAT.
BUT DOGS ARE PRETTY SMART. MAYBE LITTLE TOGO JUST FIGURED OUT IT WAS AN EASY WAY TO DEAL WITH *PESKY* HUMANS.
YIP!

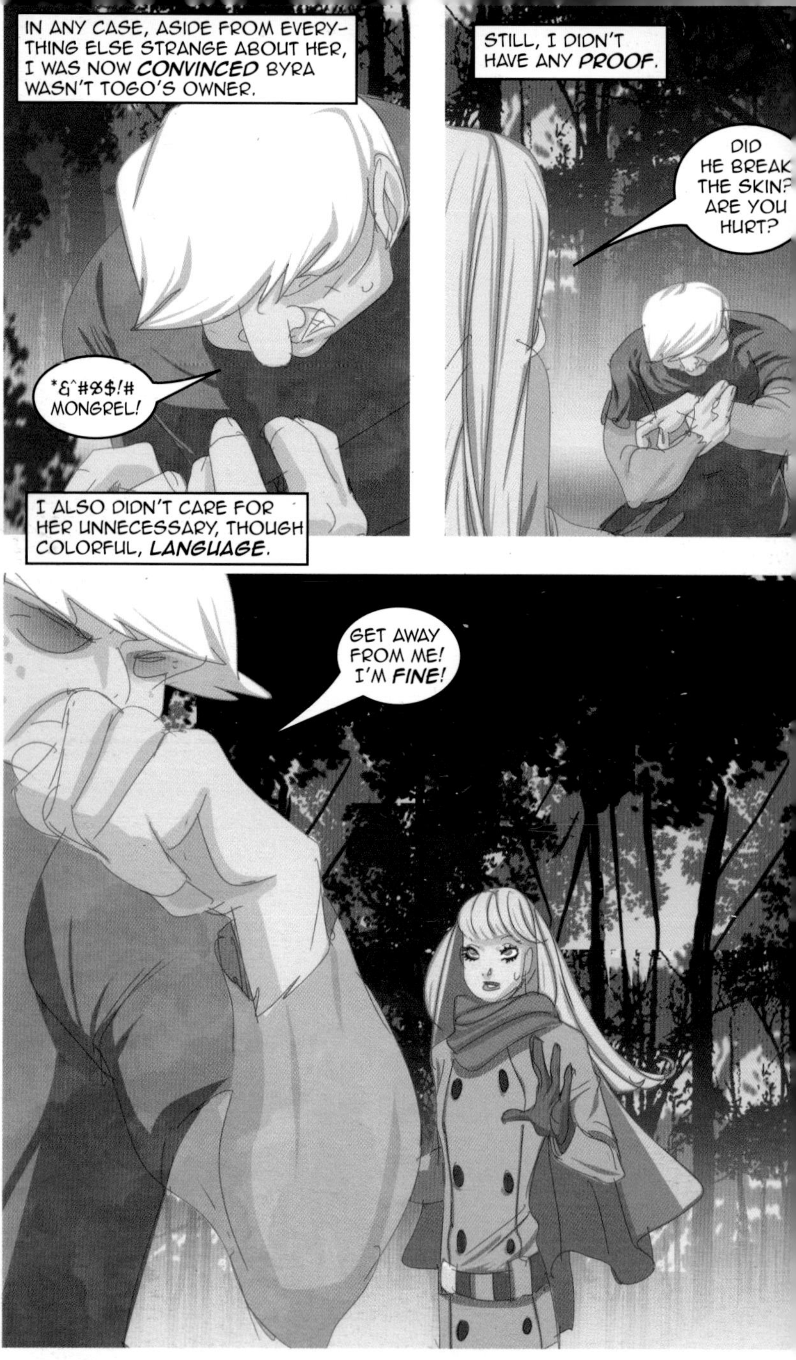
IN ANY CASE, ASIDE FROM EVERYTHING ELSE STRANGE ABOUT HER, I WAS NOW CONVINCED BYRA WASN'T TOGO'S OWNER.
*&^#%$!# MONGREL!
I ALSO DIDN'T CARE FOR HER UNNECESSARY, THOUGH COLORFUL, LANGUAGE.
STILL, I DIDN'T HAVE ANY PROOF.
DID HE BREAK THE SKIN? ARE YOU HURT?
GET AWAY FROM ME! I'M FINE!

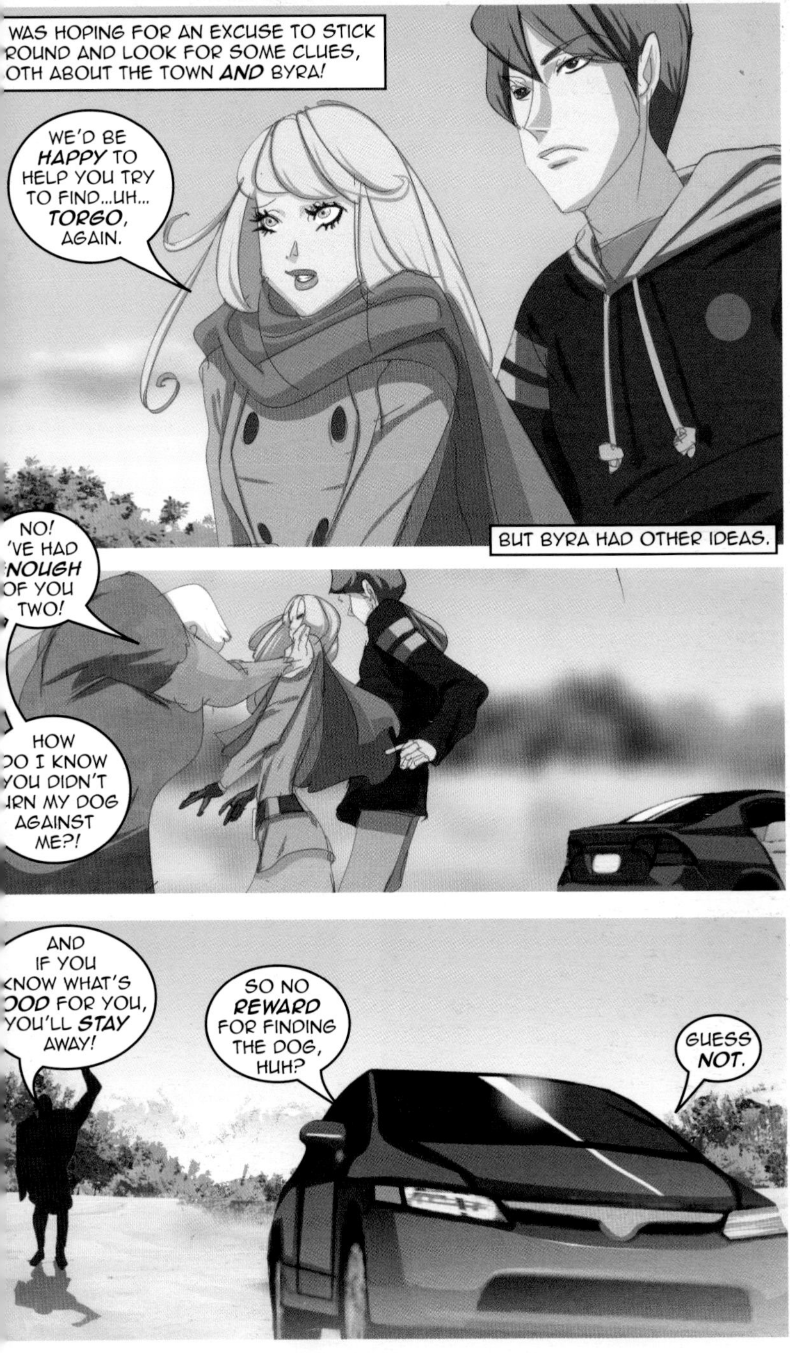
WAS HOPING FOR AN EXCUSE TO STICK
ROUND AND LOOK FOR SOME CLUES,
OTH ABOUT THE TOWN AND BYRA!
WE'D BE HAPPY TO HELP YOU TRY TO FIND...UH... TORGO, AGAIN.
BUT BYRA HAD OTHER IDEAS.
NO! 'VE HAD NOUGH OF YOU TWO!
HOW DO I KNOW YOU DIDN'T RN MY DOG AGAINST ME?!
AND IF YOU NOW WHAT'S OOD FOR YOU, YOU'LL STAY AWAY!
SO NO REWARD FOR FINDING THE DOG, HUH?
GUESS NOT.

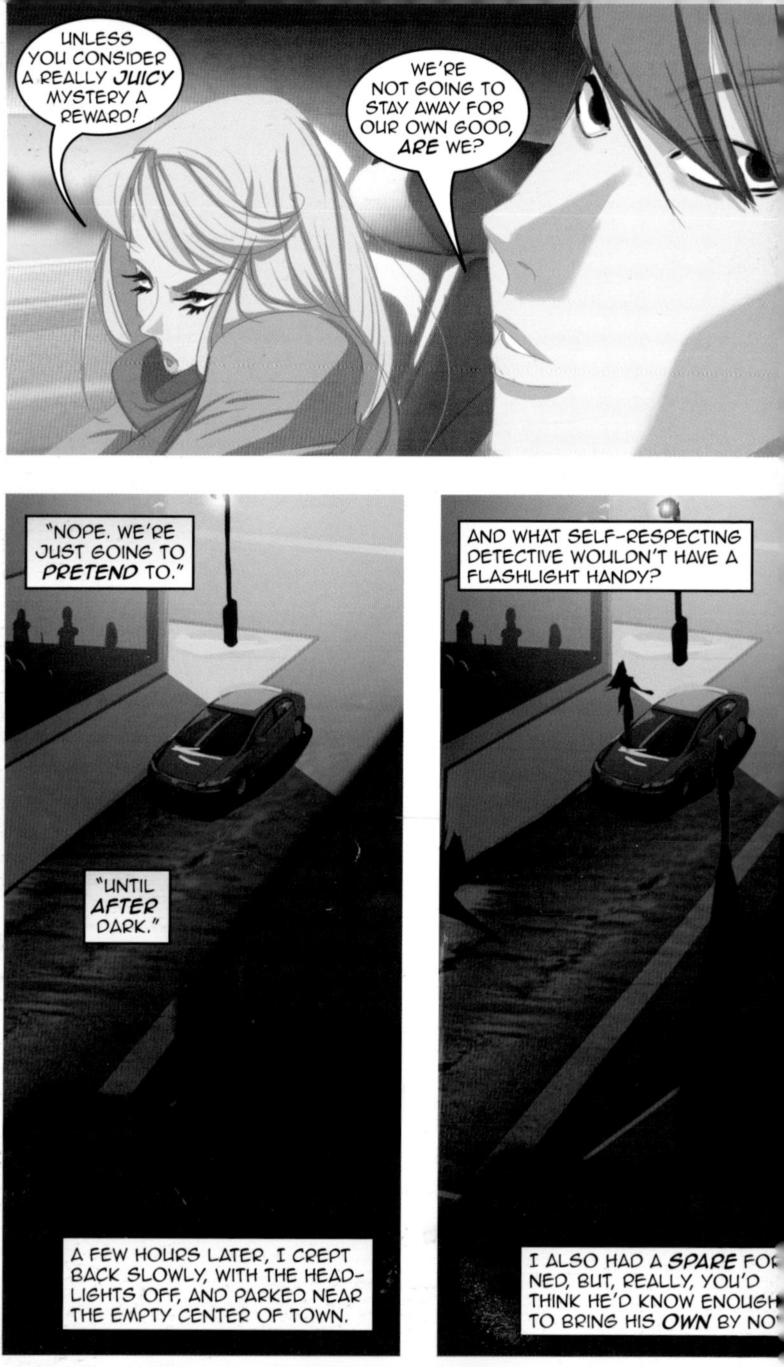
UNLESS YOU CONSIDER A REALLY *JUICY* MYSTERY A REWARD!
WE'RE NOT GOING TO STAY AWAY FOR OUR OWN GOOD, *ARE* WE?
"NOPE. WE'RE JUST GOING TO *PRETEND* TO."
"UNTIL *AFTER* DARK."
A FEW HOURS LATER, I CREPT BACK SLOWLY, WITH THE HEAD-LIGHTS OFF, AND PARKED NEAR THE EMPTY CENTER OF TOWN.
AND WHAT SELF-RESPECTING DETECTIVE WOULDN'T HAVE A FLASHLIGHT HANDY?
I ALSO HAD A *SPARE* FOR NED, BUT, REALLY, YOU'D THINK HE'D KNOW ENOUGH TO BRING HIS *OWN* BY NO

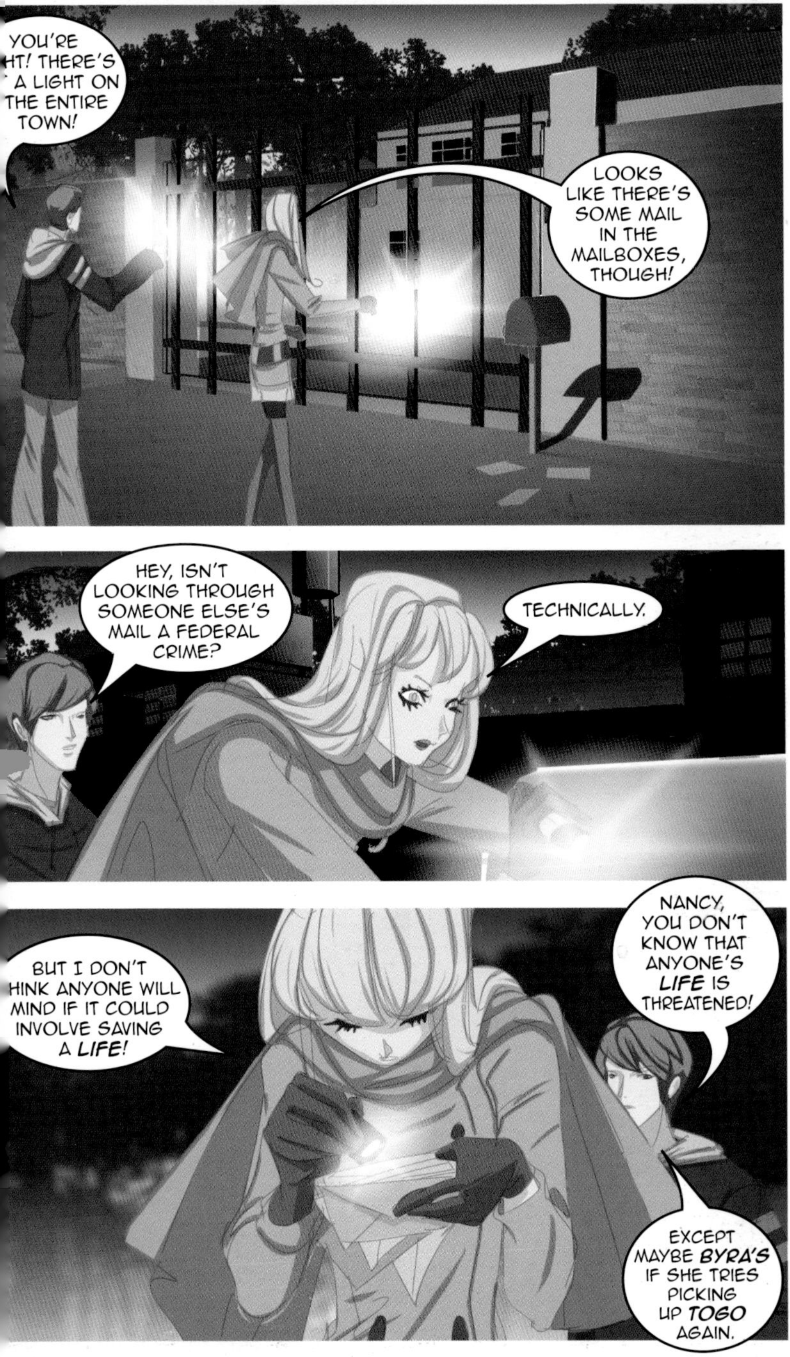
YOU'RE HT! THERE'S A LIGHT ON THE ENTIRE TOWN!
LOOKS LIKE THERE'S SOME MAIL IN THE MAILBOXES, THOUGH!
HEY, ISN'T LOOKING THROUGH SOMEONE ELSE'S MAIL A FEDERAL CRIME?
TECHNICALLY.
BUT I DON'T HINK ANYONE WILL MIND IF IT COULD INVOLVE SAVING A *LIFE*!
NANCY, YOU DON'T KNOW THAT ANYONE'S *LIFE* IS THREATENED!
EXCEPT MAYBE *BYRA'S* IF SHE TRIES PICKING UP *TOGO* AGAIN.

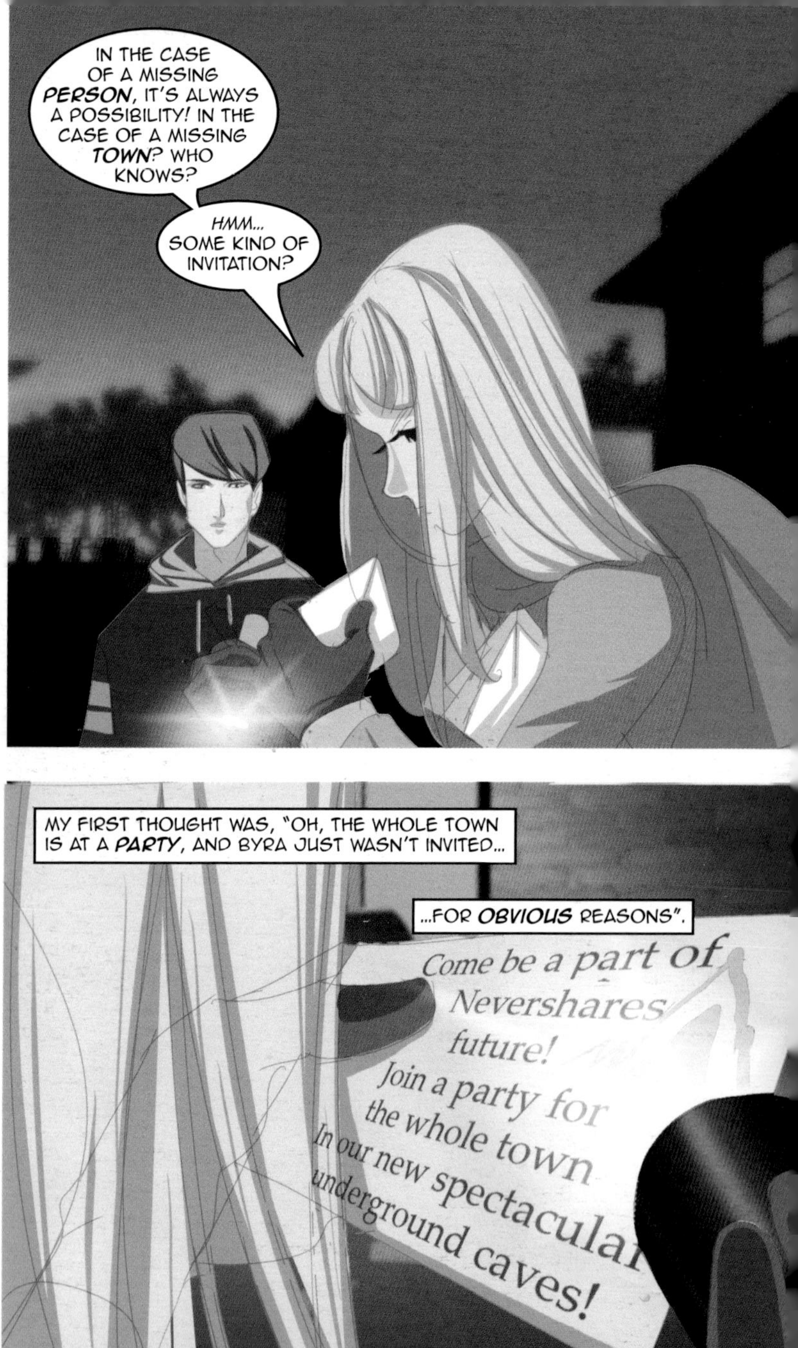

IN THE CASE OF A MISSING *PERSON*, IT'S ALWAYS A POSSIBILITY! IN THE CASE OF A MISSING *TOWN*? WHO KNOWS?
HMM... SOME KIND OF INVITATION?
MY FIRST THOUGHT WAS, "OH, THE WHOLE TOWN IS AT A *PARTY*, AND BYRA JUST WASN'T INVITED...
...FOR *OBVIOUS* REASONS".
Come be a part of Nevershares future!
Join a party for the whole town In our new spectacular underground caves!

BUT EVEN *MY* FIRST GUESSES AREN'T ALWAYS RIGHT.

AND SOON I HAD ANOTHER DISTRACTION.

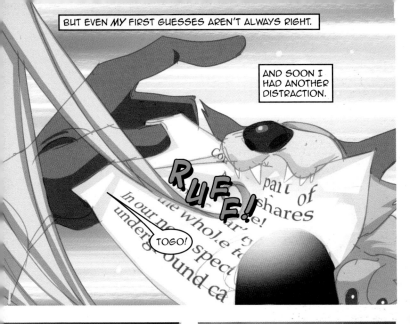

RUFF!

TOGO!

WHERE'S HE? WHERE'D HE GO?

QUIET DOWN! WE SHOULD BE ABLE TO HEAR HIS LITTLE FEET ON THE GRAVEL.

AND SURE ENOUGH, THERE HE WAS!

IF I DIDN'T KNOW BETTER, I'D SWEAR HE WAS TRYING TO LEAD US SOMEWHERE!

AND, IN POINT OF FACT, I *DIDN'T* KNOW BETTER!

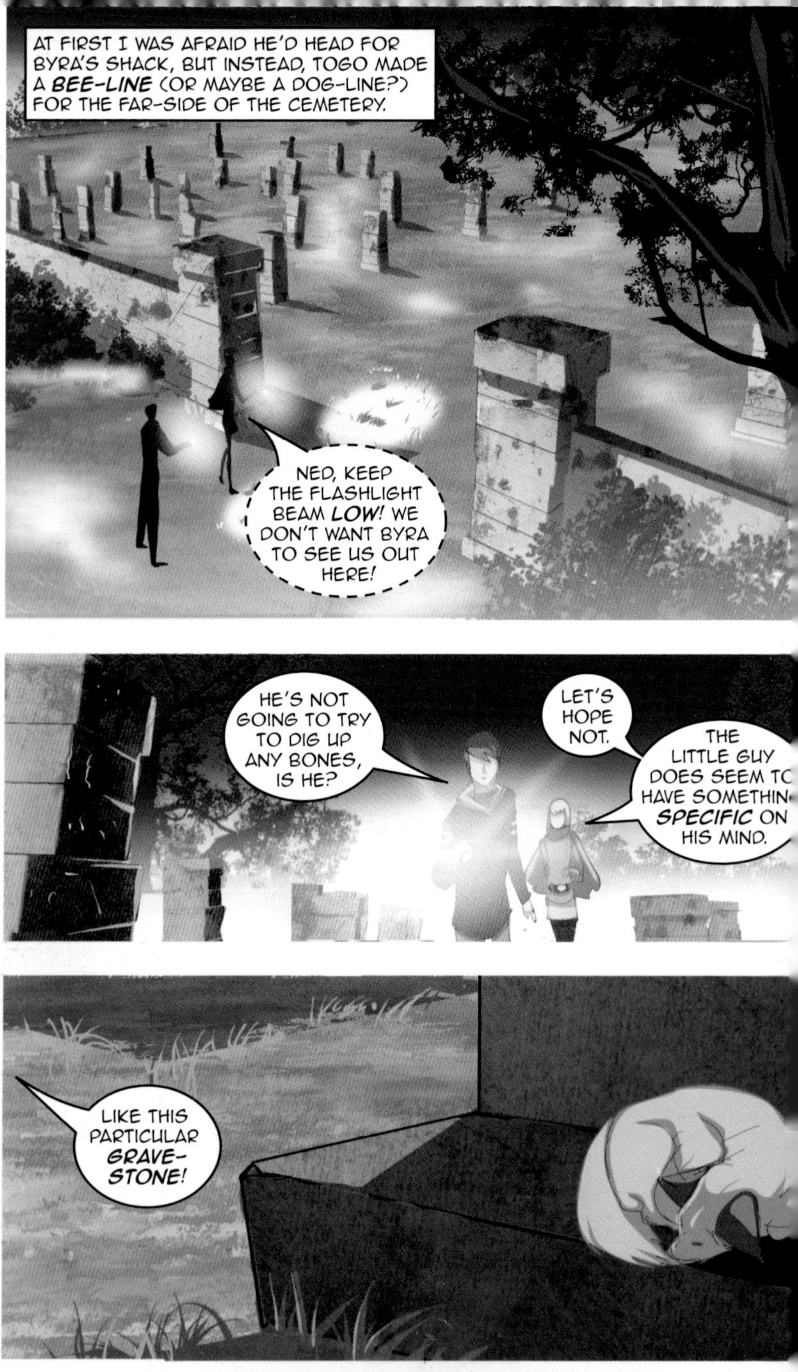
AT FIRST I WAS AFRAID HE'D HEAD FOR BYRA'S SHACK, BUT INSTEAD, TOGO MADE A **BEE-LINE** (OR MAYBE A DOG-LINE?) FOR THE FAR-SIDE OF THE CEMETERY.
NED, KEEP THE FLASHLIGHT BEAM **LOW**! WE DON'T WANT BYRA TO SEE US OUT HERE!
HE'S NOT GOING TO TRY TO DIG UP ANY BONES, IS HE?
LET'S HOPE NOT.
THE LITTLE GUY DOES SEEM TO HAVE SOMETHING **SPECIFIC** ON HIS MIND.
LIKE THIS PARTICULAR **GRAVE-STONE**!

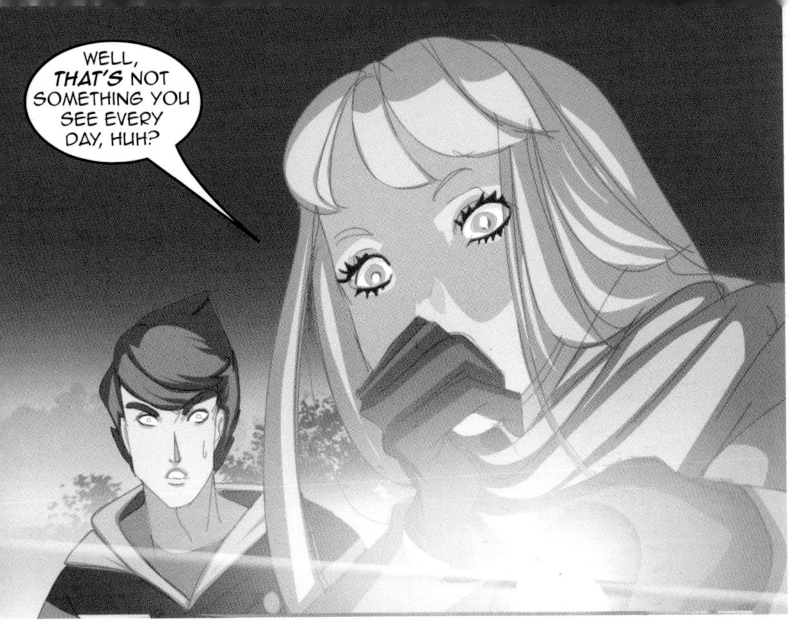
WELL, THAT'S NOT SOMETHING YOU SEE EVERY DAY, HUH?

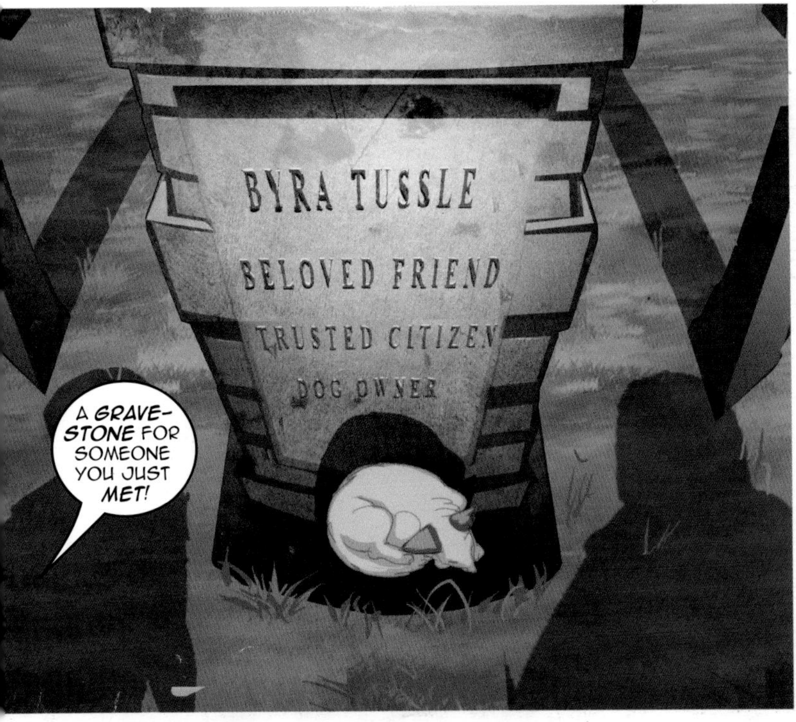
BYRA TUSSLE
BELOVED FRIEND
TRUSTED CITIZEN
DOG OWNER
A GRAVE-STONE FOR SOMEONE YOU JUST MET!

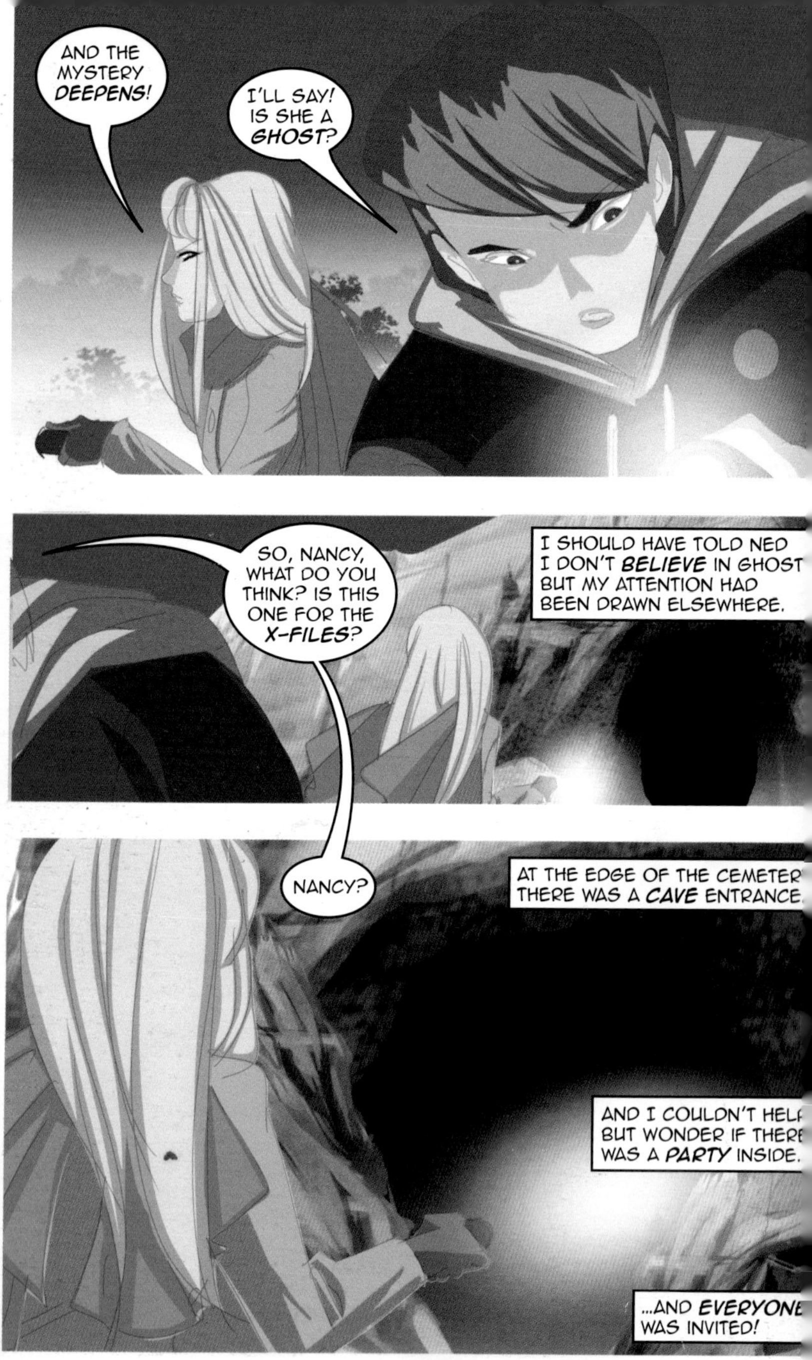
AND THE MYSTERY *DEEPENS!*
I'LL SAY! IS SHE A *GHOST?*
SO, NANCY, WHAT DO YOU THINK? IS THIS ONE FOR THE *X-FILES?*
I SHOULD HAVE TOLD NED I DON'T *BELIEVE* IN GHOST BUT MY ATTENTION HAD BEEN DRAWN ELSEWHERE.
NANCY?
AT THE EDGE OF THE CEMETER THERE WAS A *CAVE* ENTRANCE.
AND I COULDN'T HEL BUT WONDER IF THER WAS A *PARTY* INSIDE.
...AND *EVERYONE* WAS INVITED!

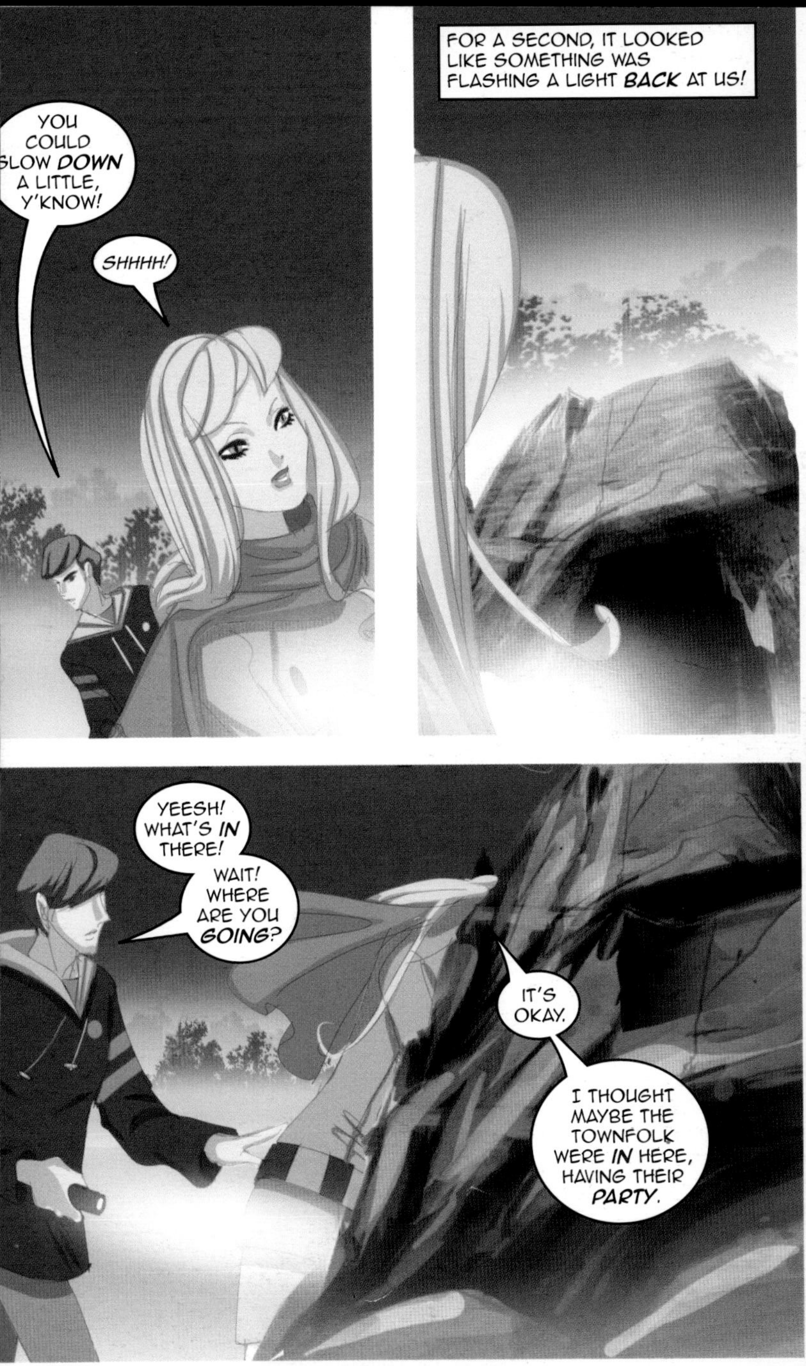
YOU COULD SLOW DOWN A LITTLE, Y'KNOW!
SHHHH!
FOR A SECOND, IT LOOKED LIKE SOMETHING WAS FLASHING A LIGHT BACK AT US!
YEESH! WHAT'S IN THERE!
WAIT! WHERE ARE YOU GOING?
IT'S OKAY.
I THOUGHT MAYBE THE TOWNFOLK WERE IN HERE, HAVING THEIR PARTY.

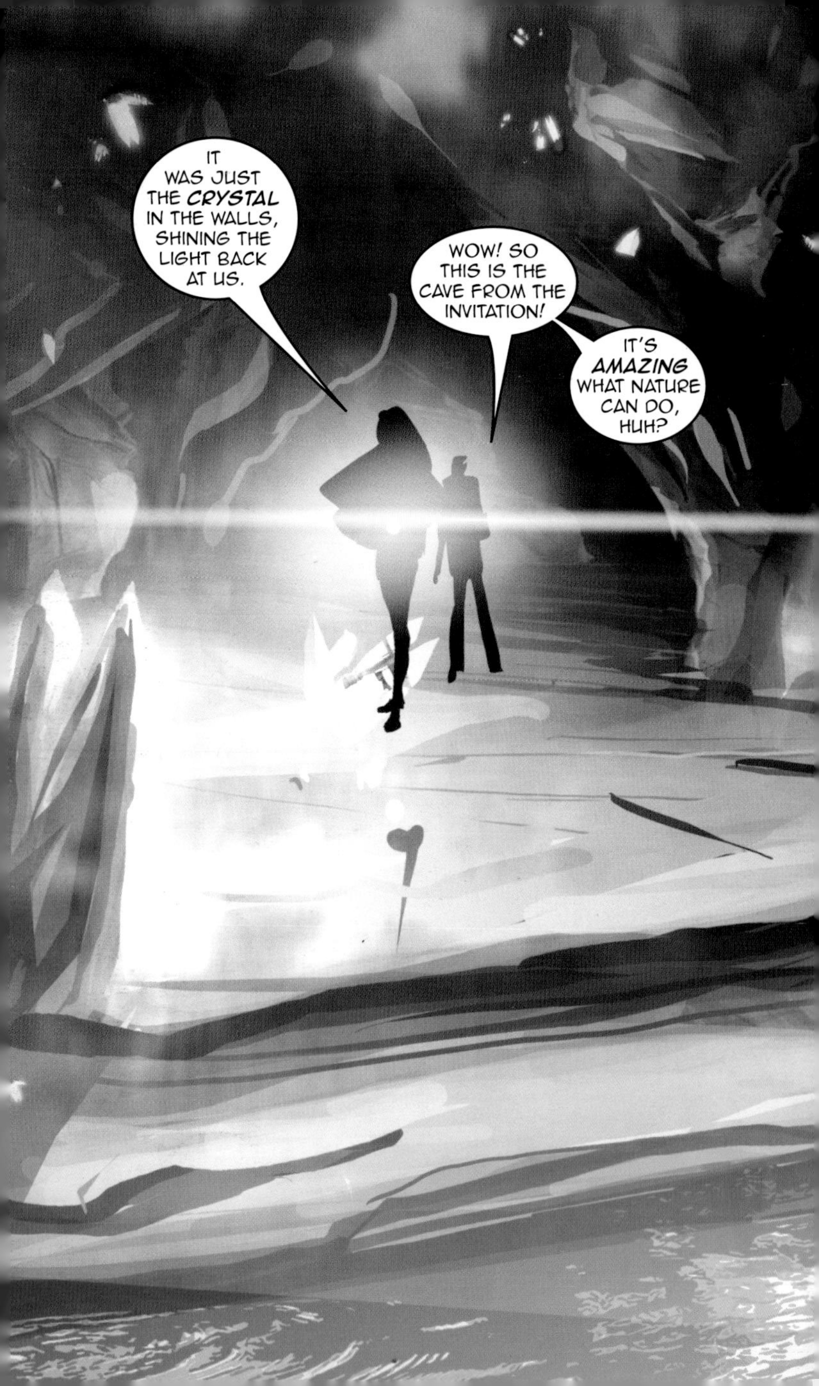
IT WAS JUST THE CRYSTAL IN THE WALLS, SHINING THE LIGHT BACK AT US.
WOW! SO THIS IS THE CAVE FROM THE INVITATION!
IT'S AMAZING WHAT NATURE CAN DO, HUH?

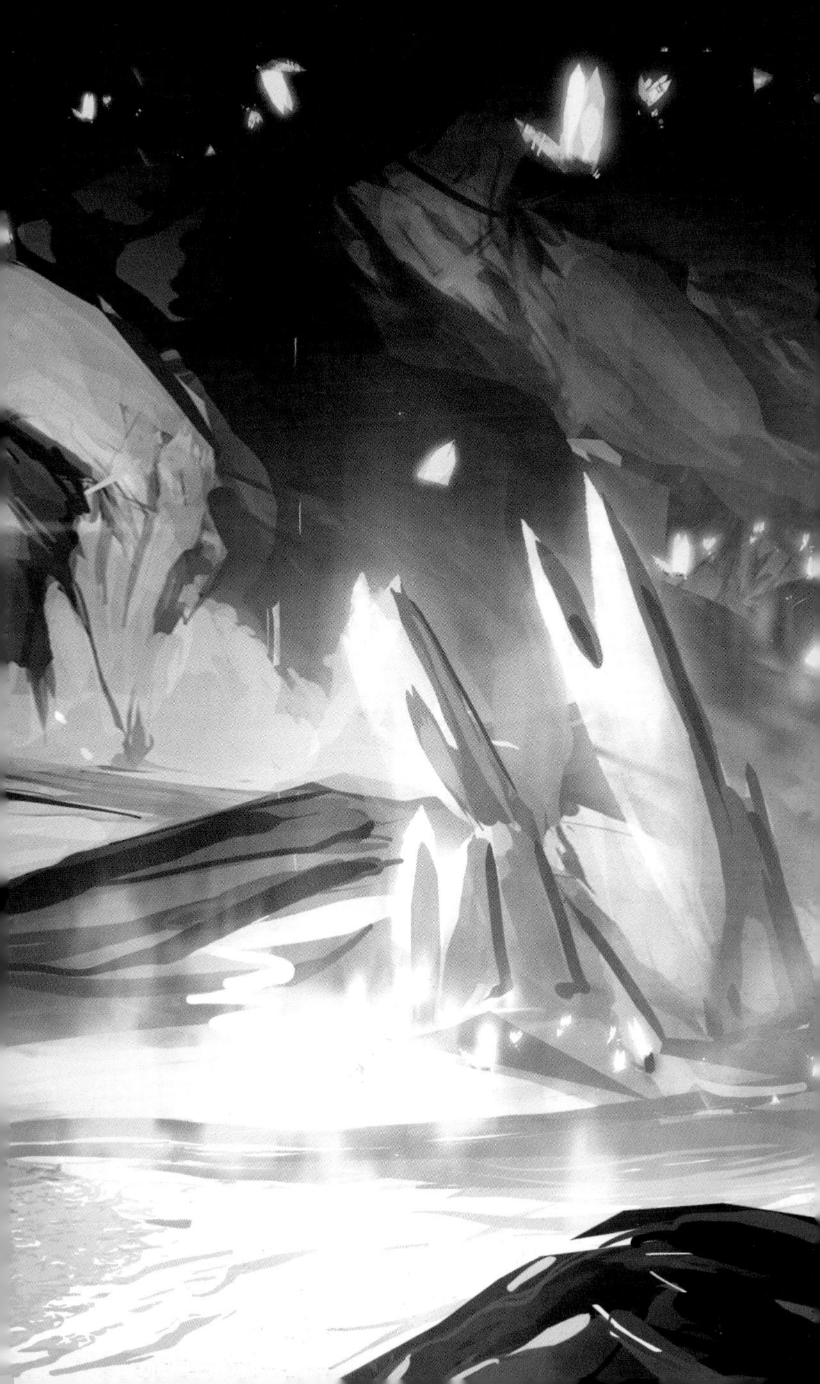

I WAS THINKING THE SAME THING, ONLY THERE WAS SOMETHING ABOUT THE CAVE THAT WAS ALMOST TOO *GOOD* TO BE TRUE!

AND THEN I NOTICED TOGO DIGGING AT THE BASE OF ONE OF THE BIGGER, MORE COLORFUL CAVE FEATURES.

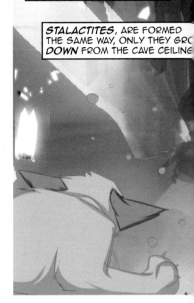

STALAGMITES RISE *UP* FROM A CAVE FLOOR, FORMED BY DRIPPING WATER, FILLED WITH MINERALS, FROM THE CEILING.

STALACTITES, ARE FORMED THE SAME WAY, ONLY THEY GRO *DOWN* FROM THE CAVE CEILING

WHATEVER TOGO WAS DIGGING AT WENT FROM THE FLOOR ALL THE WAY UP TO THE CEILING, KIND OF LIKE A *SUPPORT BEAM*.

NOW, STALACTITES AND STALAGMITES OFTEN MEET AND FORM ONE "ITE" THING, BUT THAT TAKES HUNDREDS OF THOUSANDS OF YEARS.

BESIDES, I DIDN'T THINK THE MINERALS WOULD FLAKE OFF WHITE LIKE THIS.

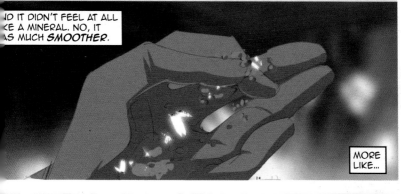

AND IT DIDN'T FEEL AT ALL LIKE A MINERAL. NO, IT WAS MUCH *SMOOTHER*.

MORE LIKE...

PLASTIC?

NED, THIS IS *PLASTIC!*

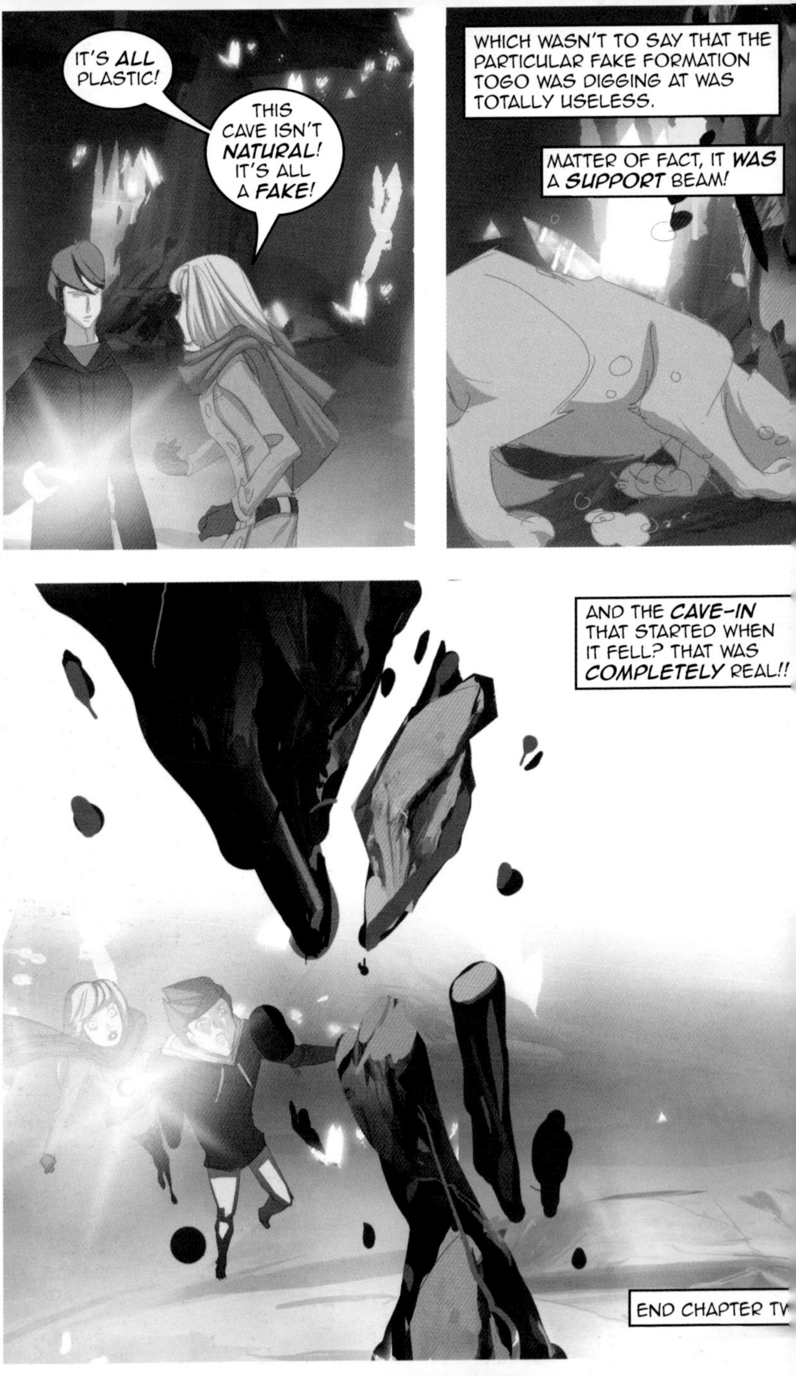
IT'S **ALL** PLASTIC!
THIS CAVE ISN'T **NATURAL!** IT'S ALL A **FAKE!**
WHICH WASN'T TO SAY THAT THE PARTICULAR FAKE FORMATION TOGO WAS DIGGING AT WAS TOTALLY USELESS.
MATTER OF FACT, IT ***WAS*** A ***SUPPORT*** BEAM!
AND THE ***CAVE-IN*** THAT STARTED WHEN IT FELL? THAT WAS ***COMPLETELY*** REAL!!
END CHAPTER TV

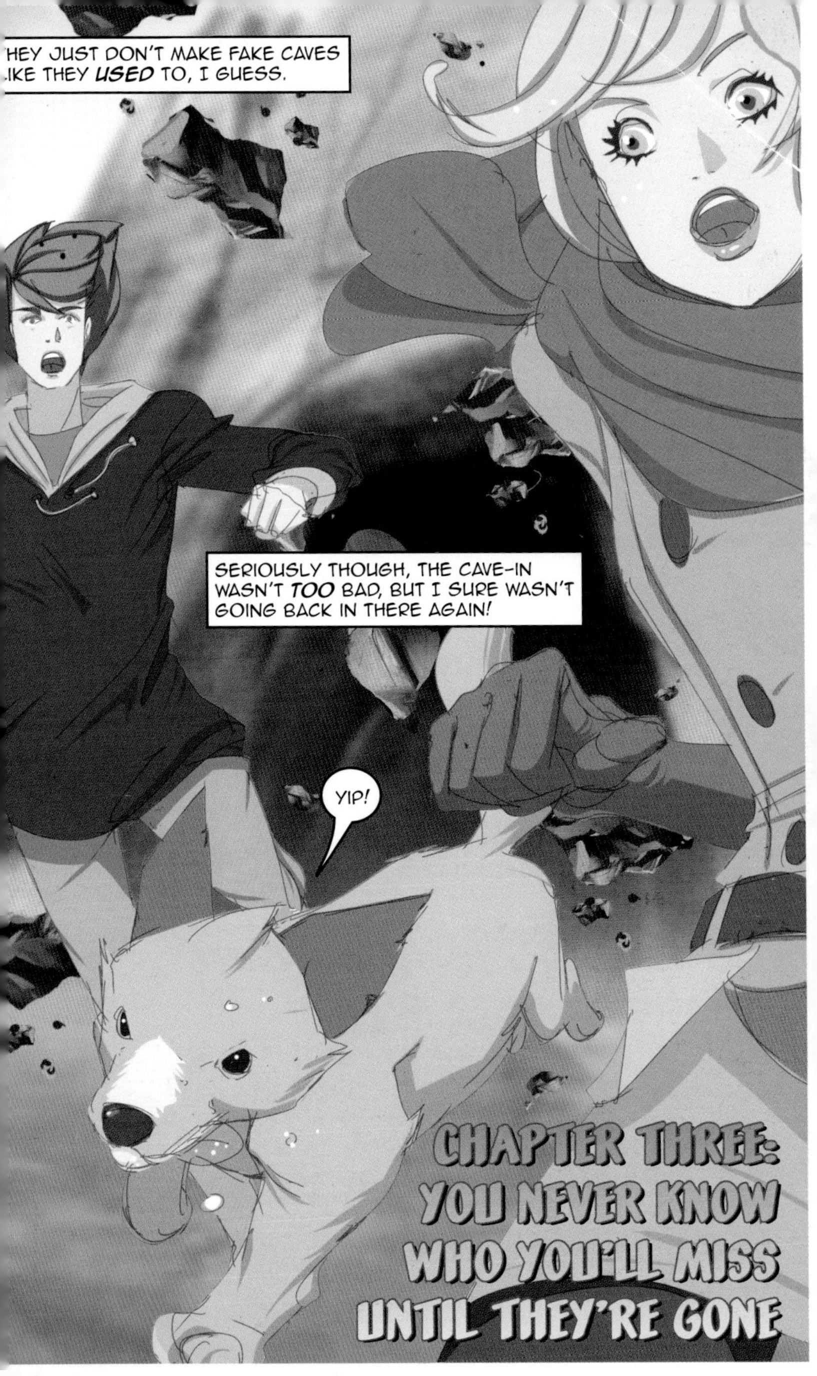
HEY JUST DON'T MAKE FAKE CAVES
IKE THEY USED TO, I GUESS.
SERIOUSLY THOUGH, THE CAVE-IN WASN'T TOO BAD, BUT I SURE WASN'T GOING BACK IN THERE AGAIN!
YIP!
CHAPTER THREE: YOU NEVER KNOW WHO YOU'LL MISS UNTIL THEY'RE GONE

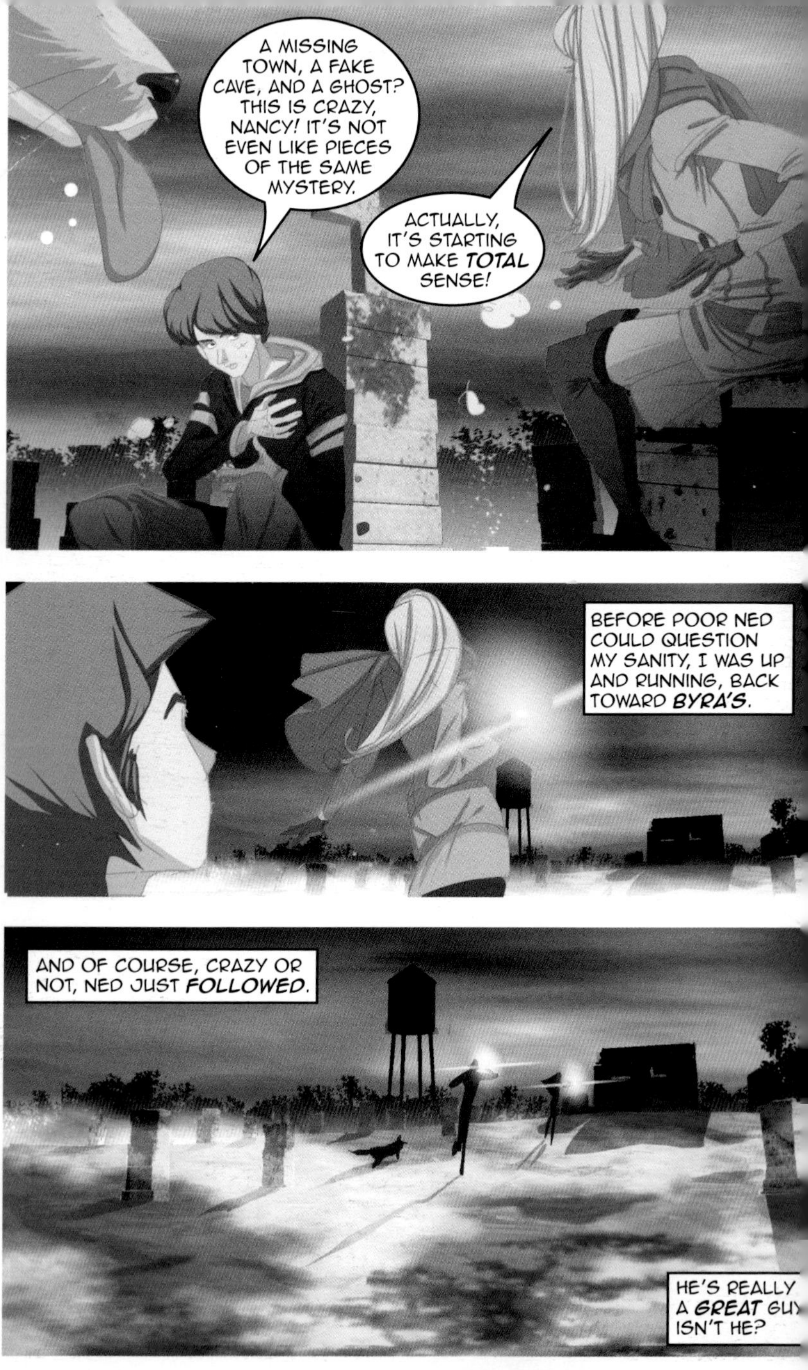
A MISSING TOWN, A FAKE CAVE, AND A GHOST? THIS IS CRAZY, NANCY! IT'S NOT EVEN LIKE PIECES OF THE SAME MYSTERY.
ACTUALLY, IT'S STARTING TO MAKE TOTAL SENSE!
BEFORE POOR NED COULD QUESTION MY SANITY, I WAS UP AND RUNNING, BACK TOWARD BYRA'S.
AND OF COURSE, CRAZY OR NOT, NED JUST FOLLOWED.
HE'S REALLY A GREAT GU
ISN'T HE?

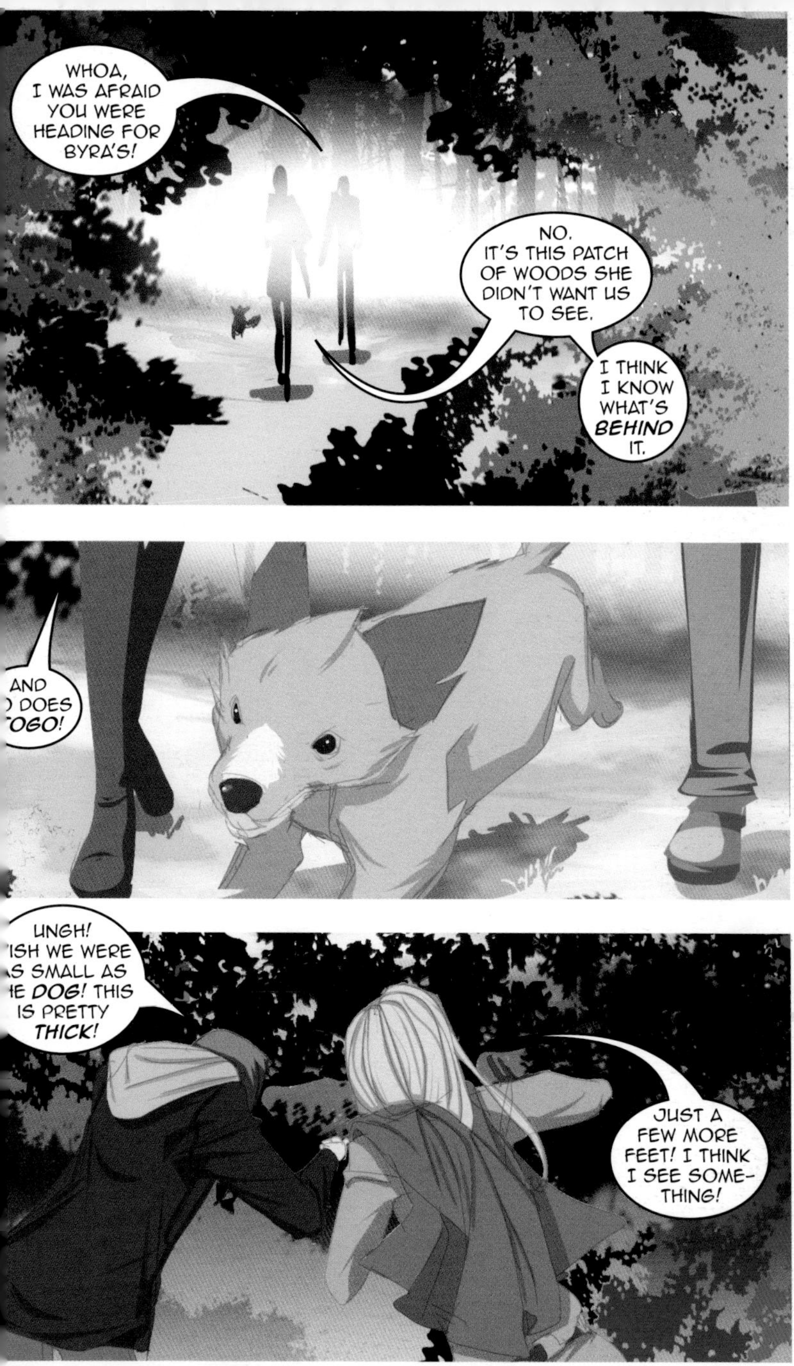
WHOA, I WAS AFRAID YOU WERE HEADING FOR BYRA'S!
NO. IT'S THIS PATCH OF WOODS SHE DIDN'T WANT US TO SEE.
I THINK I KNOW WHAT'S ***BEHIND*** IT.
AND DOES OGO!
UNGH! ISH WE WERE S SMALL AS E ***DOG!*** THIS IS PRETTY ***THICK!***
JUST A FEW MORE FEET! I THINK I SEE SOME-THING!

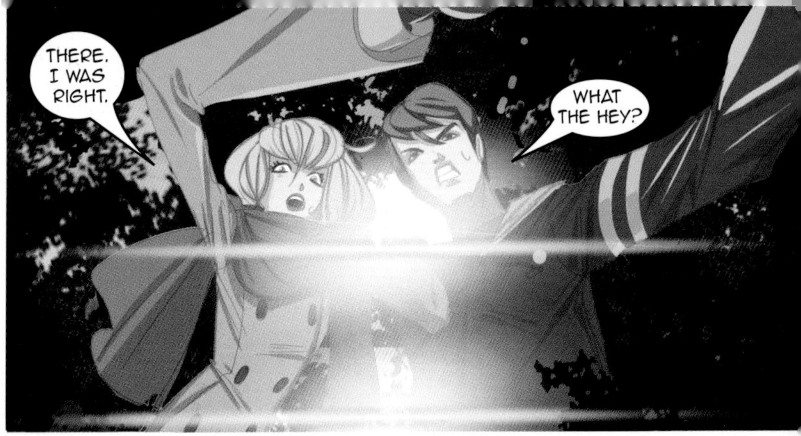
THERE. I WAS RIGHT.
WHAT THE HEY?

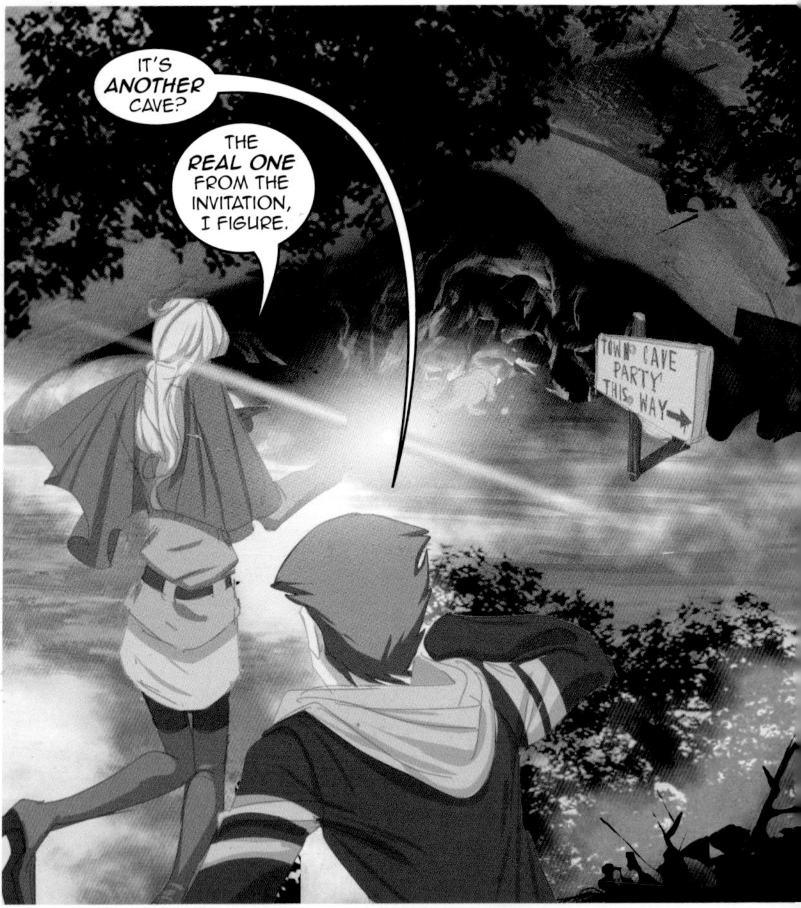
IT'S ANOTHER CAVE?
THE REAL ONE FROM THE INVITATION, I FIGURE.
TOWN CAVE PARTY THIS WAY

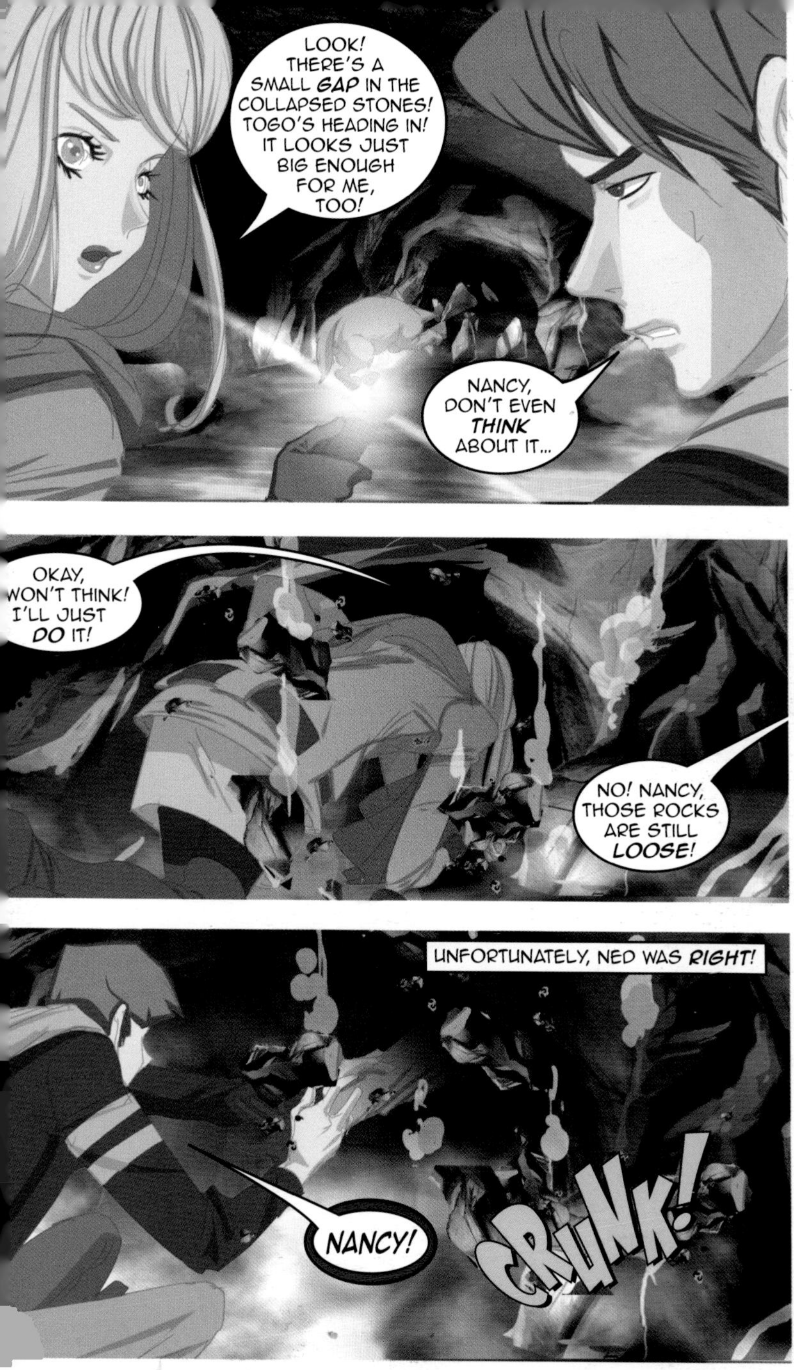
LOOK! THERE'S A SMALL GAP IN THE COLLAPSED STONES! TOGO'S HEADING IN! IT LOOKS JUST BIG ENOUGH FOR ME, TOO!
NANCY, DON'T EVEN THINK ABOUT IT...
OKAY, WON'T THINK! I'LL JUST DO IT!
NO! NANCY, THOSE ROCKS ARE STILL LOOSE!
UNFORTUNATELY, NED WAS RIGHT!
NANCY!
CRUNK!

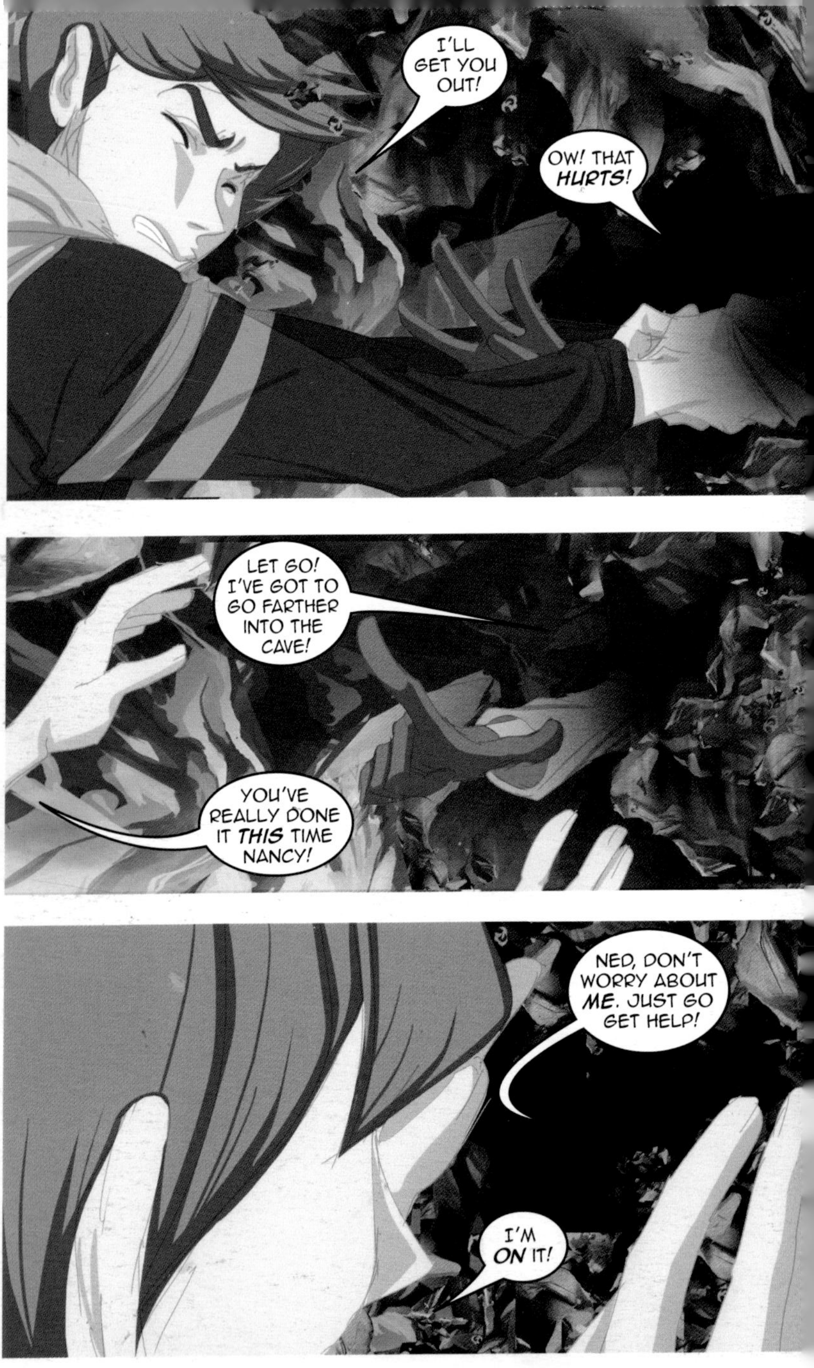
I'LL GET YOU OUT!
OW! THAT HURTS!
LET GO! I'VE GOT TO GO FARTHER INTO THE CAVE!
YOU'VE REALLY DONE IT THIS TIME NANCY!
NED, DON'T WORRY ABOUT ME. JUST GO GET HELP!
I'M ON IT!

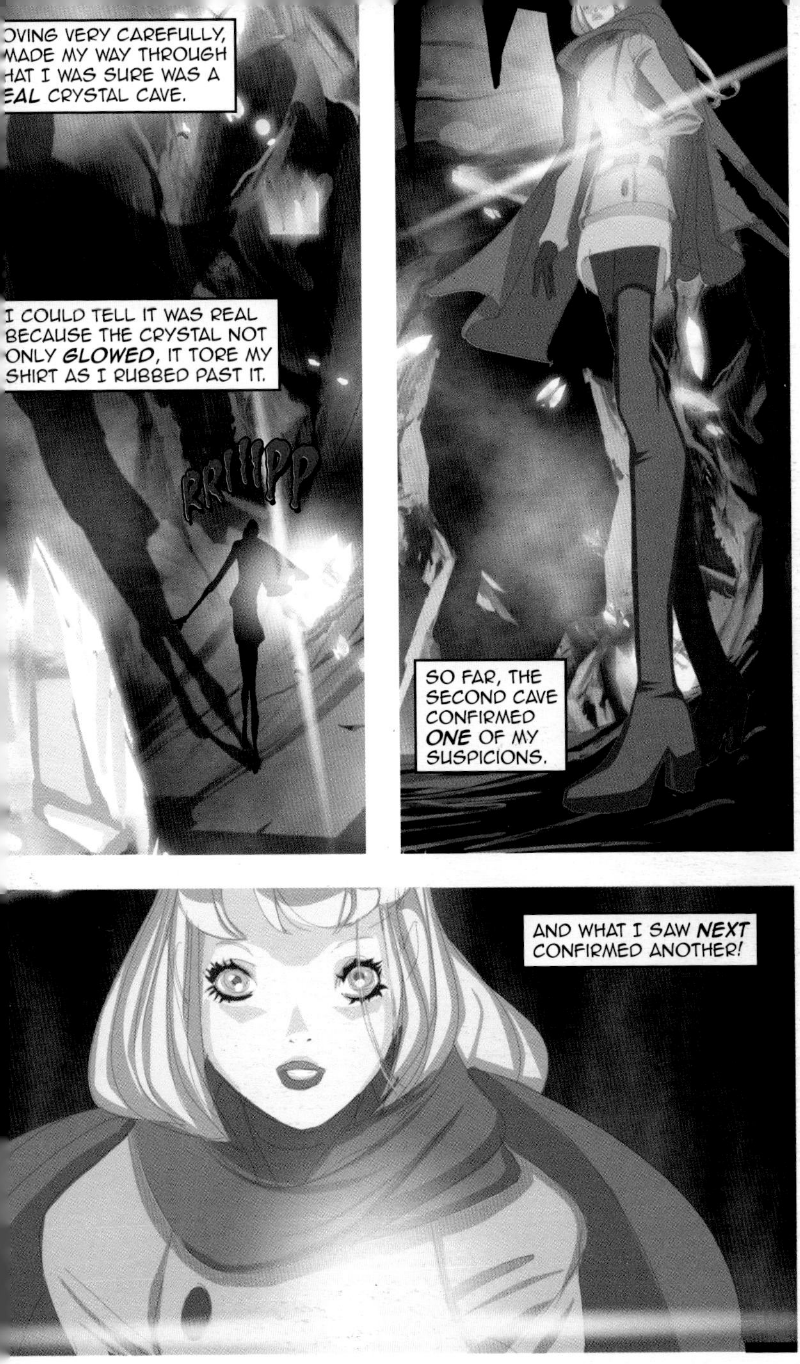
OVING VERY CAREFULLY, MADE MY WAY THROUGH HAT I WAS SURE WAS A EAL CRYSTAL CAVE.
I COULD TELL IT WAS REAL BECAUSE THE CRYSTAL NOT ONLY GLOWED, IT TORE MY SHIRT AS I RUBBED PAST IT.
RRIIIPP
SO FAR, THE SECOND CAVE CONFIRMED ONE OF MY SUSPICIONS.
AND WHAT I SAW NEXT CONFIRMED ANOTHER!

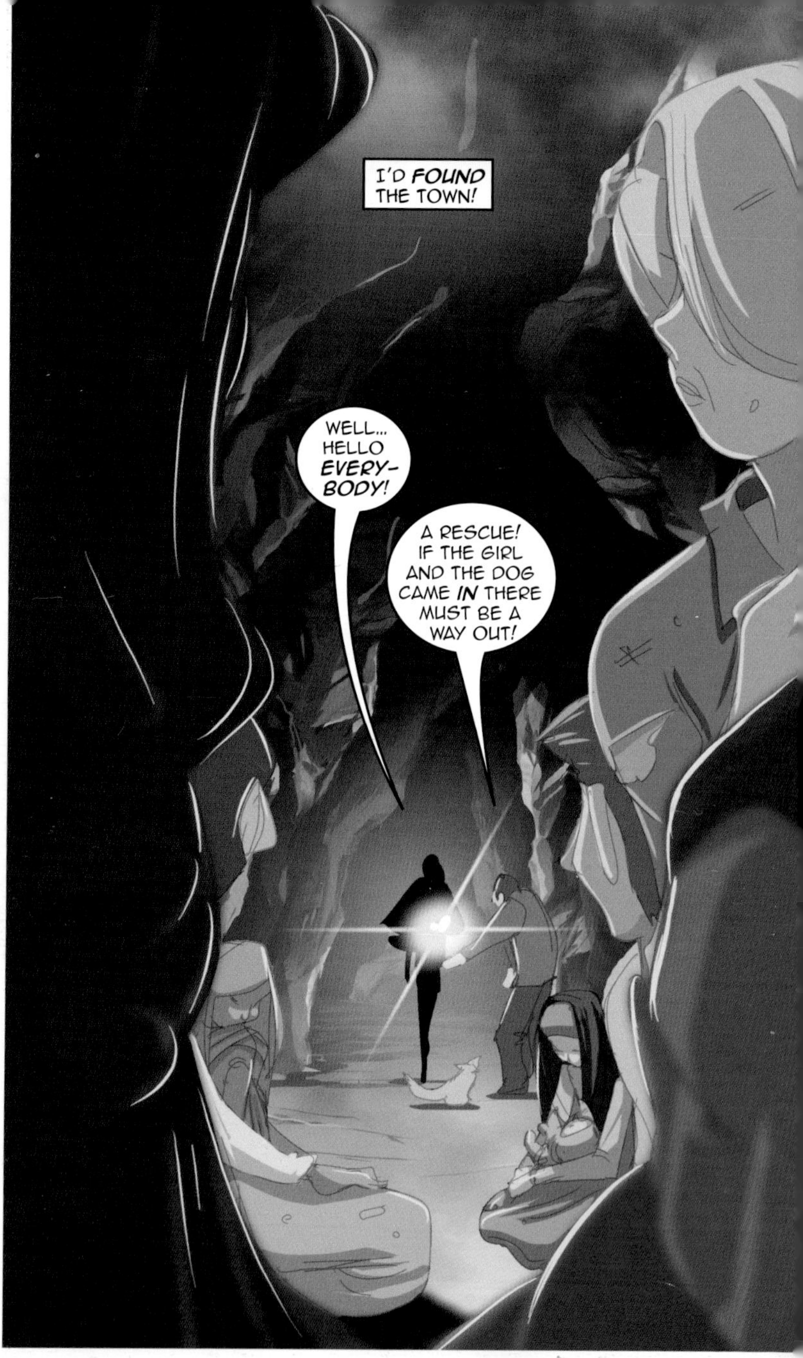
I'D FOUND THE TOWN!
WELL... HELLO EVERY-BODY!
A RESCUE! IF THE GIRL AND THE DOG CAME IN THERE MUST BE A WAY OUT!

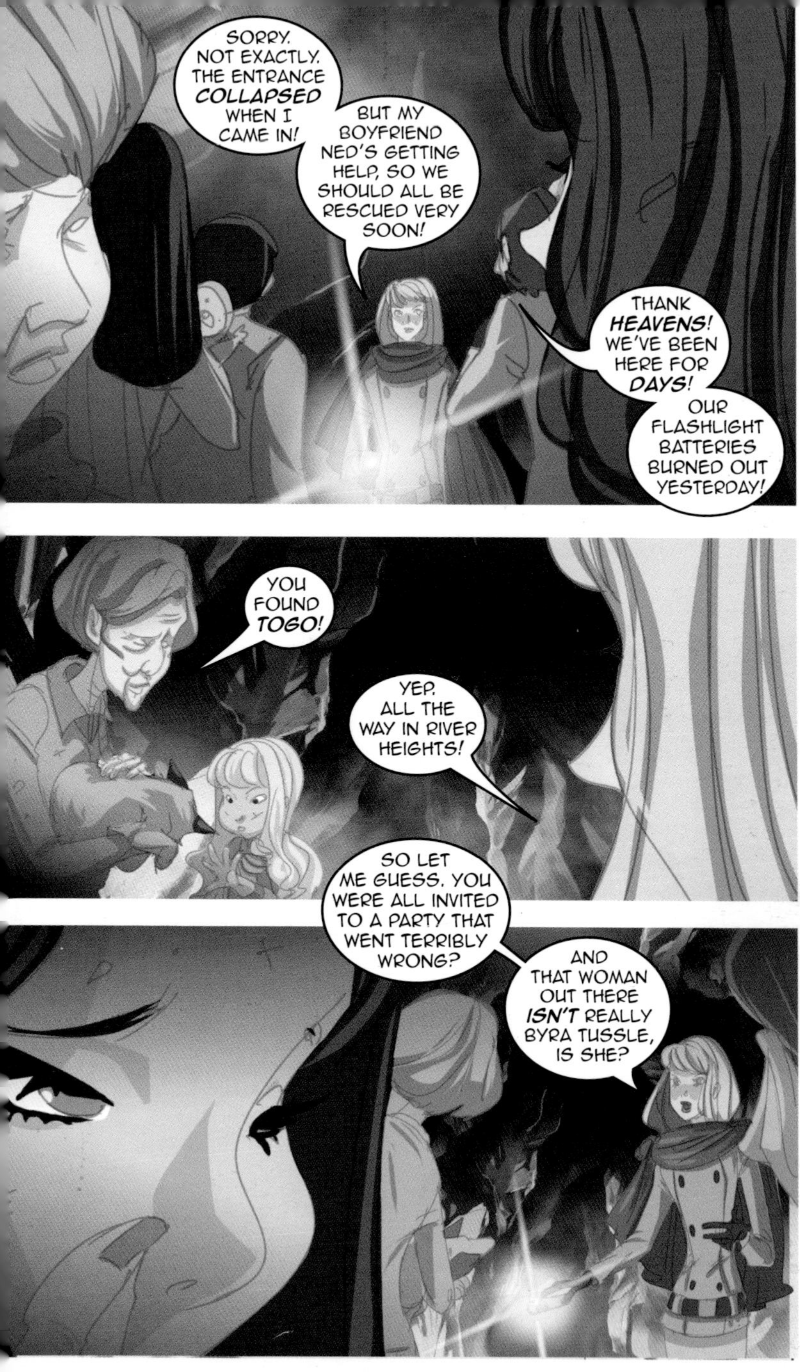
SORRY. NOT EXACTLY. THE ENTRANCE COLLAPSED WHEN I CAME IN!
BUT MY BOYFRIEND NED'S GETTING HELP, SO WE SHOULD ALL BE RESCUED VERY SOON!
THANK HEAVENS! WE'VE BEEN HERE FOR DAYS!
OUR FLASHLIGHT BATTERIES BURNED OUT YESTERDAY!
YOU FOUND TOGO!
YEP. ALL THE WAY IN RIVER HEIGHTS!
SO LET ME GUESS. YOU WERE ALL INVITED TO A PARTY THAT WENT TERRIBLY WRONG?
AND THAT WOMAN OUT THERE ISN'T REALLY BYRA TUSSLE, IS SHE?

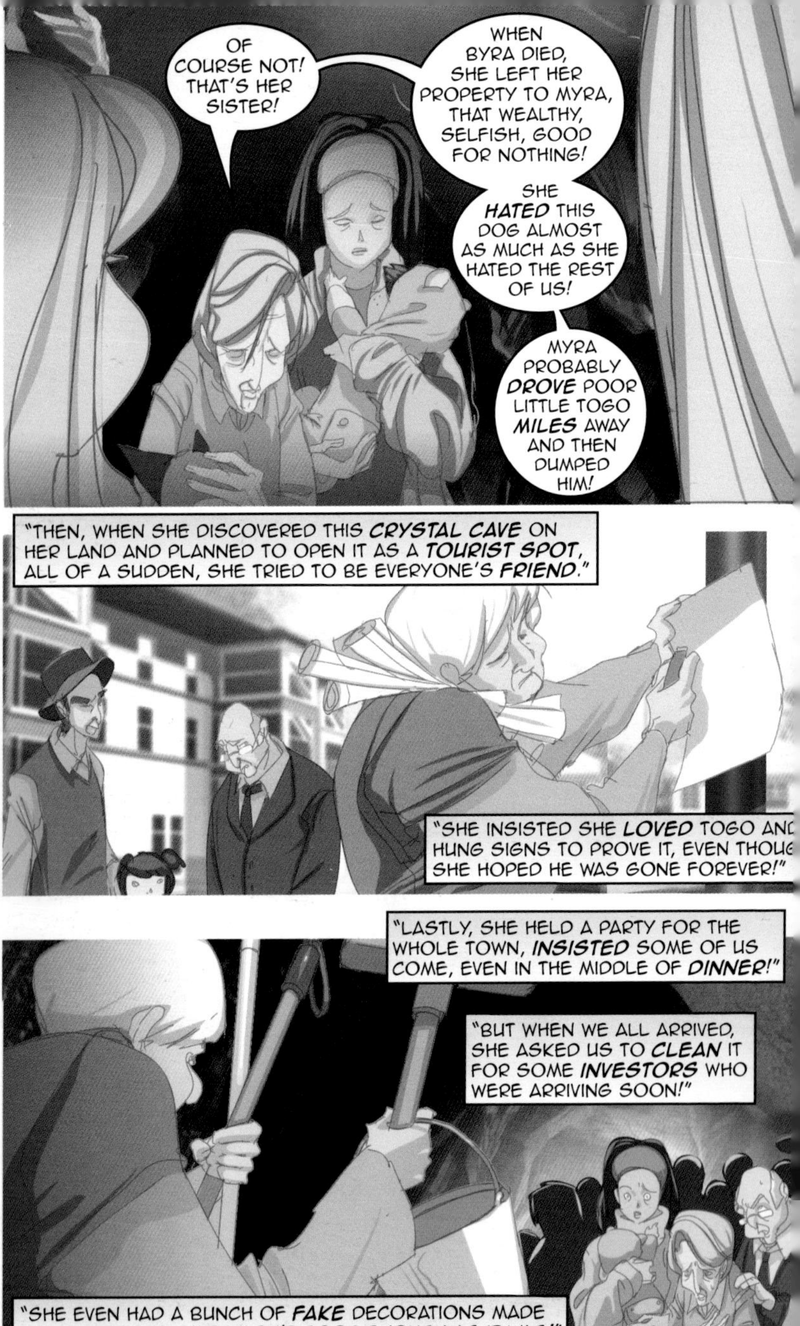

OF COURSE NOT! THAT'S HER SISTER!
WHEN BYRA DIED, SHE LEFT HER PROPERTY TO MYRA, THAT WEALTHY, SELFISH, GOOD FOR NOTHING!
SHE HATED THIS DOG ALMOST AS MUCH AS SHE HATED THE REST OF US!
MYRA PROBABLY DROVE POOR LITTLE TOGO MILES AWAY AND THEN DUMPED HIM!
"THEN, WHEN SHE DISCOVERED THIS CRYSTAL CAVE ON HER LAND AND PLANNED TO OPEN IT AS A TOURIST SPOT, ALL OF A SUDDEN, SHE TRIED TO BE EVERYONE'S FRIEND."
"SHE INSISTED SHE LOVED TOGO AND HUNG SIGNS TO PROVE IT, EVEN THOUG SHE HOPED HE WAS GONE FOREVER!"
"LASTLY, SHE HELD A PARTY FOR THE WHOLE TOWN, INSISTED SOME OF US COME, EVEN IN THE MIDDLE OF DINNER!"
"BUT WHEN WE ALL ARRIVED, SHE ASKED US TO CLEAN IT FOR SOME INVESTORS WHO WERE ARRIVING SOON!"
"SHE EVEN HAD A BUNCH OF FAKE DECORATIONS MADE UP, IN CASE THE CAVE WASN'T GOOD ENOUGH AS IT WAS!"

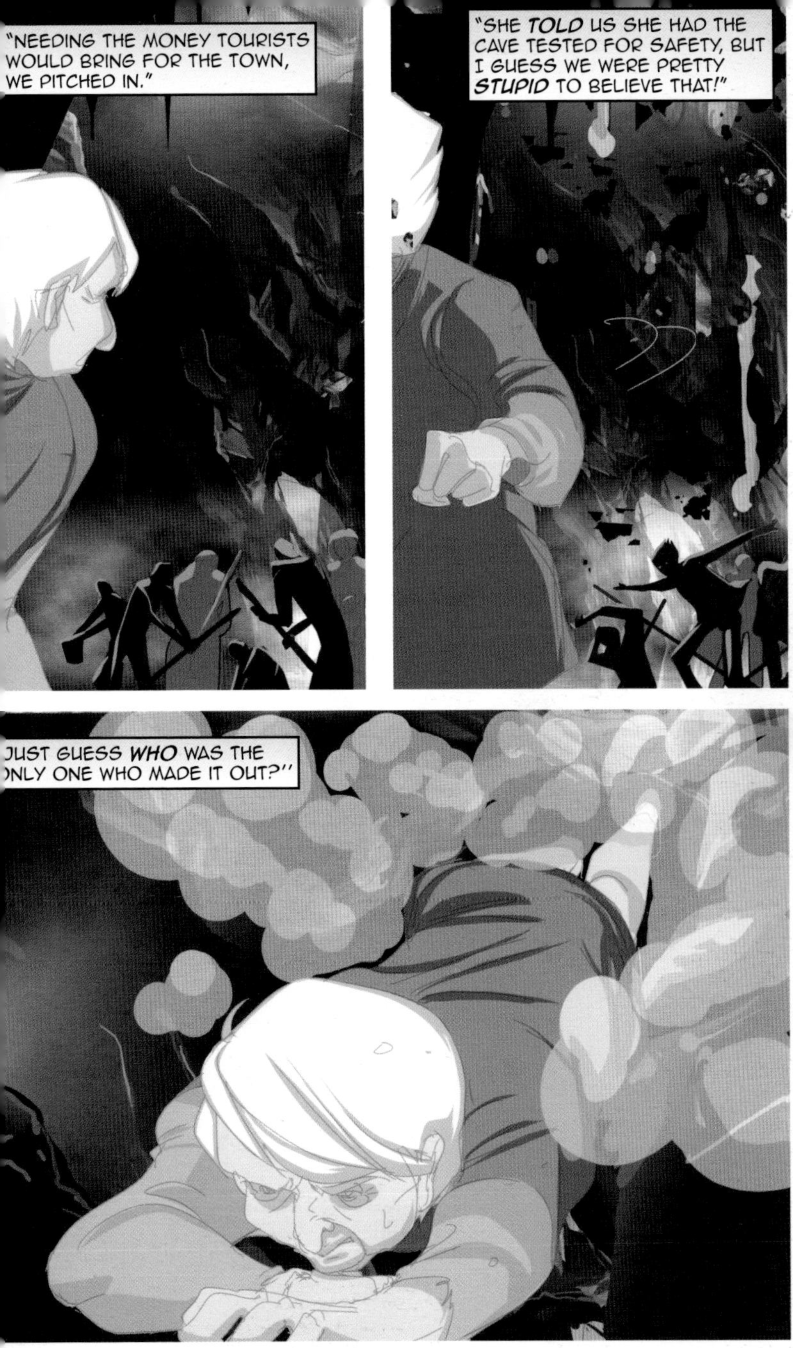
"NEEDING THE MONEY TOURISTS WOULD BRING FOR THE TOWN, WE PITCHED IN."
"SHE TOLD US SHE HAD THE CAVE TESTED FOR SAFETY, BUT I GUESS WE WERE PRETTY STUPID TO BELIEVE THAT!"
JUST GUESS WHO WAS THE ONLY ONE WHO MADE IT OUT?"

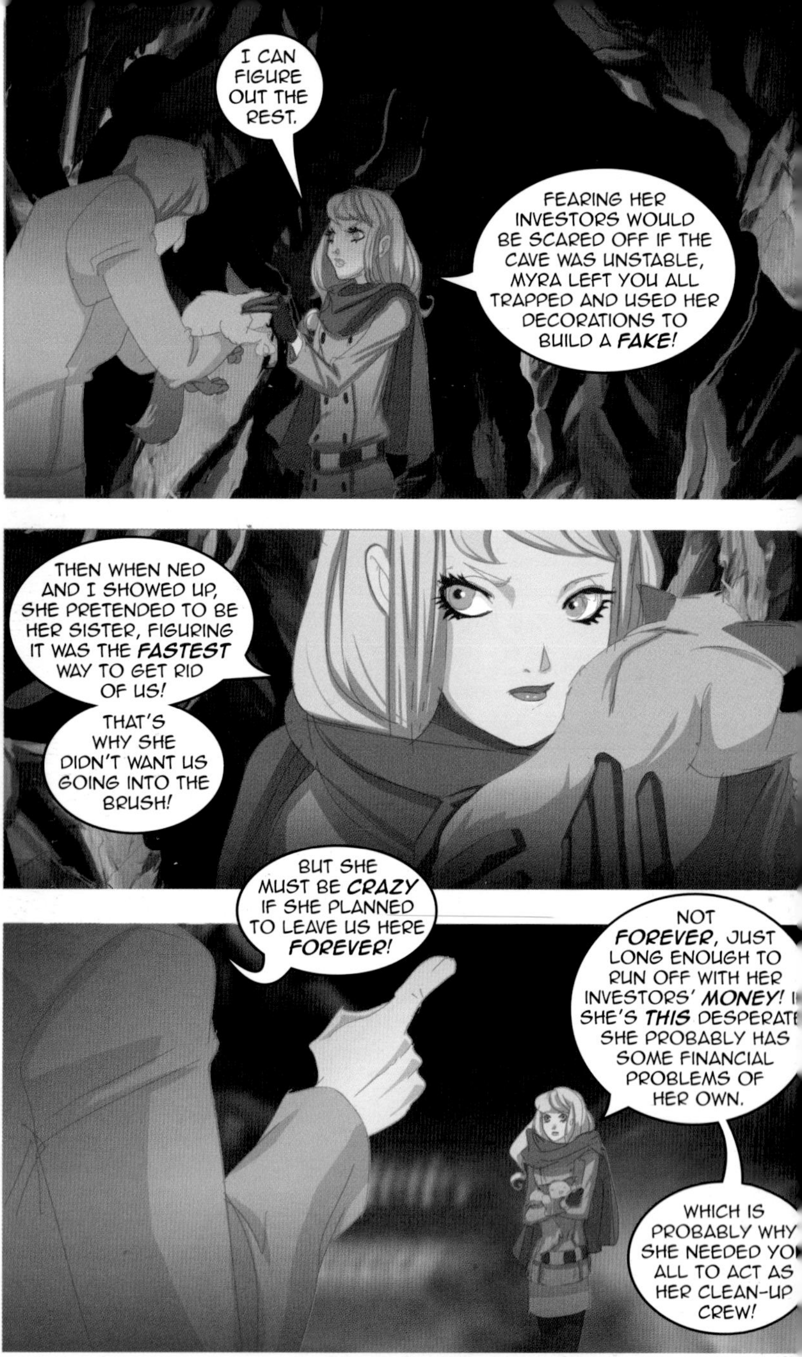
I CAN FIGURE OUT THE REST.
FEARING HER INVESTORS WOULD BE SCARED OFF IF THE CAVE WAS UNSTABLE, MYRA LEFT YOU ALL TRAPPED AND USED HER DECORATIONS TO BUILD A *FAKE*!
THEN WHEN NED AND I SHOWED UP, SHE PRETENDED TO BE HER SISTER, FIGURING IT WAS THE *FASTEST* WAY TO GET RID OF US!
THAT'S WHY SHE DIDN'T WANT US GOING INTO THE BRUSH!
BUT SHE MUST BE *CRAZY* IF SHE PLANNED TO LEAVE US HERE *FOREVER*!
NOT *FOREVER*, JUST LONG ENOUGH TO RUN OFF WITH HER INVESTORS' *MONEY*! I SHE'S *THIS* DESPERATE SHE PROBABLY HAS SOME FINANCIAL PROBLEMS OF HER OWN.
WHICH IS PROBABLY WHY SHE NEEDED YO ALL TO ACT AS HER CLEAN-UP CREW!

I HAVE TO WARN ED ABOUT MYRA-BYRA!

BUT THE CAVE WALLS ARE BLOCKING MY SIGNAL.

HMM? THAT'S NO CRYSTAL REFLECTION. IT'S MOON-LIGHT.

BUT WHERE'S IT COMING FROM?

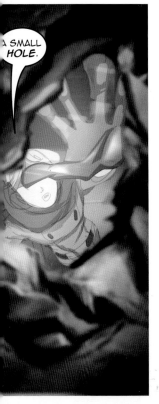

A SMALL HOLE.

NOT BIG ENOUGH FOR A PERSON.

THOUGH I BET IT LOOKED KIND OF CREEPY FROM THE OUTSIDE, LIKE TALES FROM THE CRYPT.

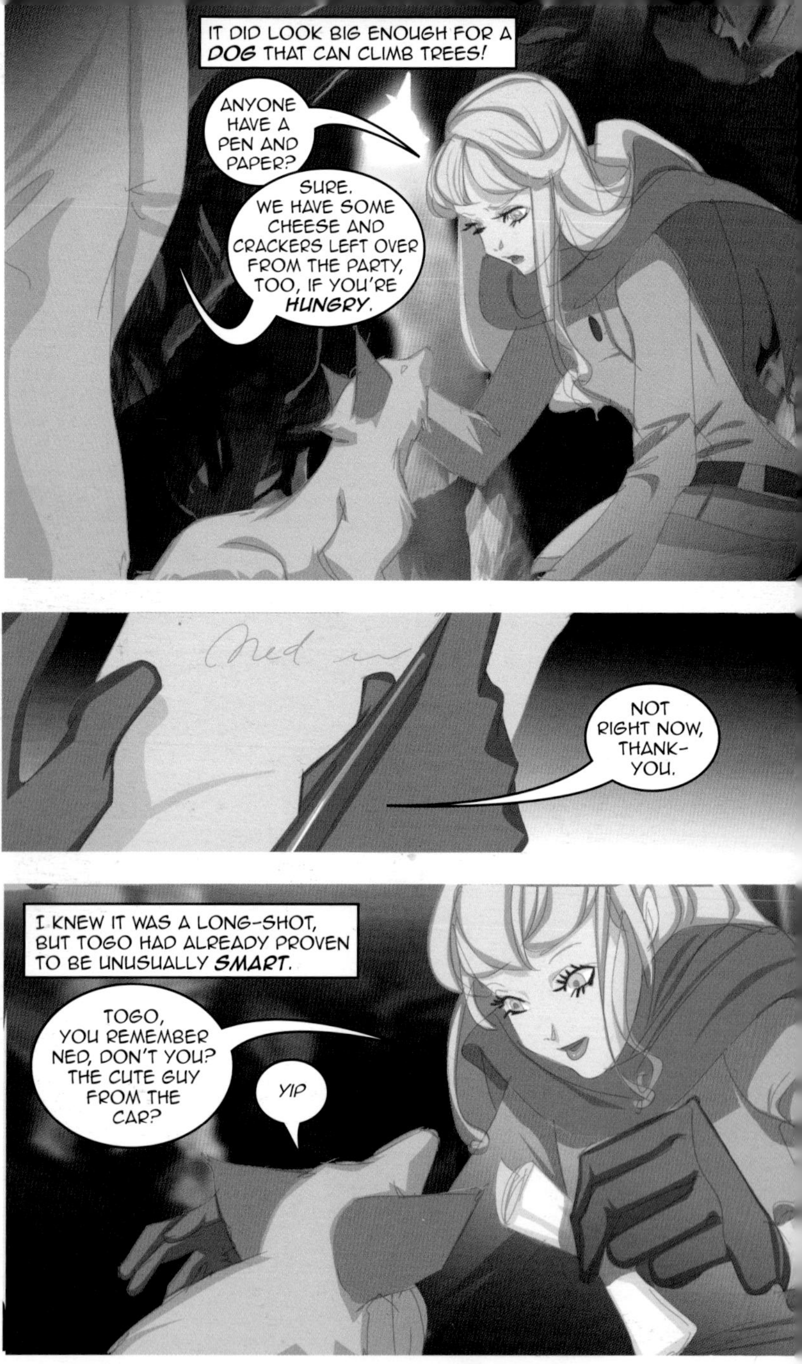
IT DID LOOK BIG ENOUGH FOR A DOG THAT CAN CLIMB TREES!
ANYONE HAVE A PEN AND PAPER?
SURE. WE HAVE SOME CHEESE AND CRACKERS LEFT OVER FROM THE PARTY, TOO, IF YOU'RE HUNGRY.
Ned
NOT RIGHT NOW, THANK-YOU.
I KNEW IT WAS A LONG-SHOT, BUT TOGO HAD ALREADY PROVEN TO BE UNUSUALLY SMART.
TOGO, YOU REMEMBER NED, DON'T YOU? THE CUTE GUY FROM THE CAR?
YIP

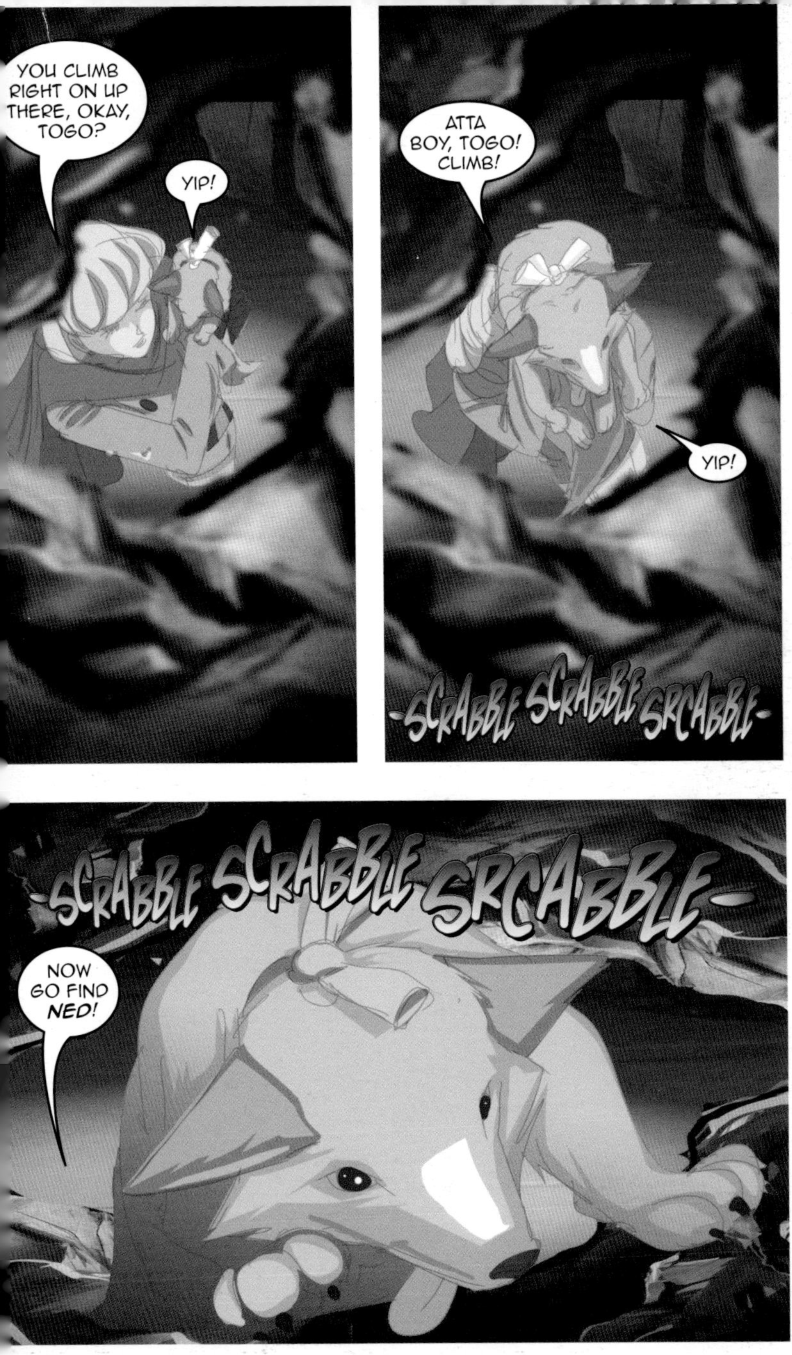
YOU CLIMB RIGHT ON UP THERE, OKAY, TOGO?
YIP!
ATTA BOY, TOGO! CLIMB!
YIP!
-SCRABBLE SCRABBLE SRCABBLE-
-SCRABBLE SCRABBLE SRCABBLE-
NOW GO FIND NED!

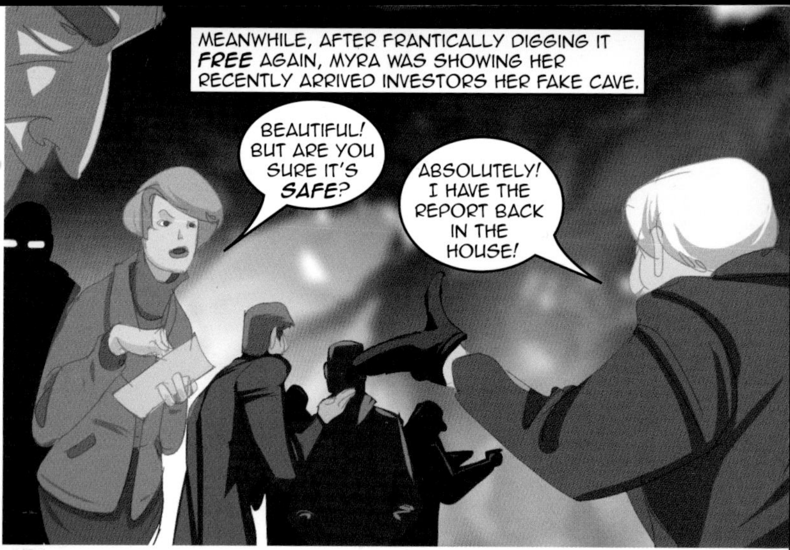
MEANWHILE, AFTER FRANTICALLY DIGGING IT FREE AGAIN, MYRA WAS SHOWING HER RECENTLY ARRIVED INVESTORS HER FAKE CAVE.
BEAUTIFUL! BUT ARE YOU SURE IT'S SAFE?
ABSOLUTELY! I HAVE THE REPORT BACK IN THE HOUSE!

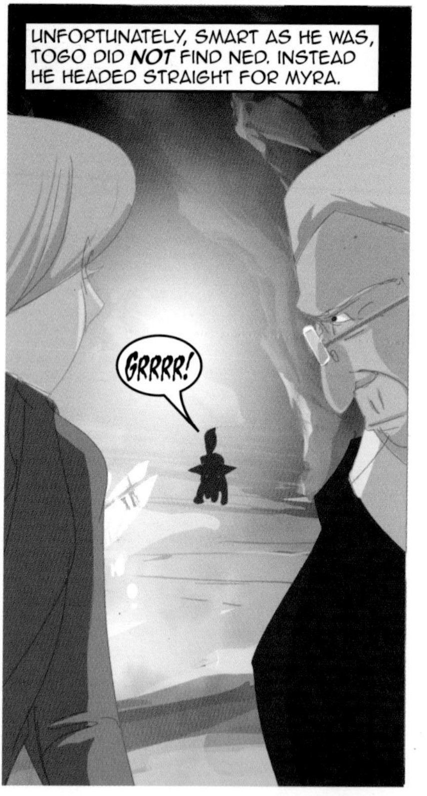
UNFORTUNATELY, SMART AS HE WAS, TOGO DID NOT FIND NED. INSTEAD HE HEADED STRAIGHT FOR MYRA.
GRRRR!

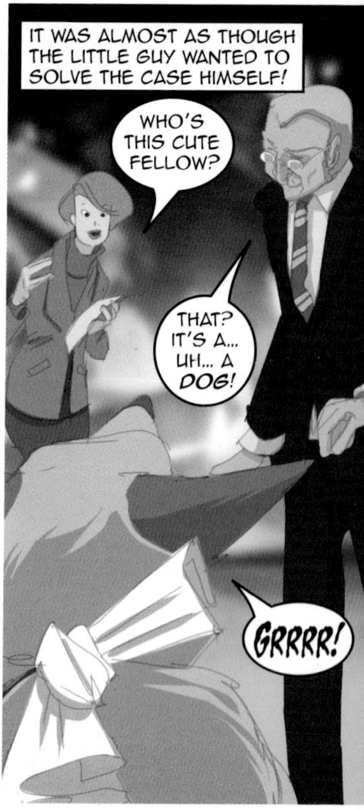
IT WAS ALMOST AS THOUGH THE LITTLE GUY WANTED TO SOLVE THE CASE HIMSELF!
WHO'S THIS CUTE FELLOW?
THAT? IT'S A... UH... A DOG!
GRRRR!

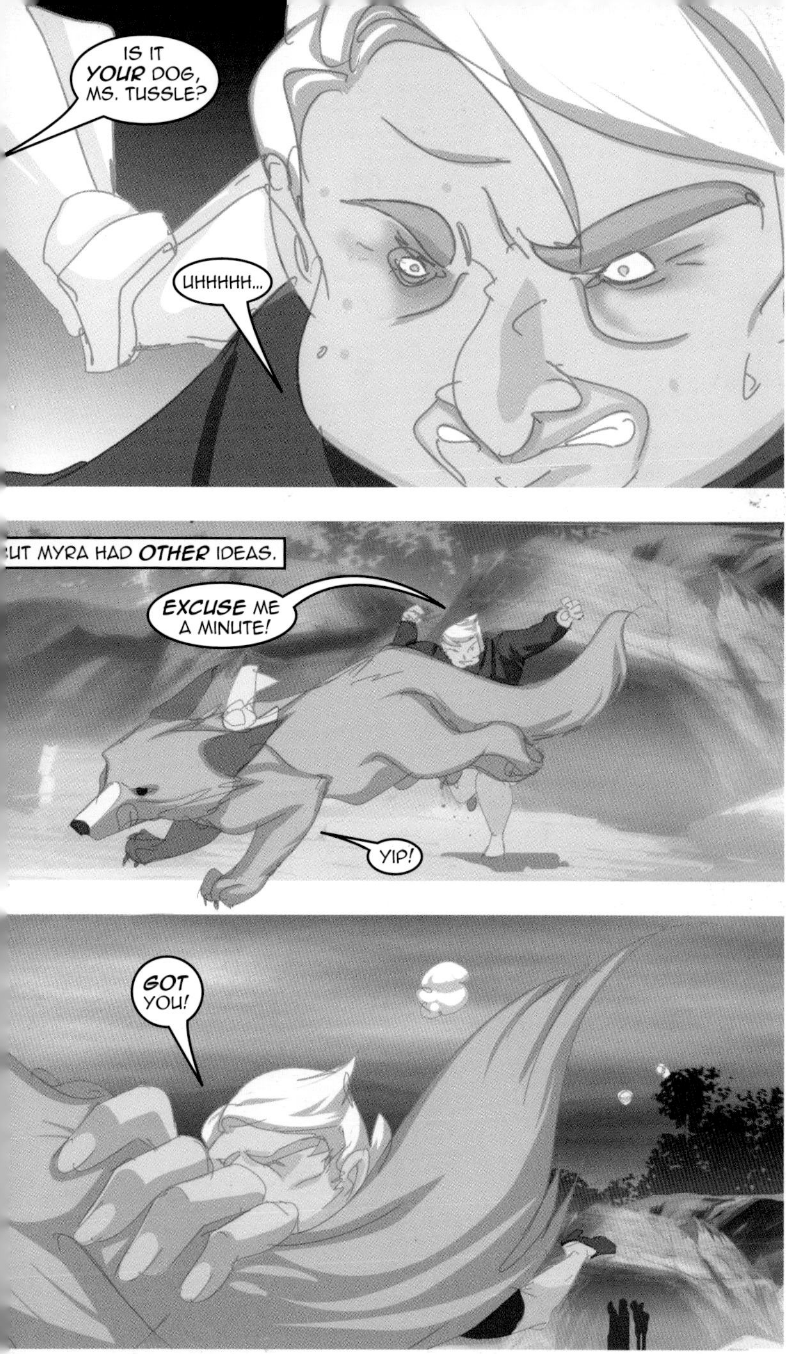
IS IT YOUR DOG, MS. TUSSLE?
UHHHHH...
UT MYRA HAD OTHER IDEAS.
EXCUSE ME A MINUTE!
YIP!
GOT YOU!

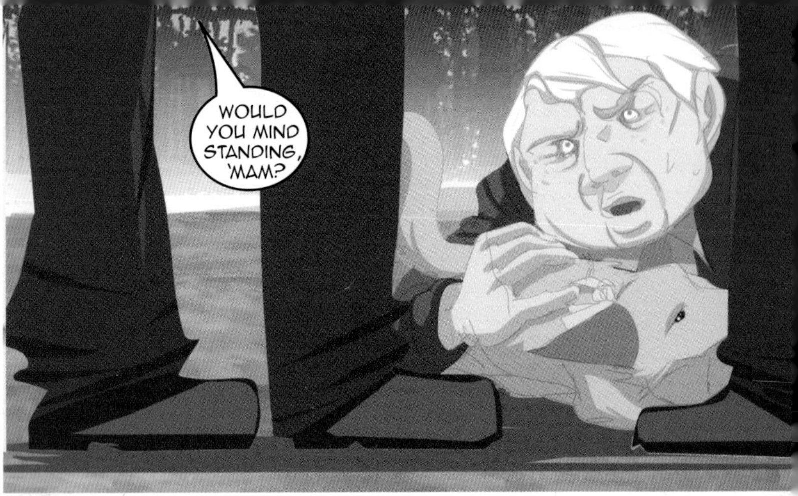
WOULD YOU MIND STANDING, 'MAM?

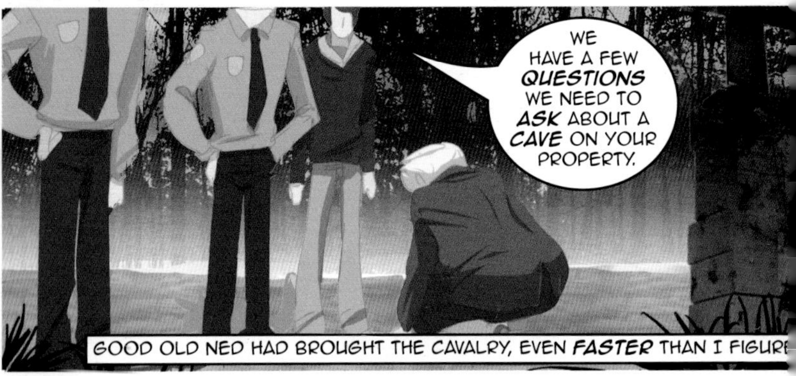
WE HAVE A FEW **QUESTIONS** WE NEED TO **ASK** ABOUT A **CAVE** ON YOUR PROPERTY.
GOOD OLD NED HAD BROUGHT THE CAVALRY, EVEN **FASTER** THAN I FIGURE

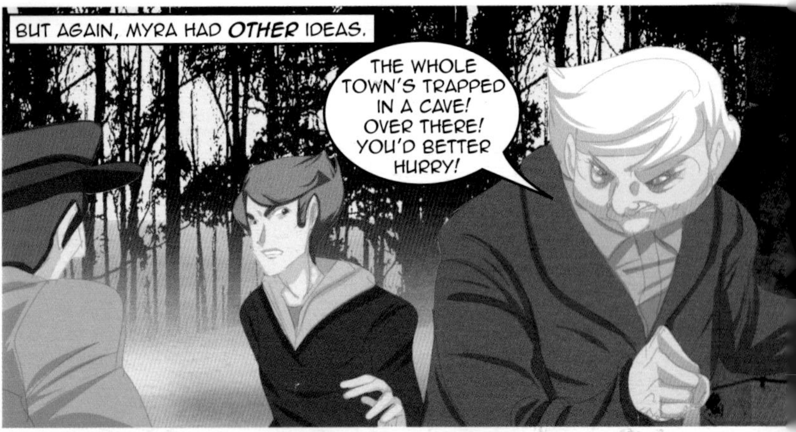
BUT AGAIN, MYRA HAD **OTHER** IDEAS.
THE WHOLE TOWN'S TRAPPED IN A CAVE! OVER THERE! YOU'D BETTER HURRY!

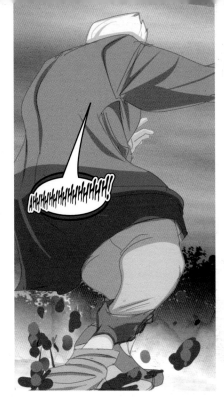

SHE HEADED STRAIGHT FOR THE CEMETERY. I GUESS SHE WAS THINKING SHE MIGHT BE ABLE TO ESCAPE IF SHE REACHED THE **WOODS** ON THE OTHER SIDE.

WHICH PROVIDED A VERY **INTERESTING** OPPORTUNITY FOR ME.

AAHHHHHHHHHHHHH!!

BYRA, NO! YOU'RE **DEAD!** LET GO! LET GO!

SEE? I **TOLD** YOU IT LOOKED PRETTY CREEPY.

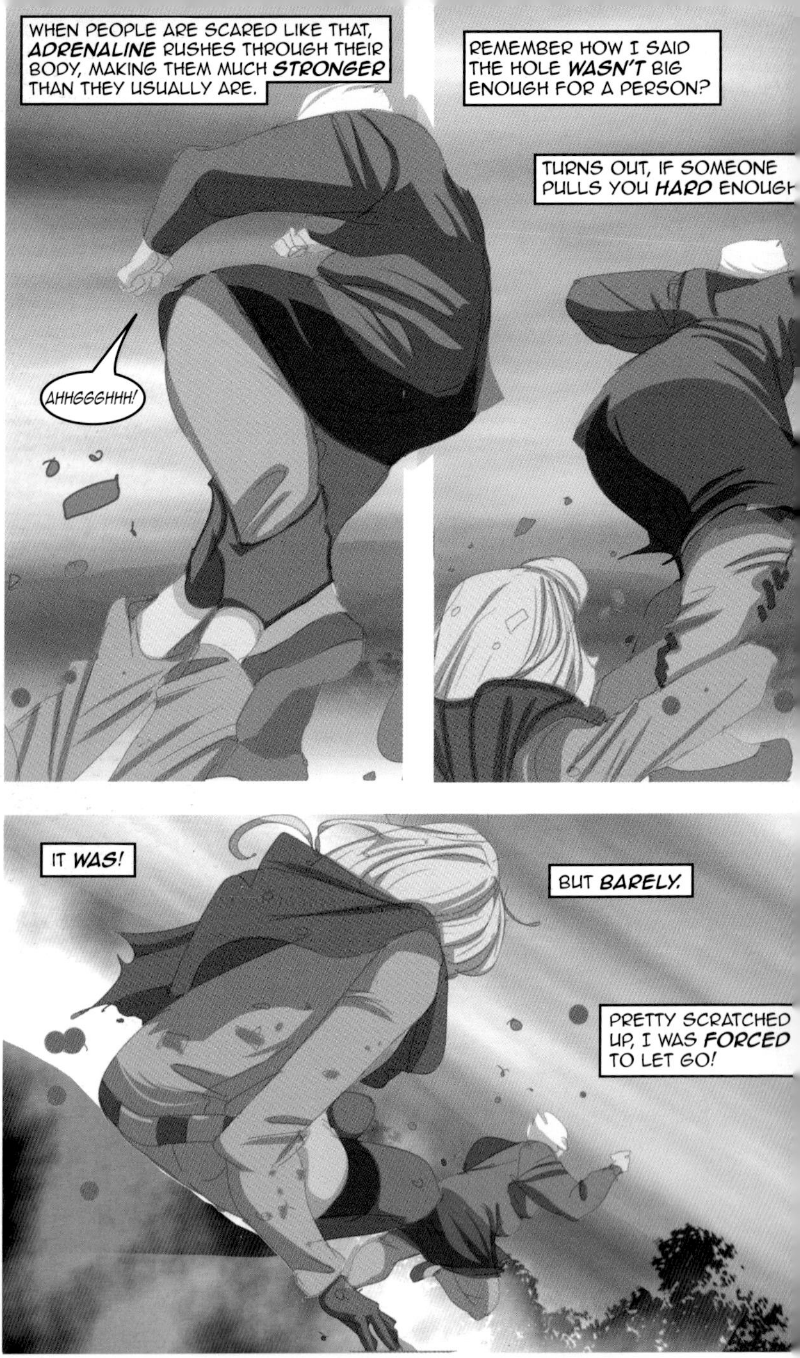
WHEN PEOPLE ARE SCARED LIKE THAT, ADRENALINE RUSHES THROUGH THEIR BODY, MAKING THEM MUCH STRONGER THAN THEY USUALLY ARE.
AHHGGGHHH!
REMEMBER HOW I SAID THE HOLE WASN'T BIG ENOUGH FOR A PERSON?
TURNS OUT, IF SOMEONE PULLS YOU HARD ENOUGH
IT WAS!
BUT BARELY.
PRETTY SCRATCHED UP, I WAS FORCED TO LET GO!

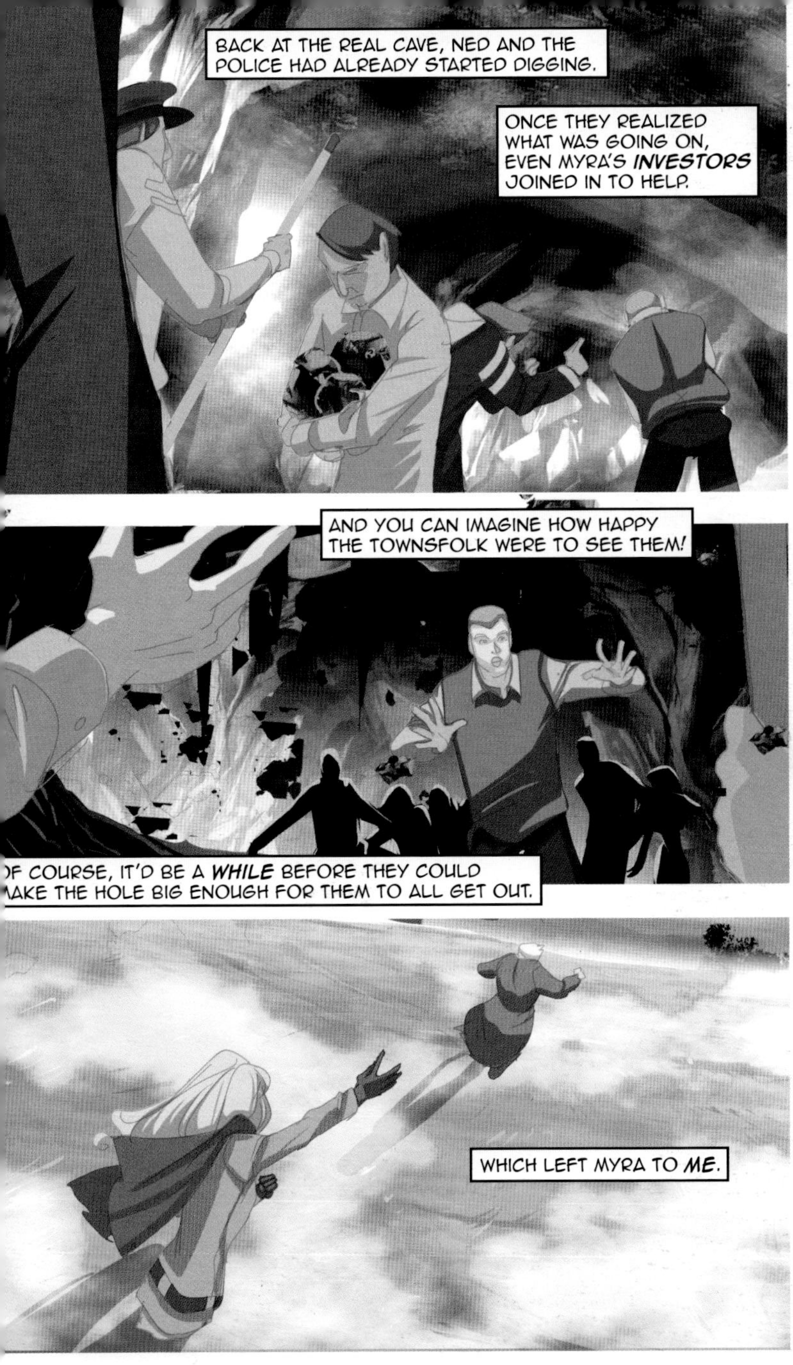
BACK AT THE REAL CAVE, NED AND THE POLICE HAD ALREADY STARTED DIGGING.
ONCE THEY REALIZED WHAT WAS GOING ON, EVEN MYRA'S ***INVESTORS*** JOINED IN TO HELP.
AND YOU CAN IMAGINE HOW HAPPY THE TOWNSFOLK WERE TO SEE THEM!
OF COURSE, IT'D BE A ***WHILE*** BEFORE THEY COULD MAKE THE HOLE BIG ENOUGH FOR THEM TO ALL GET OUT.
WHICH LEFT MYRA TO ***ME***.

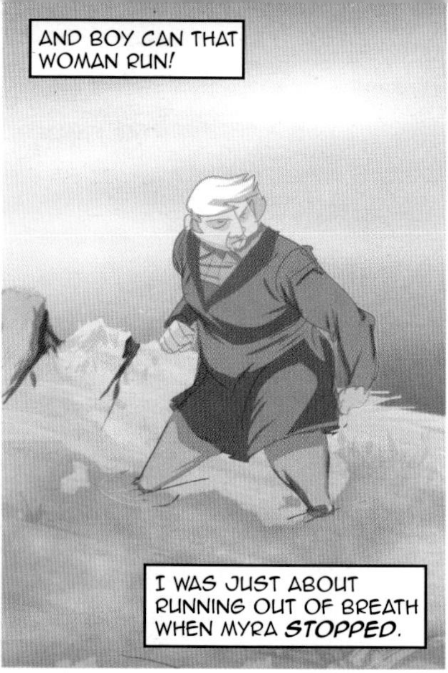
AND BOY CAN THAT WOMAN RUN!
I WAS JUST ABOUT RUNNING OUT OF BREATH WHEN MYRA **STOPPED**.

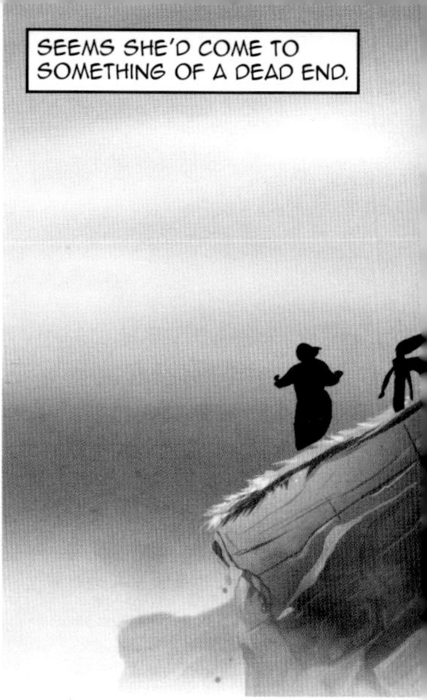
SEEMS SHE'D COME TO SOMETHING OF A DEAD END.

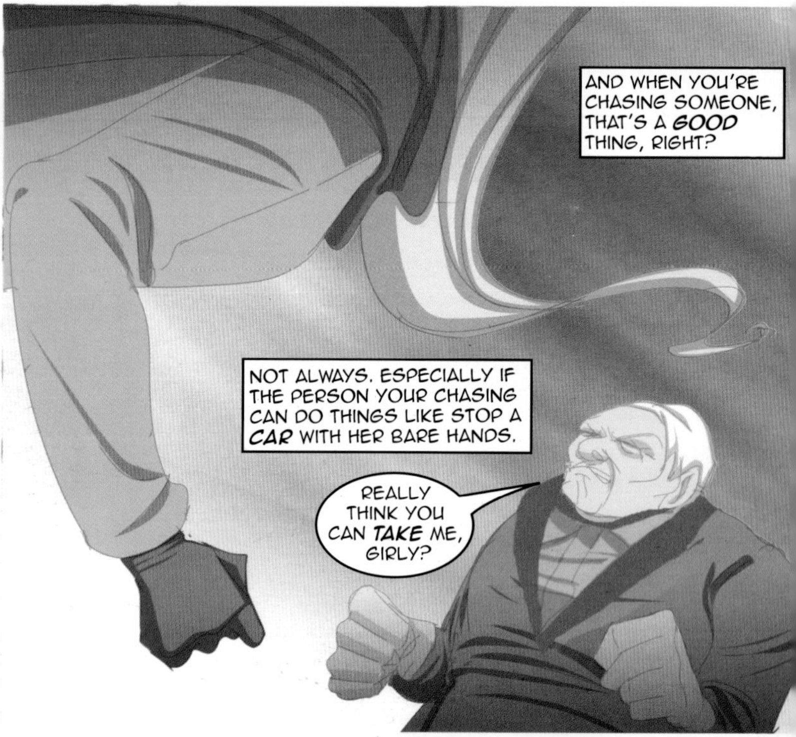
AND WHEN YOU'RE CHASING SOMEONE, THAT'S A **GOOD** THING, RIGHT?
NOT ALWAYS. ESPECIALLY IF THE PERSON YOUR CHASING CAN DO THINGS LIKE STOP A **CAR** WITH HER BARE HANDS.
REALLY THINK YOU CAN **TAKE** ME, GIRLY?

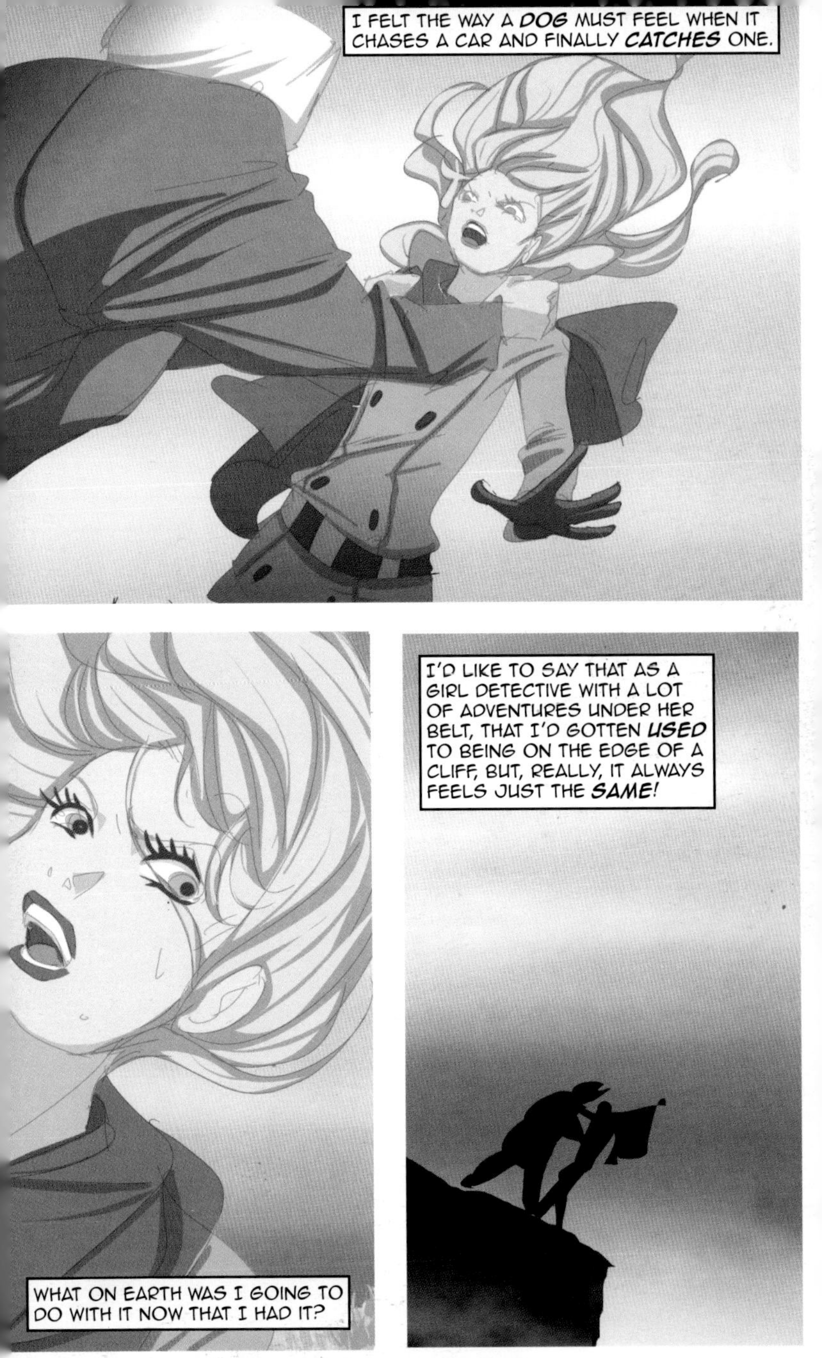
I FELT THE WAY A *DOG* MUST FEEL WHEN IT CHASES A CAR AND FINALLY *CATCHES* ONE.
WHAT ON EARTH WAS I GOING TO DO WITH IT NOW THAT I HAD IT?
I'D LIKE TO SAY THAT AS A GIRL DETECTIVE WITH A LOT OF ADVENTURES UNDER HER BELT, THAT I'D GOTTEN *USED* TO BEING ON THE EDGE OF A CLIFF, BUT, REALLY, IT ALWAYS FEELS JUST THE *SAME*!

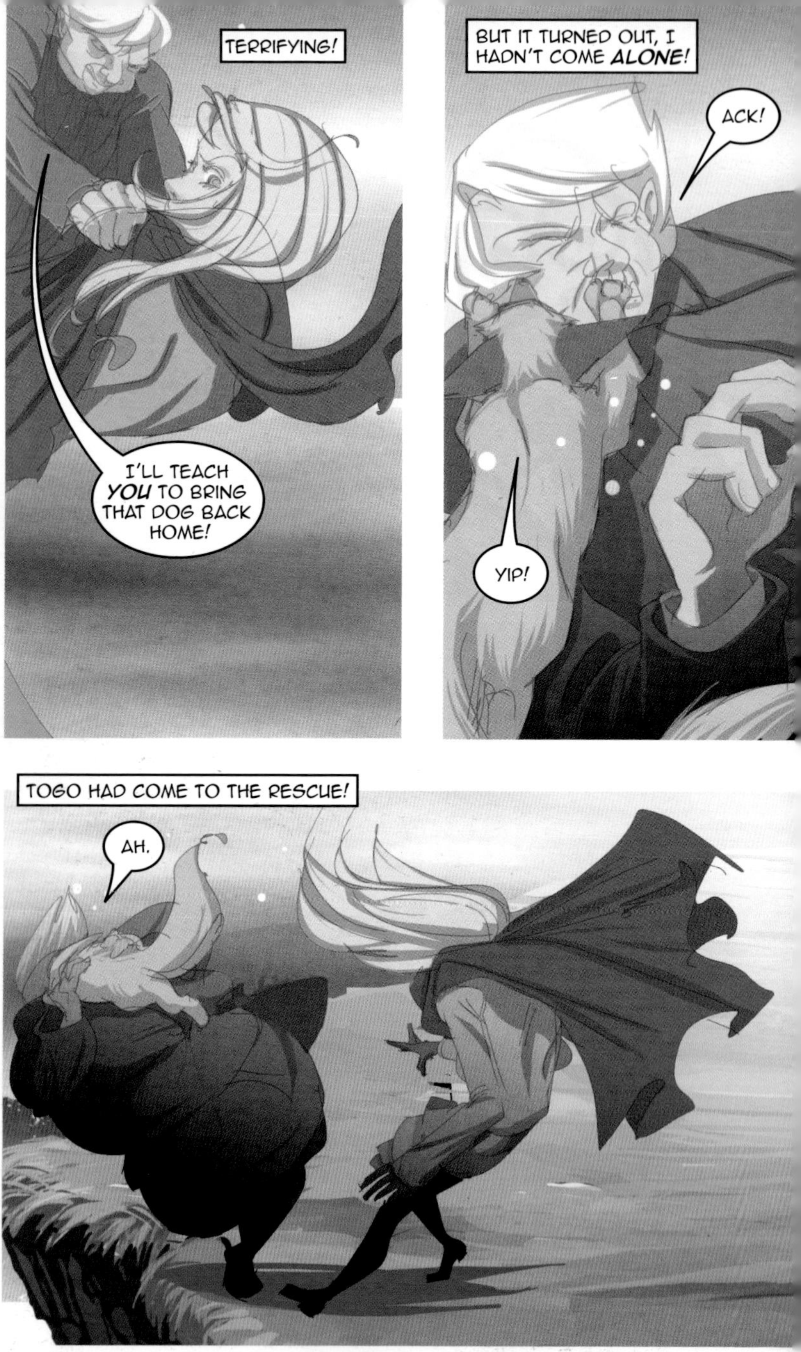
TERRIFYING!
I'LL TEACH YOU TO BRING THAT DOG BACK HOME!
BUT IT TURNED OUT, I HADN'T COME ALONE!
ACK!
YIP!
TOGO HAD COME TO THE RESCUE!
AH.

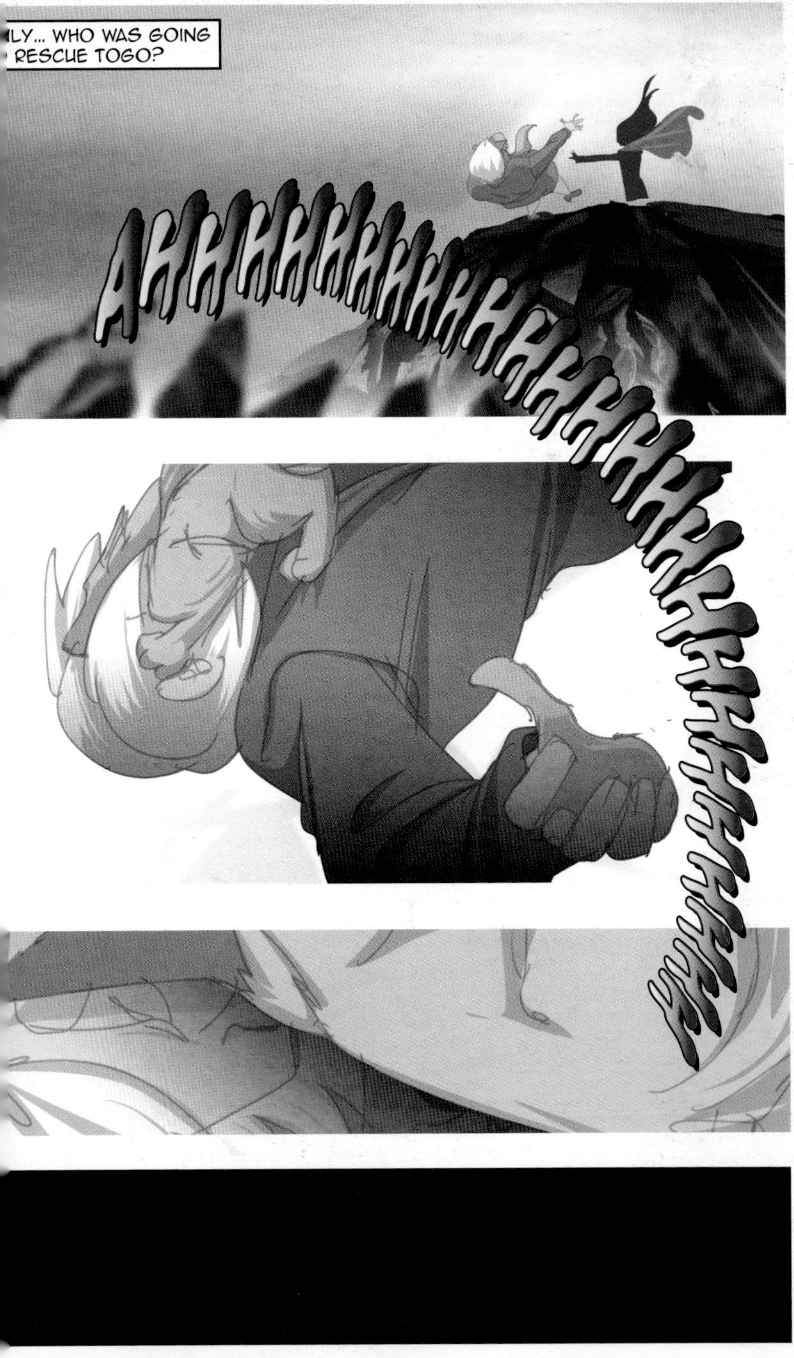
LY... WHO WAS GOING
RESCUE TOGO?
AHHHHHHHHHHHHHHHHHHHHHHHHHHHHHH

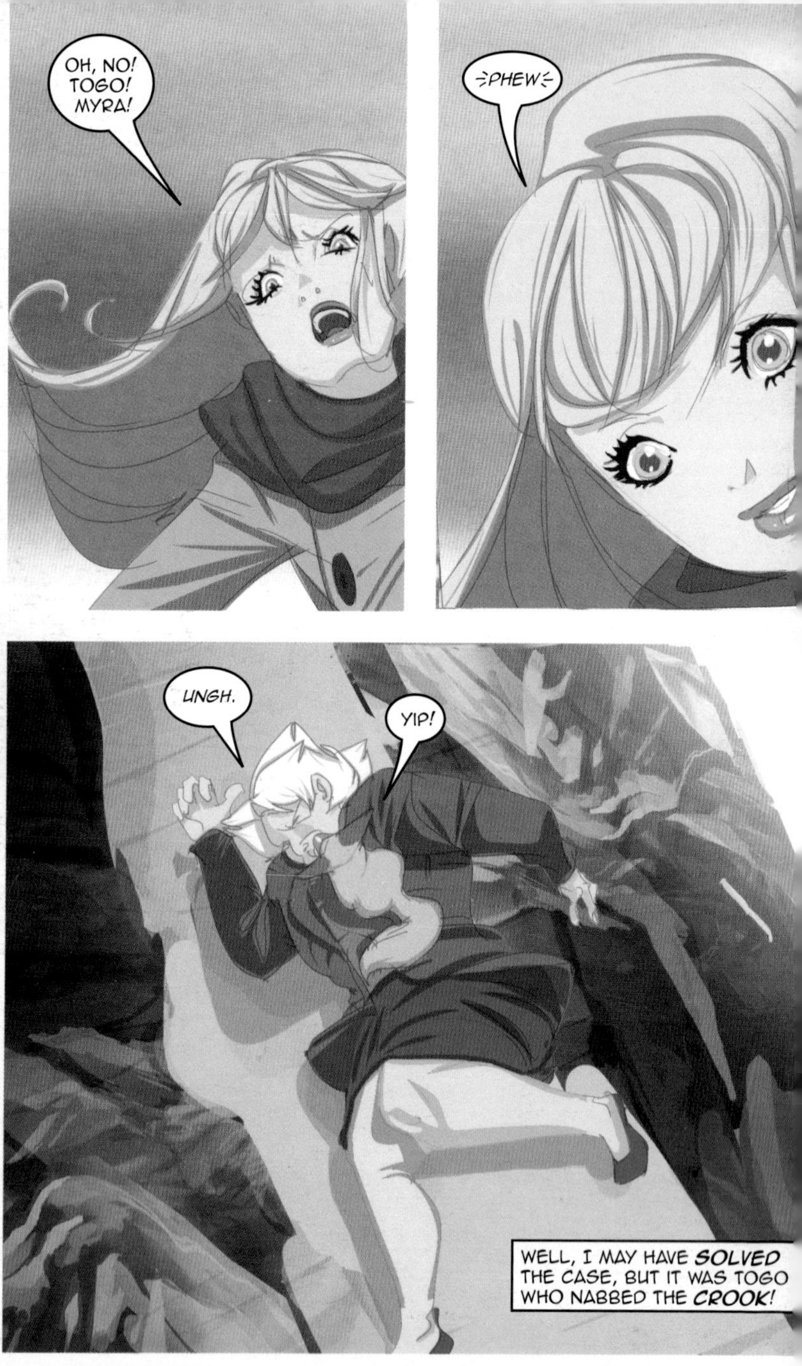
OH, NO! TOGO! MYRA!
PHEW
UNGH.
YIP!
WELL, I MAY HAVE SOLVED THE CASE, BUT IT WAS TOGO WHO NABBED THE CROOK!

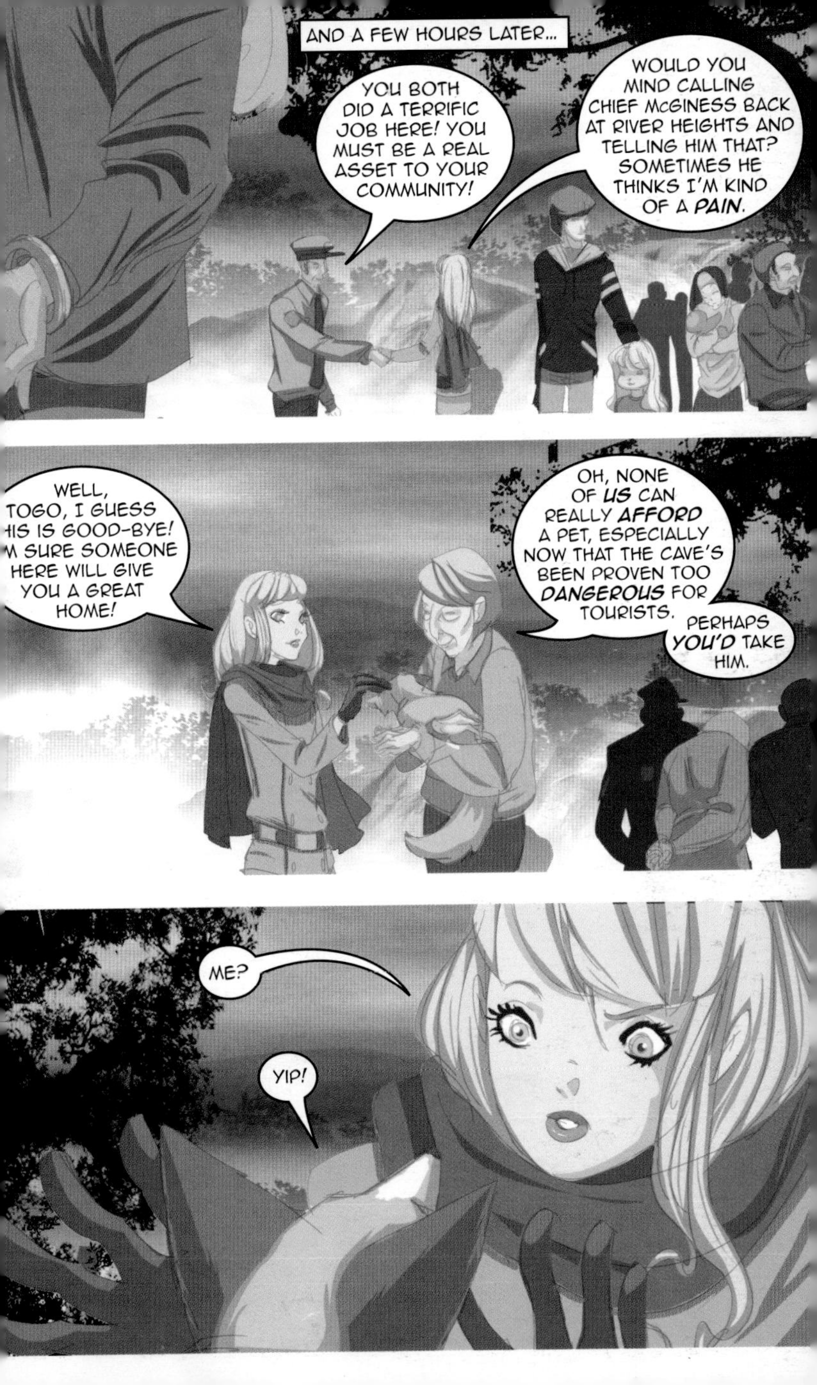
AND A FEW HOURS LATER...
YOU BOTH DID A TERRIFIC JOB HERE! YOU MUST BE A REAL ASSET TO YOUR COMMUNITY!
WOULD YOU MIND CALLING CHIEF McGINESS BACK AT RIVER HEIGHTS AND TELLING HIM THAT? SOMETIMES HE THINKS I'M KIND OF A PAIN.
WELL, TOGO, I GUESS HIS IS GOOD-BYE! M SURE SOMEONE HERE WILL GIVE YOU A GREAT HOME!
OH, NONE OF US CAN REALLY AFFORD A PET, ESPECIALLY NOW THAT THE CAVE'S BEEN PROVEN TOO DANGEROUS FOR TOURISTS.
PERHAPS YOU'D TAKE HIM.
ME?
YIP!

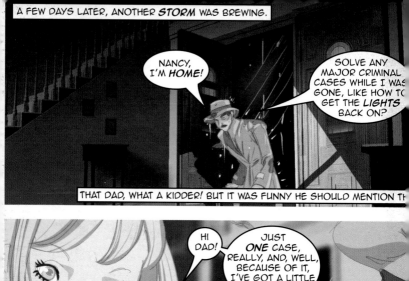

A FEW DAYS LATER, ANOTHER **STORM** WAS BREWING.

NANCY, I'M **HOME**!

SOLVE ANY MAJOR CRIMINAL CASES WHILE I WAS GONE, LIKE HOW TO GET THE **LIGHTS** BACK ON?

THAT DAD, WHAT A KIDDER! BUT IT WAS FUNNY HE SHOULD MENTION TH

HI DAD!

JUST **ONE** CASE, REALLY, AND, WELL, BECAUSE OF IT, I'VE GOT A LITTLE **SURPRISE**!

REALLY? WHAT SORT OF SURPRISE?

AT LEAST HE DIDN'T RUN **SCREAMING** LIKE HANNAH DID. THOUGH IN A COUPLE OF WEEK EVEN **SHE** WARMED TO HIM, AND TOGO WAS PRACTICALLY ONE OF THE FAMILY!

YIP!

AGHH!

THE EN

This Fall, take the mystery with you
on your Nintendo DS™ system!

NANCY DREW™
The Deadly Secret of Olde World Park

- Play as Nancy Drew, the world's most recognizable teen sleuth
- Solve puzzles and discover clues left by a slew of suspicious characters
- Use the Touch Screen to play detective mini-games and access tasks, maps and inventory
- Unravel 15 intriguing chapters filled with challenging missions and interrogations

NINTENDO DS™

GORILLA

MAJESCO
ENTERTAINMENT

www.majescoentertainment.com

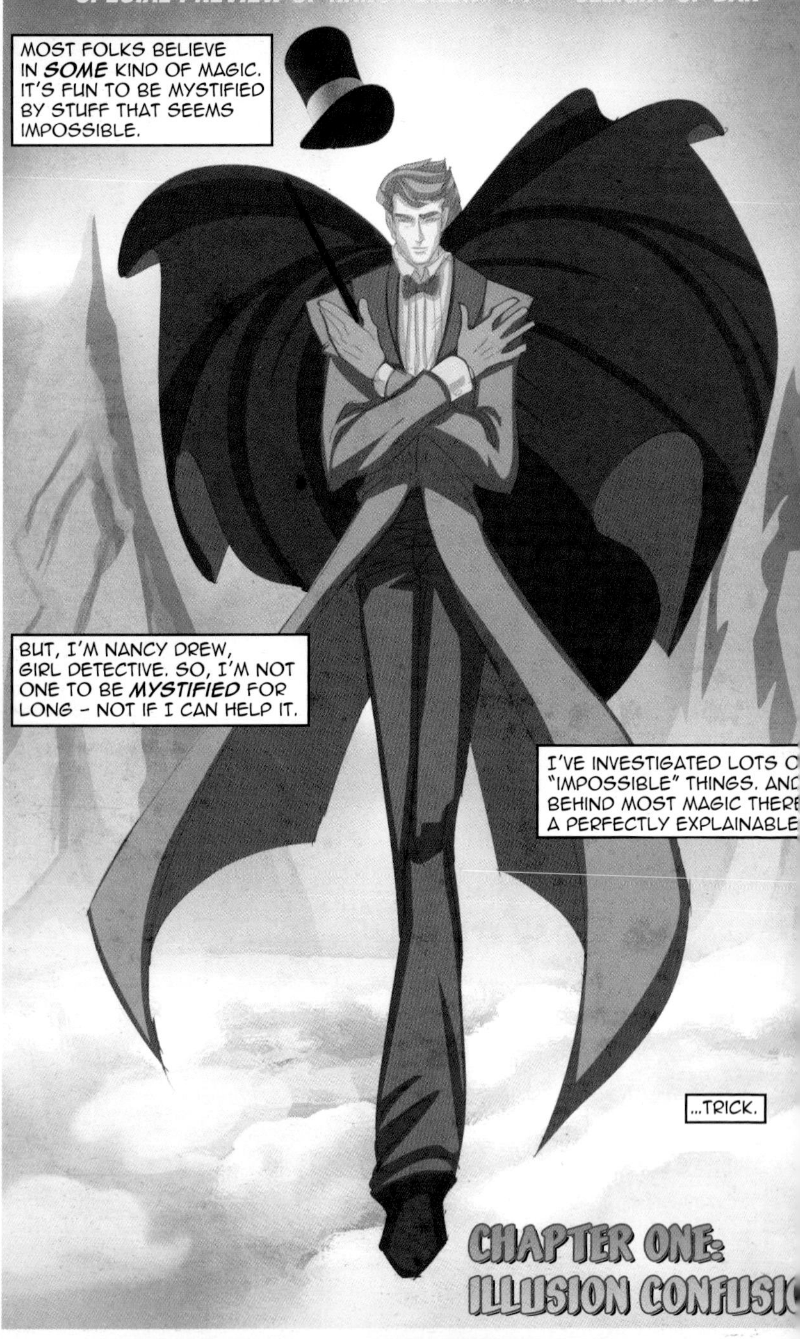
MOST FOLKS BELIEVE IN SOME KIND OF MAGIC. IT'S FUN TO BE MYSTIFIED BY STUFF THAT SEEMS IMPOSSIBLE.
BUT, I'M NANCY DREW, GIRL DETECTIVE. SO, I'M NOT ONE TO BE MYSTIFIED FOR LONG - NOT IF I CAN HELP IT.
I'VE INVESTIGATED LOTS O "IMPOSSIBLE" THINGS. AND BEHIND MOST MAGIC THERE A PERFECTLY EXPLAINABLE
...TRICK.
CHAPTER ONE: ILLUSION CONFUSIO

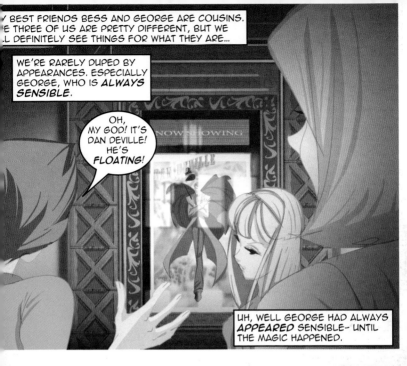

MY BEST FRIENDS BESS AND GEORGE ARE COUSINS. THE THREE OF US ARE PRETTY DIFFERENT, BUT WE ALL DEFINITELY SEE THINGS FOR WHAT THEY ARE...

WE'RE RARELY DUPED BY APPEARANCES. ESPECIALLY GEORGE, WHO IS *ALWAYS SENSIBLE*.

OH, MY GOD! IT'S DAN DEVILLE! HE'S *FLOATING*!

UH, WELL GEORGE HAD ALWAYS *APPEARED* SENSIBLE- UNTIL THE MAGIC HAPPENED.

EEIIII!!

GEORGE? ARE YOU ALL RIGHT?

DON'T TELL ME *YOU'RE* A... A *FAN*?!

⇒PANT⇐ OKAY! AFTER MY PARENTS TOLD ME THE EASTER BUNNY WASN'T REAL, I WAS DEVASTATED. I WANTED TO BELIEVE IN MAGIC SO BAD.

SO, THEY TOOK ME TO SEE DAN DEVILLE – HE WAS THE MOST AMAZING MAGICIAN I'VE EVER SEEN!

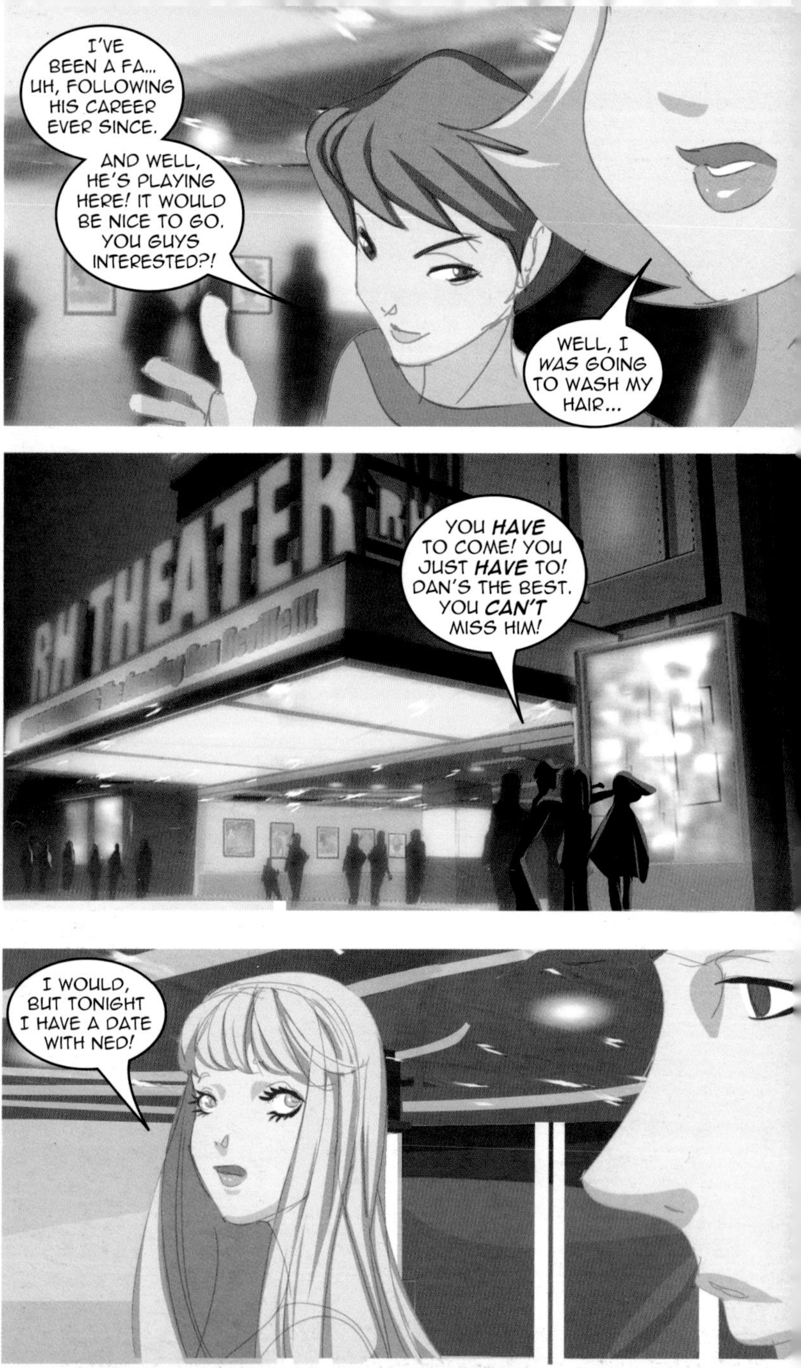
I'VE BEEN A FA... UH, FOLLOWING HIS CAREER EVER SINCE.
AND WELL, HE'S PLAYING HERE! IT WOULD BE NICE TO GO. YOU GUYS INTERESTED?!
WELL, I WAS GOING TO WASH MY HAIR...
RH THEATER
YOU HAVE TO COME! YOU JUST HAVE TO! DAN'S THE BEST. YOU CAN'T MISS HIM!
I WOULD, BUT TONIGHT I HAVE A DATE WITH NED!

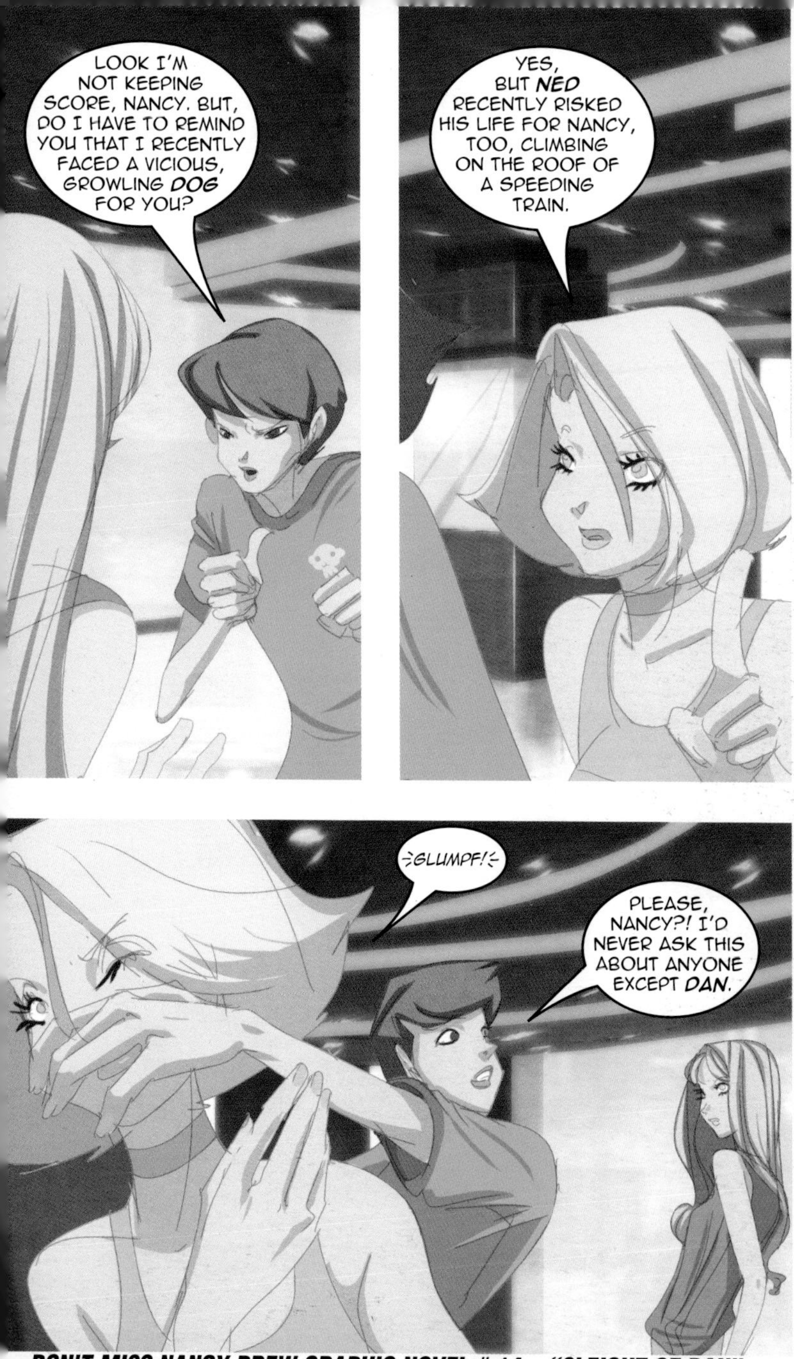
LOOK I'M NOT KEEPING SCORE, NANCY. BUT, DO I HAVE TO REMIND YOU THAT I RECENTLY FACED A VICIOUS, GROWLING DOG FOR YOU?
YES, BUT NED RECENTLY RISKED HIS LIFE FOR NANCY, TOO, CLIMBING ON THE ROOF OF A SPEEDING TRAIN.
GLUMPF!
PLEASE, NANCY?! I'D NEVER ASK THIS ABOUT ANYONE EXCEPT DAN.

DON'T MISS NANCY DREW GRAPHIC NOVEL # 14 – "SLEIGHT OF DAN"

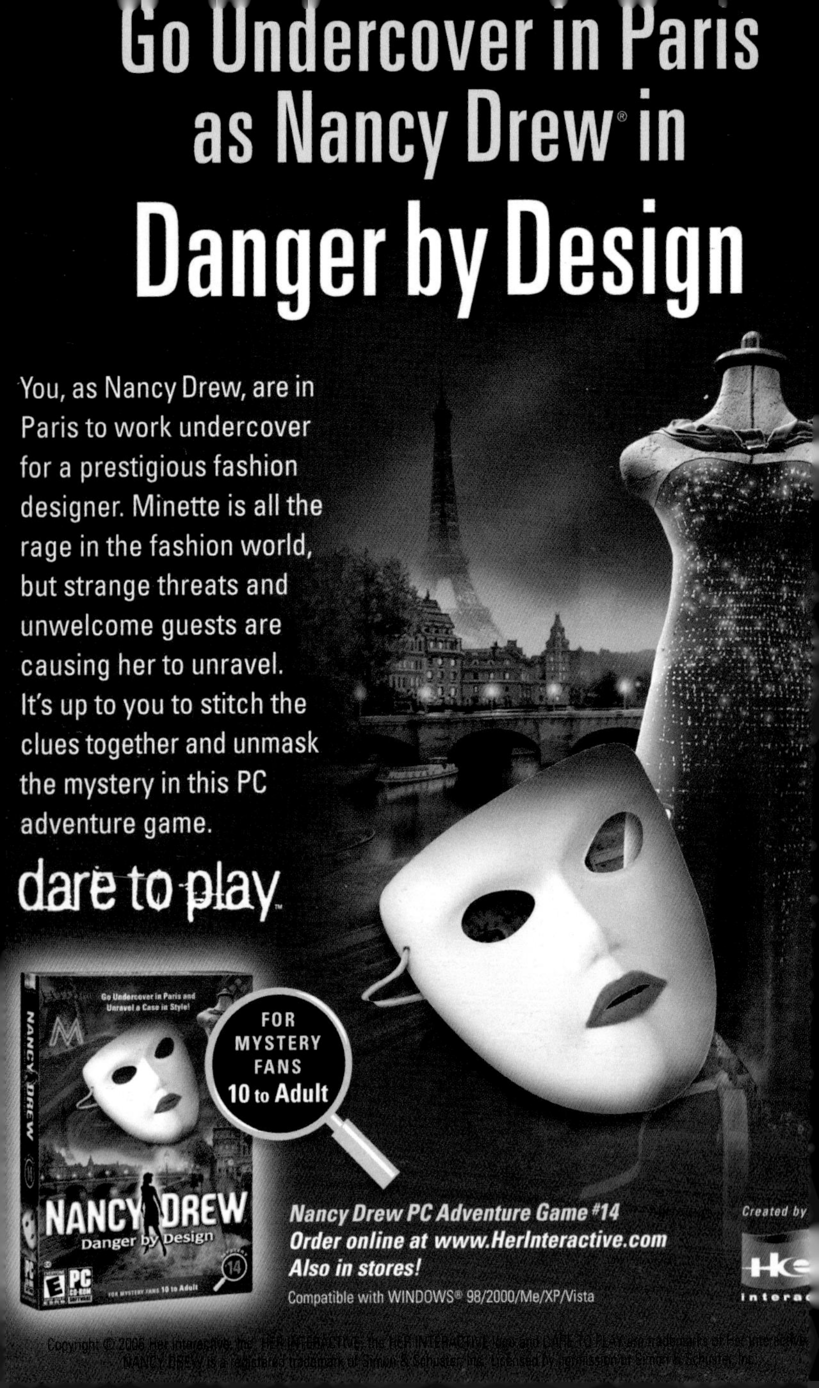

Go Undercover in Paris
as Nancy Drew® in
Danger by Design
You, as Nancy Drew, are in Paris to work undercover for a prestigious fashion designer. Minette is all the rage in the fashion world, but strange threats and unwelcome guests are causing her to unravel. It's up to you to stitch the clues together and unmask the mystery in this PC adventure game.
dare to play™
Go Undercover in Paris and Unravel a Case in Style!
NANCY DREW
NANCY DREW
Danger by Design
14
PC CD-ROM
FOR MYSTERY FANS 10 to Adult
FOR MYSTERY FANS 10 to Adult
Nancy Drew PC Adventure Game #14
Order online at www.HerInteractive.com
Also in stores!
Compatible with WINDOWS® 98/2000/Me/XP/Vista
Created by

THE HARDY BOYS®

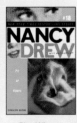

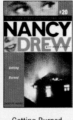

WATCH OUT FOR PAPERCUTZ™

If this is your very first Papercutz graphic novel, then allow me, Jim Salicrup, your humble and lovable Editor-in-Chief, to welcome you to the Papercutz Backpages where we check out what's happening in the ever-expanding Papercutz Universe! If you're a long-time Papercutz fan, then welcome back, friend!

Things really have been popping at Papercutz! In the last few editions of the Backpages we've announced new titles such as TALES FROM THE CRYPT, CLASSICS ILLUSTRATED, and CLASSICS ILLUSTRATED DELUXE. Well, guess what? The tradition continues, and we're announcing yet another addition to our line-up of blockbuster titles. So, what is our latest and greatest title? We'll give you just one hint -- the stars of the next Papercutz graphic novel series just happen to be the biggest, most exciting line of constructible action figures ever created! That's right -- BIONICLE is coming! Check out the power-packed preview pages ahead!

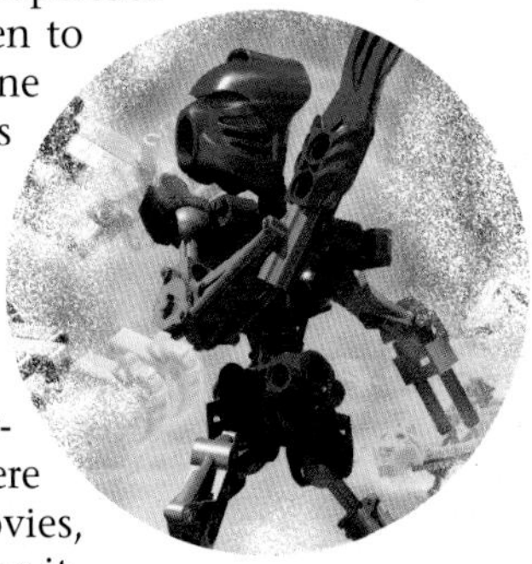

Before I run out of room, let me say that we're always interested in what you think! Are there characters, TV shows, movies, books, videogames, you-name-it, that you'd like to see Papercutz turn into graphic novels? Don't be shy, let's us know! You can contact me at salicrup@papercutz.com or Jim Salicrup, PAPERCUTZ, 40 Exchange Place, Ste. 1308, New York, NY 10005 and let us know how we're doing. After all, we want you to be as excited about Papercutz as we are!

Thanks,

Jim

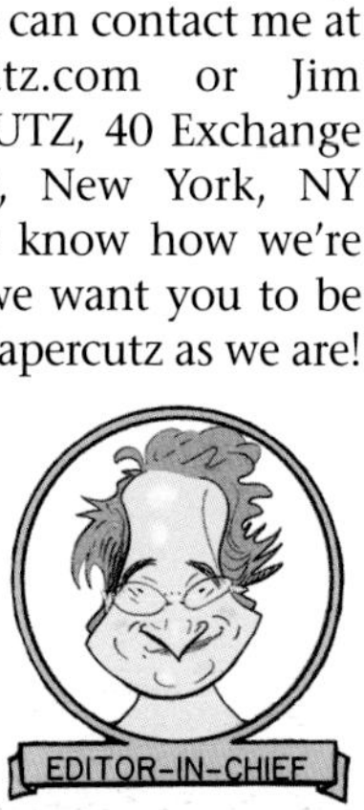
EDITOR-IN-CHIEF

Caricature drawn by Steve Brodner at the MoCCA Art Fest.

TWO DOZEN TEEN DETECTIVE GRAPHIC NOVELS NOW IN PRINT!

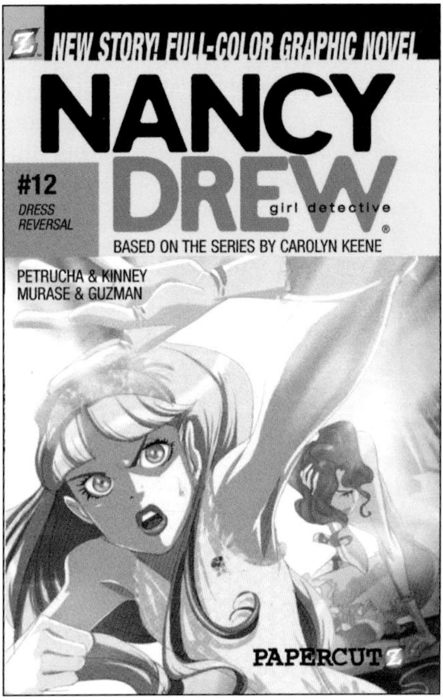
NEW STORY! FULL-COLOR GRAPHIC NOVEL
NANCY DREW
girl detective
#12
DRESS REVERSAL
BASED ON THE SERIES BY CAROLYN KEENE
PETRUCHA & KINNEY
MURASE & GUZMAN
PAPERCUTZ

You know, while it's exciting to be adding so many new titles, we don't want anyone to think we've forgotten any of our previous Papercutz publications! For example, can you believe there are now two dozen all-new, full-color graphic novels starring America's favorite teen sleuths?! Let's check out what's happening in the 12th volume of NANCY DREW...

Writers Stefan Petrucha and Sarah Kinney and artists Sho Murase and Carlos Jose Guzman present Nancy's latest case, "Dress Reversal." After showing up at River Height's social event of the year, in the identical dress as the party's hostess, Deirdre Shannon, things get worse for Nancy when she's suddenly kidnapped! That leaves Bess, George, and Ned to solve the mystery of the missing Girl Detective.

That's all in NANCY DREW #12 "Dress Reversal," on sale sale at bookstores everywhere and online booksellers.

Behold. . .

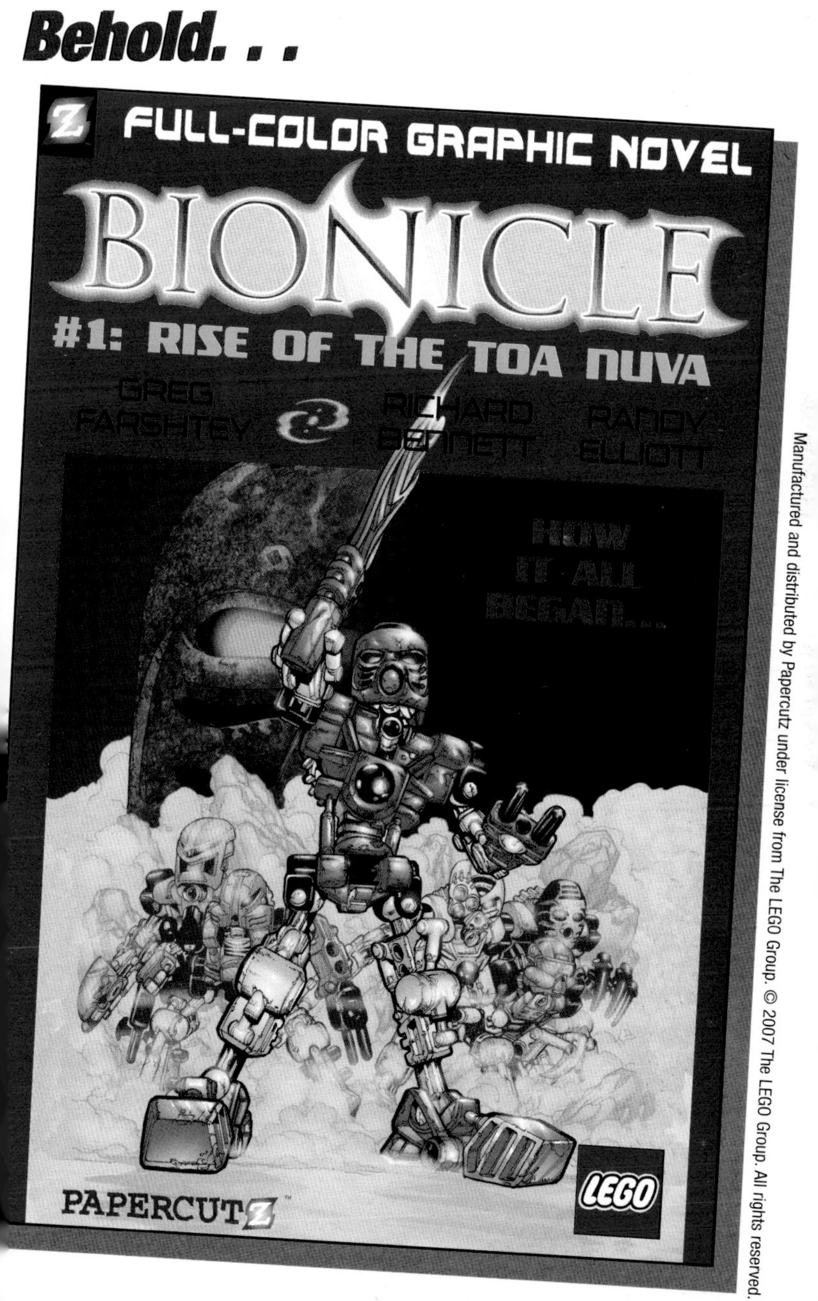
FULL-COLOR GRAPHIC NOVEL
BIONICLE
#1: RISE OF THE TOA NUVA
GREG FARSHTEY
RICHARD BENNETT
RANDY ELLIOTT
HOW IT ALL BEGAN...
PAPERCUTZ
LEGO

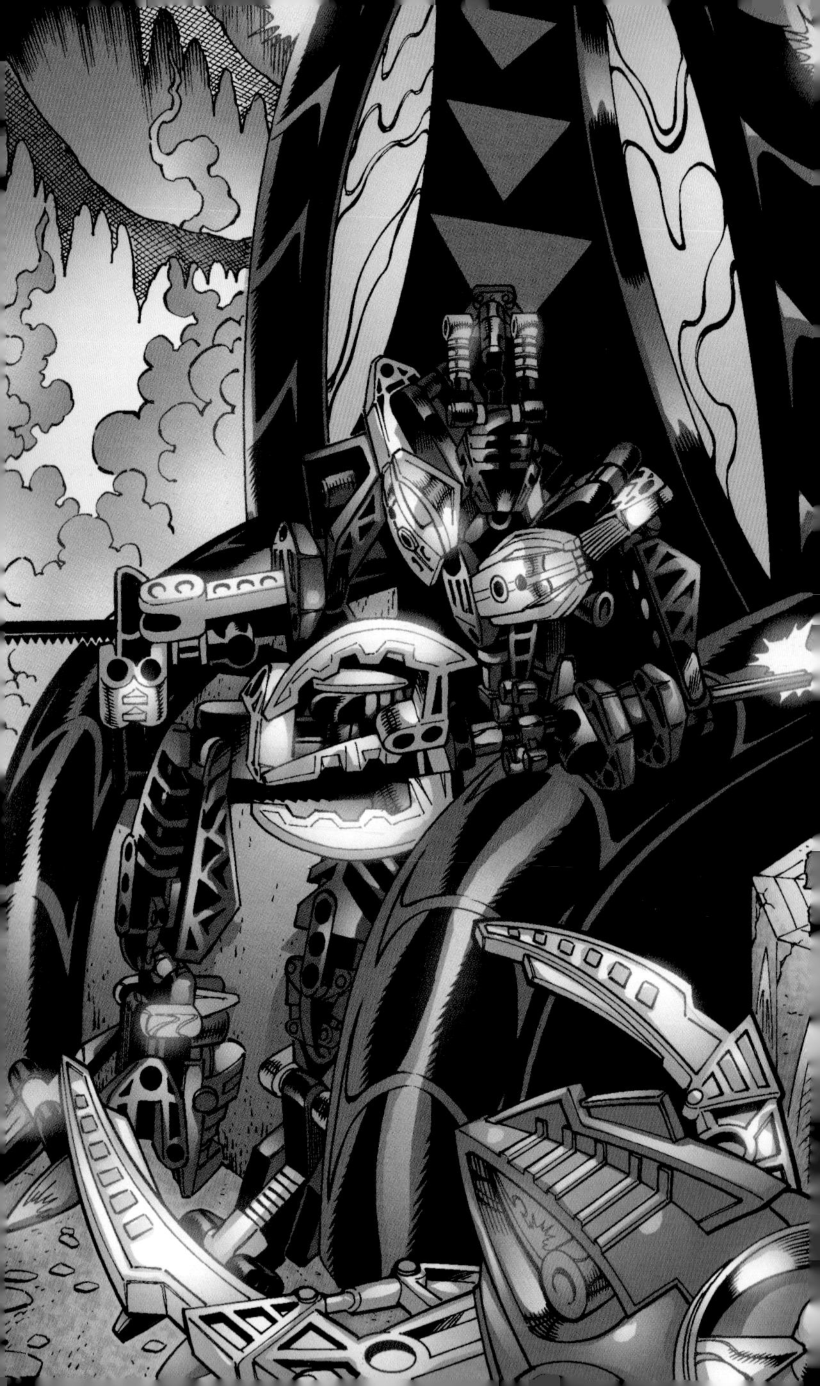

At the start of the new millennium, a new line of toys from LEGO
made their dramatic debut. Originally released in six color-coded can-
isters, each containing a constructible, fully-poseable, articulated char-
acter, BIONICLE was an instant hit!

The BIONICLE figures were incredibly intriguing. With their exotic
names hinting at a complex history, fans were curious to discover more
about these captivating characters. Even now, over six years later, there
are still many unanswered questions surrounding every facet of the
ever-expanding BIONICLE universe.

A comicbook, written by leading BIONICLE expert and author of
most of the BIONICLE novels Greg Farshtey, was created by DC Comics
and given away to members of the BIONICLE fan club. The action-
packed comics revealed much about these mysterious biomechanical
(part biological, part mechanical) beings and the world they inhabited.
A world filled with many races, most prominent being the Matoran. A
world once protected millennia ago by a Great Spirit known as Mata
Nui, who has fallen asleep. A world that has begun to decay as its
inhabitants must defend themselves from the evil forces of Makuta.

The first story arc of the comics called "The BIONICLE Chronicles,"
begins when six heroic beings known as Toa arrive on a tropical-like
island which is also named Mata Nui. The Toa may just be the saviors
the people of Mata Nui need, if they can avoid fighting with them-
selves, not to mention the Bohrok and the Rahkshise early comics are
incredibly hard-to-find, and many new BIONICLE fans have never seen
these all-important early chapters in this epic science fantasy. But soon,
those comics will be collected as the first two volumes in the Papercutz
series of BIONICLE graphic novels.

These early comics are incredibly hard-to-find, and many new BION-
ICLE fans have never seen these all-important early chapters in this
epic science fantasy. But soon, those comics will be collected as the first
two volumes in the Papercutz series of BIONICLE graphic novels.

In the following pages, enjoy a special preview of BIONICLE
graphic novel #1...

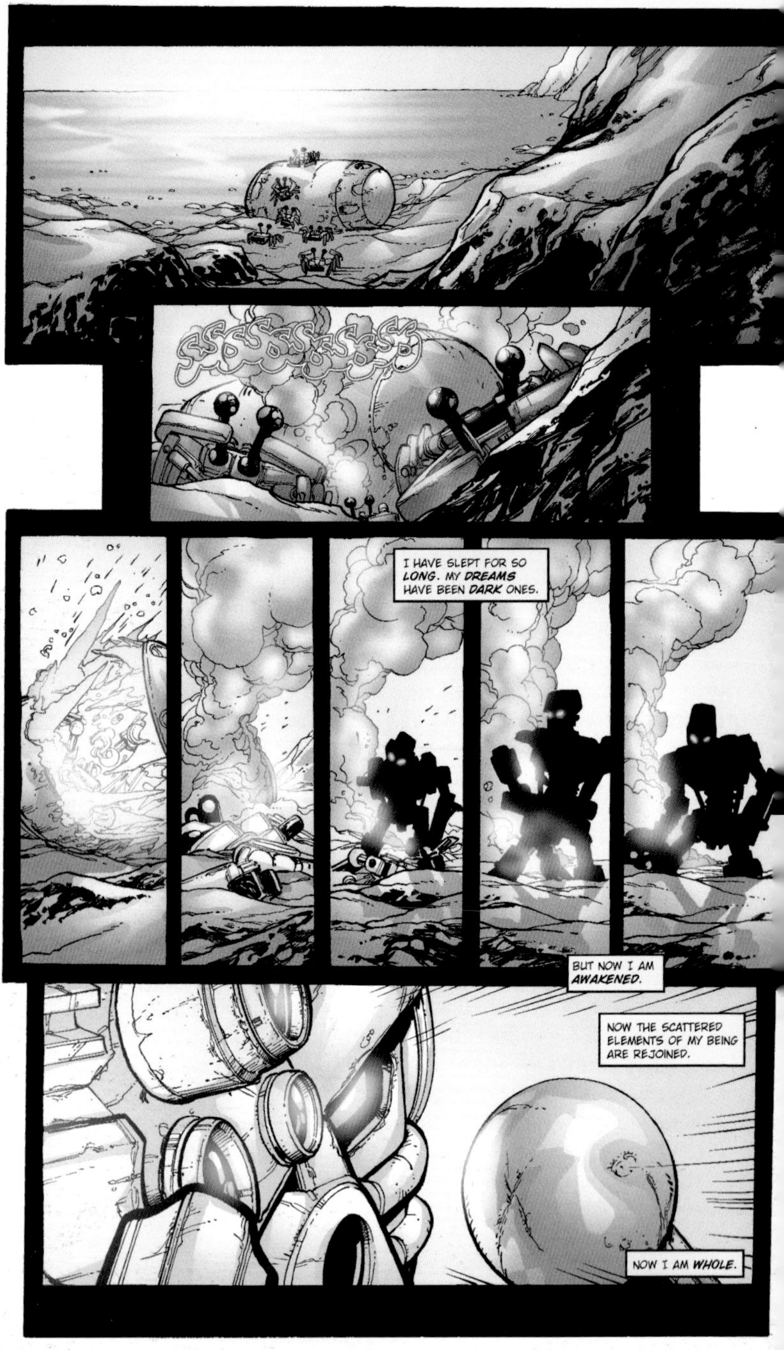
SSSSSSSSSSS
I HAVE SLEPT FOR SO LONG. MY DREAMS HAVE BEEN DARK ONES.
BUT NOW I AM AWAKENED.
NOW THE SCATTERED ELEMENTS OF MY BEING ARE REJOINED.
NOW I AM WHOLE.

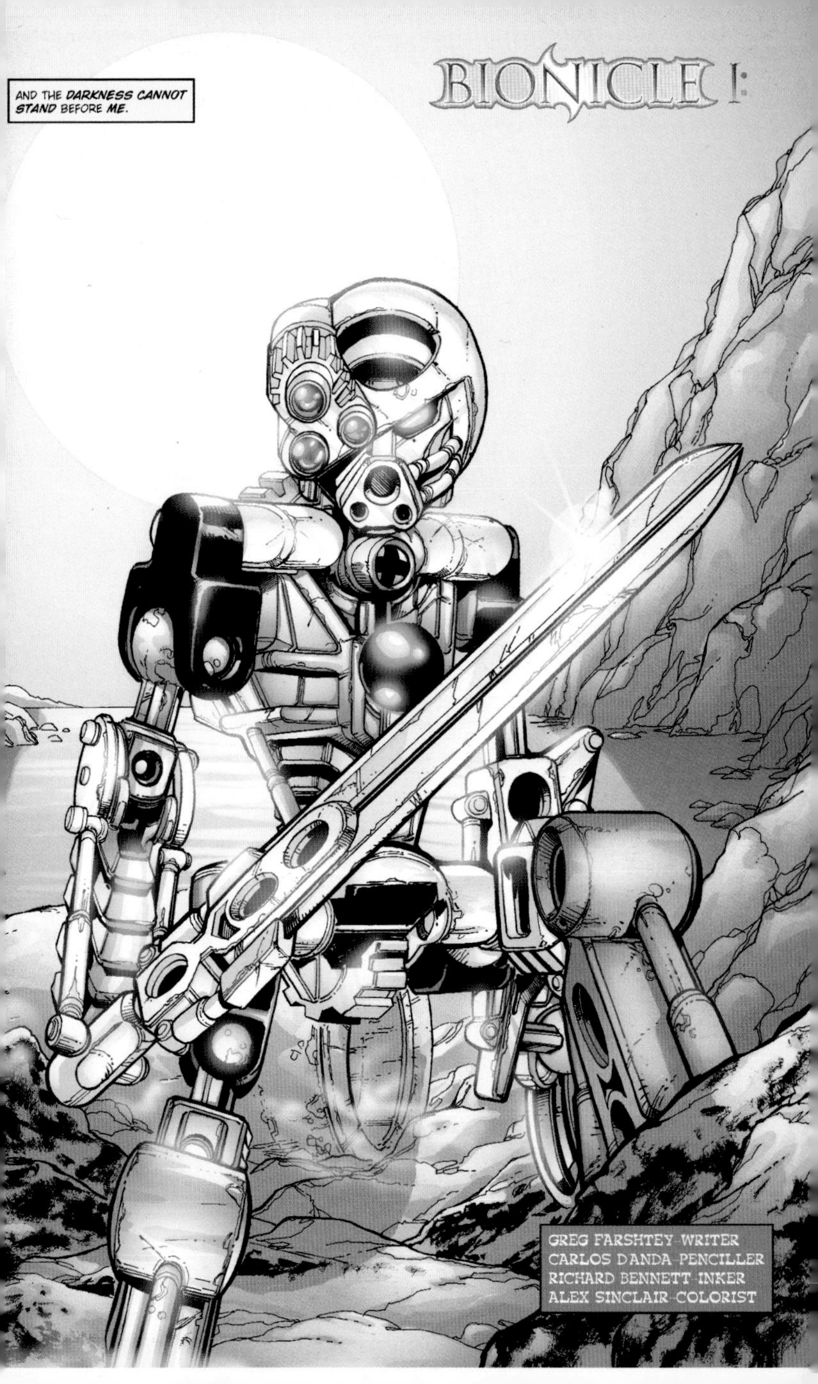
AND THE DARKNESS CANNOT STAND BEFORE ME.
BIONICLE I:
GREG FARSHTEY-WRITER
CARLOS D'ANDA-PENCILLER
RICHARD BENNETT-INKER
ALEX SINCLAIR-COLORIST

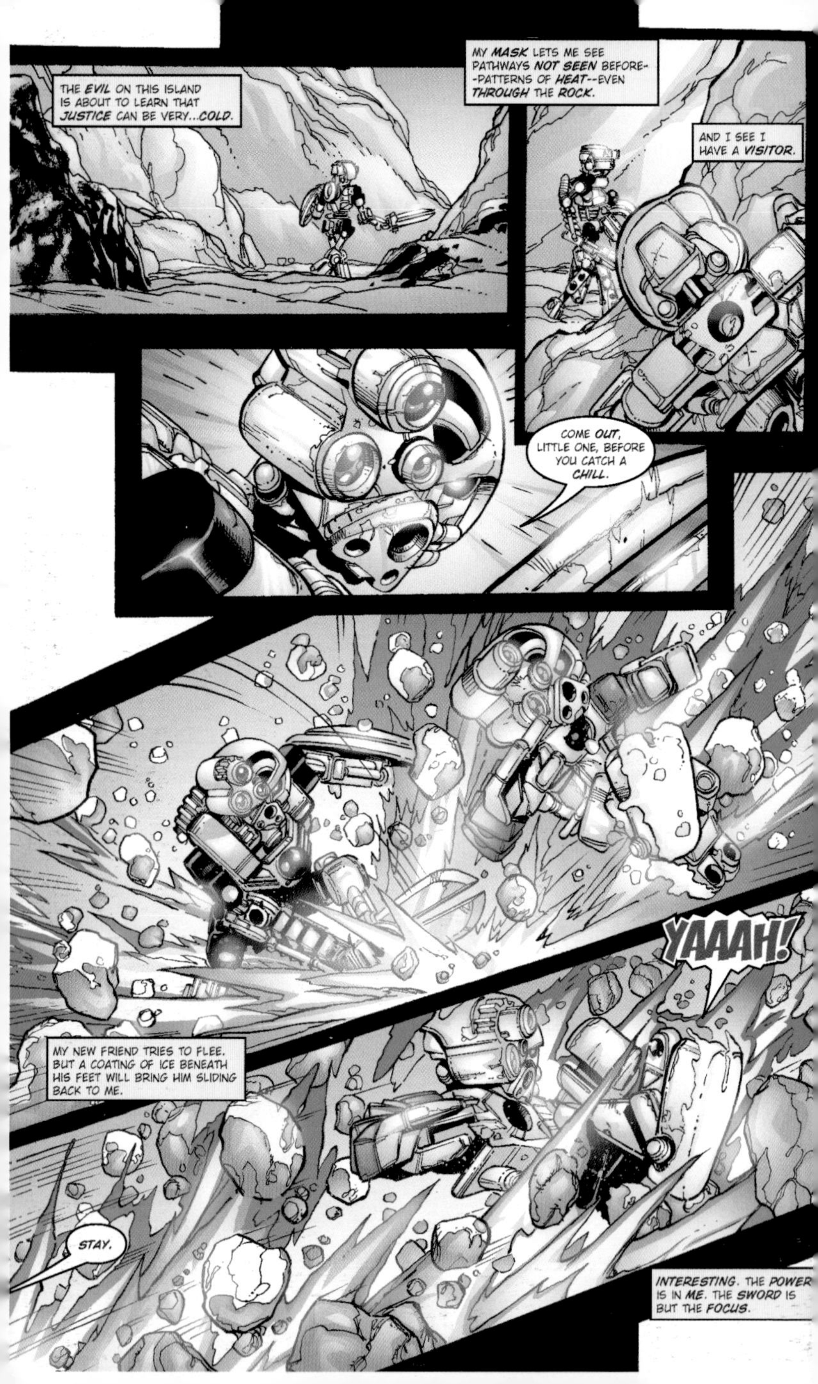

THE EVIL ON THIS ISLAND IS ABOUT TO LEARN THAT JUSTICE CAN BE VERY...COLD.
MY MASK LETS ME SEE PATHWAYS NOT SEEN BEFORE--PATTERNS OF HEAT--EVEN THROUGH THE ROCK.
AND I SEE I HAVE A VISITOR.
COME OUT, LITTLE ONE, BEFORE YOU CATCH A CHILL.
YAAAH!
MY NEW FRIEND TRIES TO FLEE. BUT A COATING OF ICE BENEATH HIS FEET WILL BRING HIM SLIDING BACK TO ME.
STAY.
INTERESTING. THE POWER IS IN ME. THE SWORD IS BUT THE FOCUS.

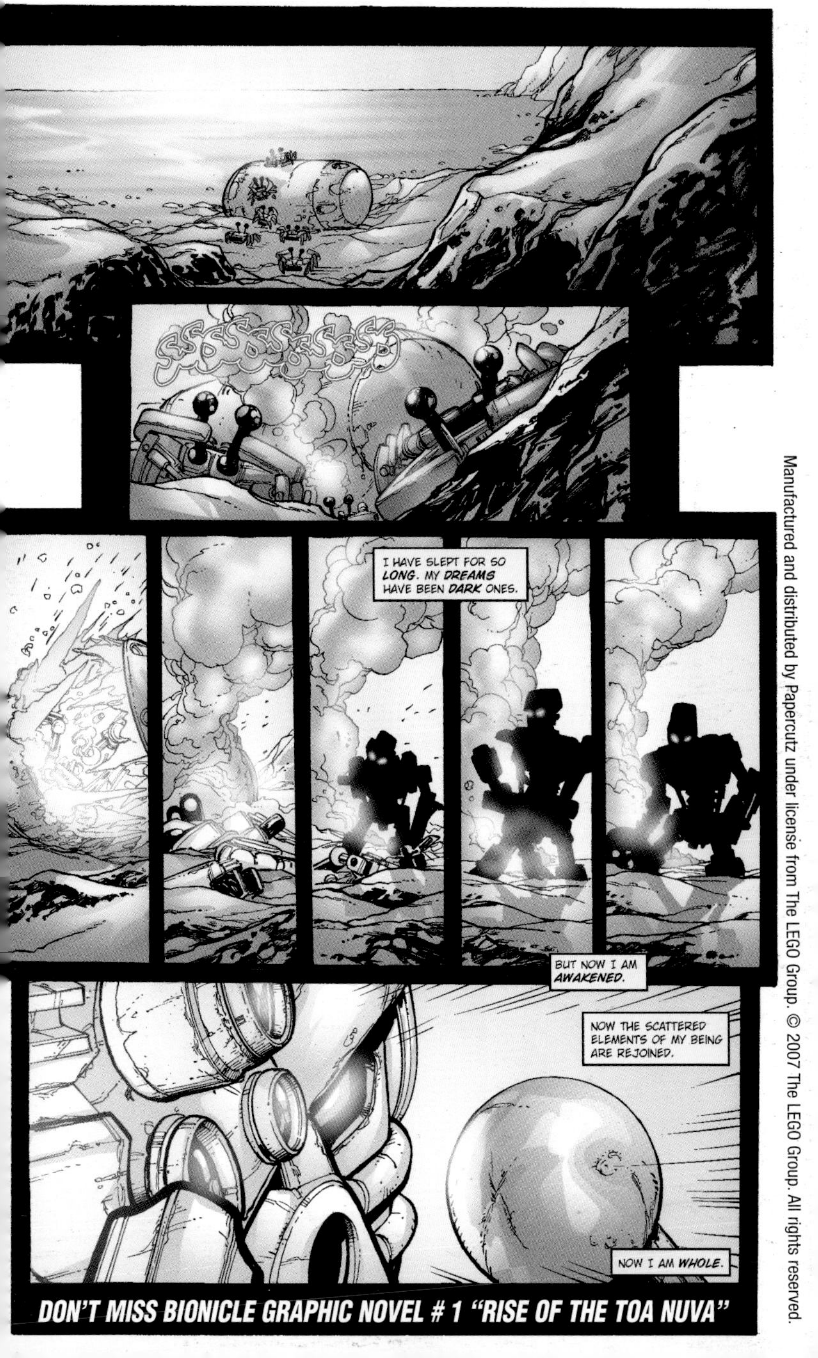
I HAVE SLEPT FOR SO LONG. MY DREAMS HAVE BEEN DARK ONES.
BUT NOW I AM AWAKENED.
NOW THE SCATTERED ELEMENTS OF MY BEING ARE REJOINED.
NOW I AM WHOLE.

DON'T MISS BIONICLE GRAPHIC NOVEL # 1 "RISE OF THE TOA NUVA"

CLASSICS *Illustrated*

Featuring Stories by the World's Greatest Authors

Returns in two new series from Papercutz!

The original, best-selling series of comics adaptations of the world's greatest literature, CLASSICS ILLUSTRATED, returns in two new formats--the original, featuring abridged adaptations of classic novels, and CLASSICS ILLUSTRATED DELUXE, featuring longer, more expansive adaptations-from graphic novel publisher Papercutz. "We're very proud to say that Papercutz has received such an enthusiastic reception from librarians and school teachers for its NANCY DREW and HARDY BOYS graphic novels as well as THE LIFE OF POPE JOHN PAUL II...*IN COMICS!*, that it only seemed logical for us to bring back the original CLASSICS ILLUSTRATED comicbook series beloved by parents, educators, and librarians," explained Papercutz Publisher, Terry Nantier. "We can't thank the enlightened librarians and teachers who have supported Papercutz enough. And we're thrilled that they're so excited about CLASSICS ILLUSTRATED."

Upcoming titles include The Invisible Man, Tales from the Brothers Grimm, and Robinson Crusoe.

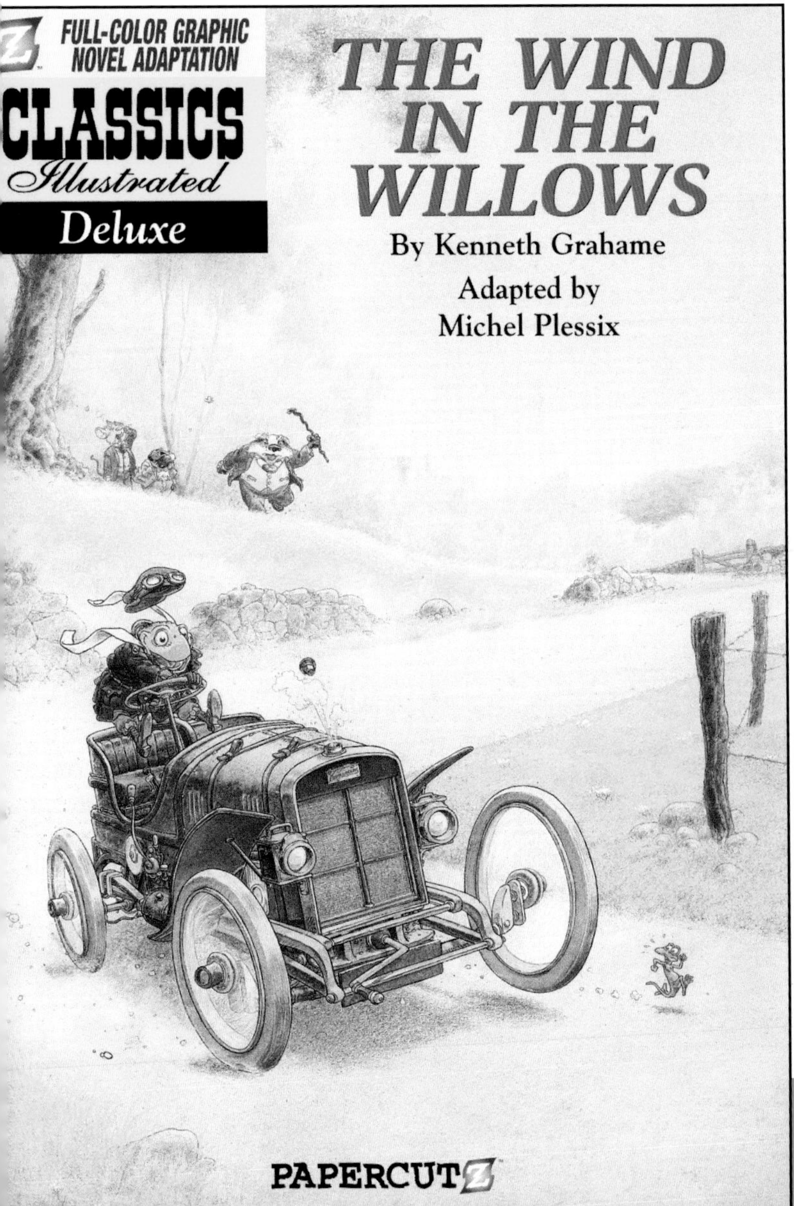
FULL-COLOR GRAPHIC NOVEL ADAPTATION
CLASSICS Illustrated
Deluxe
THE WIND IN THE WILLOWS
By Kenneth Grahame
Adapted by Michel Plessix
PAPERCUTZ

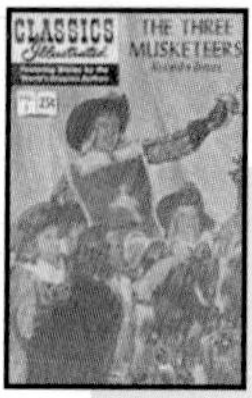
CLASSICS Illustrated
THE THREE MUSKETEERS
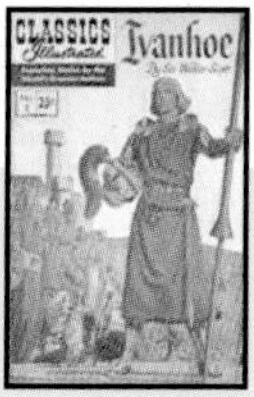
CLASSICS Illustrated
Ivanhoe
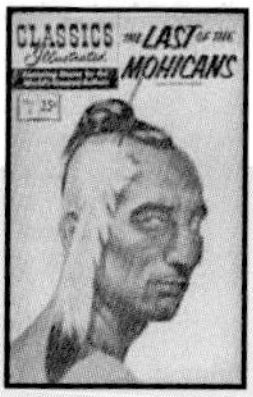
CLASSICS Illustrated
THE LAST OF THE MOHICANS
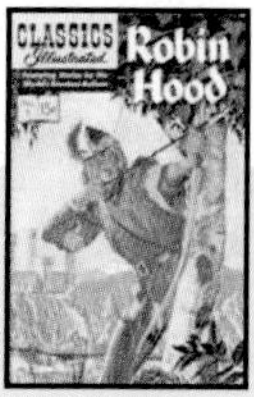
CLASSICS Illustrated
Robin Hood
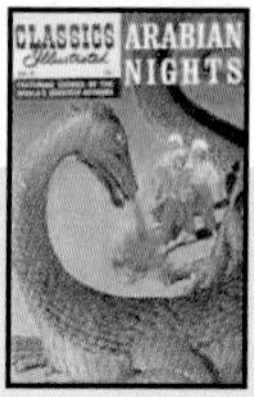
CLASSICS Illustrated
ARABIAN NIGHTS
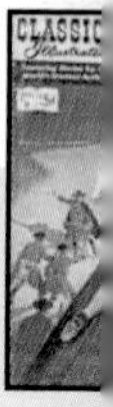

A Short History of CLASSICS ILLUSTRATED...

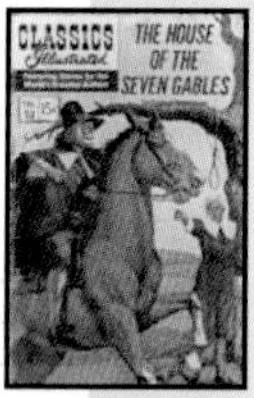
CLASSICS Illustrated
THE HOUSE OF THE SEVEN GABLES
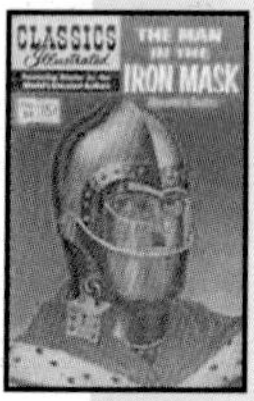
CLASSICS Illustrated
THE MAN IN THE IRON MASK
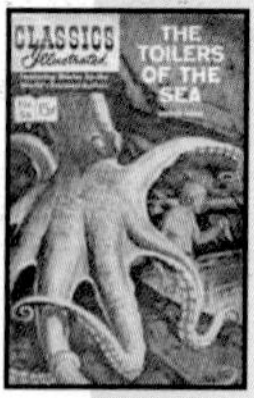
CLASSICS Illustrated
THE TOILERS OF THE SEA
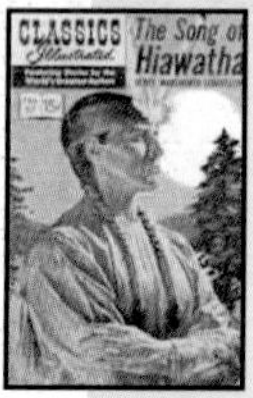
CLASSICS Illustrated
The Song of Hiawatha

William B. Jones Jr. is the author of Classics Illustrated: A Cultural History, which offers a comprehensive overview of the original comic-book series and the writers, artists, editors, and publishers behind-the-scenes. With Mr. Jones Jr.'s kind permission, here's a very short overview of the history of CLASSICS ILLUSTRATED adapted from his 2005 essay on Albert Kanter.

CLASSICS ILLUSTRATED was the creation of Albert Lewis Kanter, a visionary publisher, who from 1941 to 1971, introduced young readers worldwide to the realms of literature, history, folklore, mythology, and science in over 200 titles in such comicbook series as CLASSICS ILLUSTRATED and CLASSICS ILLUSTRATED JUNIOR. Kanter, inspired by the success of the first comicbooks published in the early 30s and late 40s, believed he

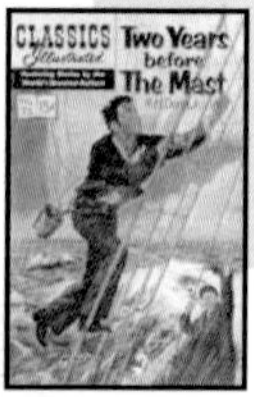
CLASSICS Illustrated
Two Years before The Mast
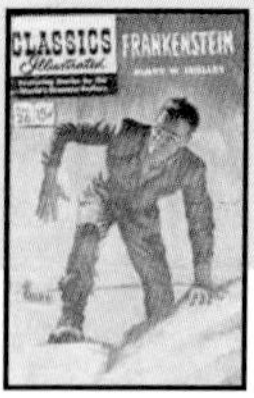
CLASSICS Illustrated
FRANKENSTEIN
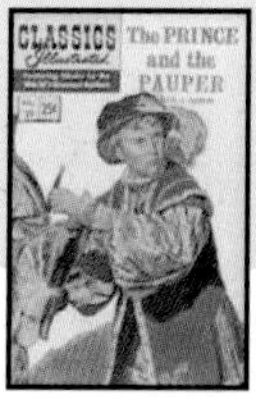
CLASSICS Illustrated
The PRINCE and the PAUPER
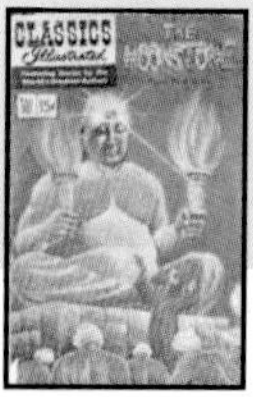
CLASSICS Illustrated
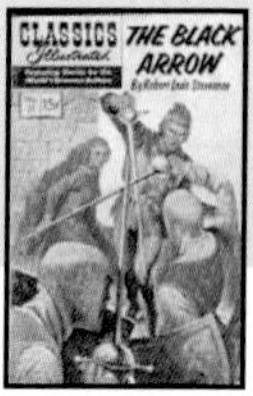
CLASSICS Illustrated
THE BLACK ARROW
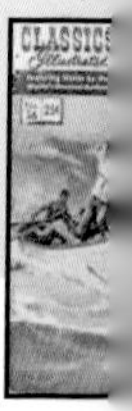

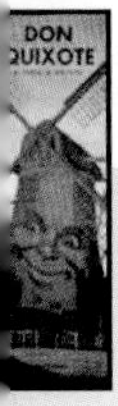
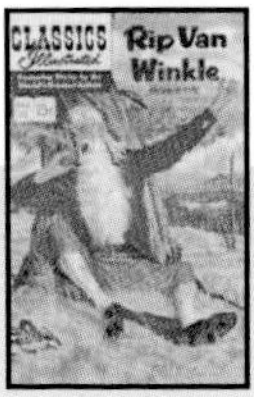
CLASSICS Illustrated
Rip Van Winkle
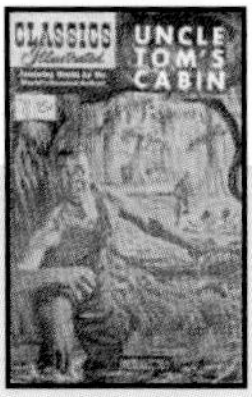
CLASSICS Illustrated
UNCLE TOM'S CABIN
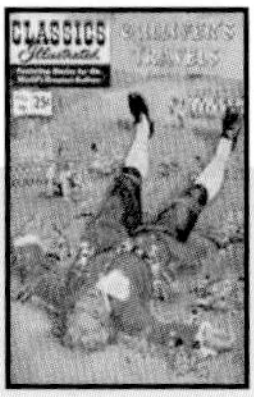
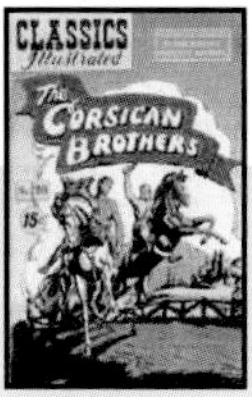
CLASSICS Illustrated
The CORSICAN BROTHERS
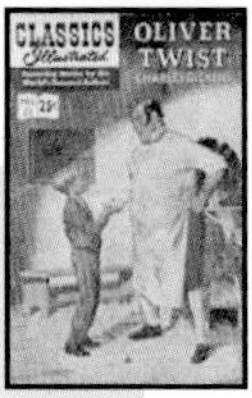
CLASSICS Illustrated
OLIVER TWIST

could use the same medium to introduce young readers to the world of great literature. CLASSIC COMICS (later changed to CLASSICS ILLUSTRATED in 1947) was launched in 1941, and soon the comicbook adaptations of Shakespeare, Stevenson, Twain, Verne, and other authors, were being used in schools and endorsed by educators.

CLASSICS ILLUSTRATED was translated and distributed in countries such as Canada, Great Britain, the Netherlands, Greece, Brazil, Mexico, and Australia. The genial publisher was hailed abroad as "Papa Kassiker." By the beginning of the 1960s, CLASSICS ILLUSTRATED was the largest childrens publication in the world. The original CLASSICS ILLUSTRATED series adapted into comics 169 titles; among these were Frankenstein, 20,000 Leagues Under the Sea, Treasure Island, Julius Caesar, and Faust.

Albert L. Kanter died, March 17, 1973, leaving behind a rich legacy for the millions of readers whose imaginations were awakened by CLASSICS ILLUSTRATED.

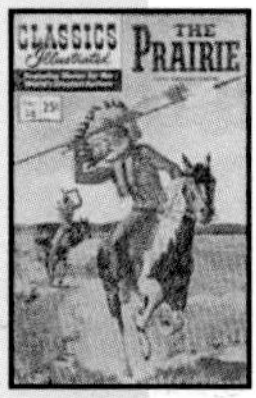
CLASSICS Illustrated
THE PRAIRIE
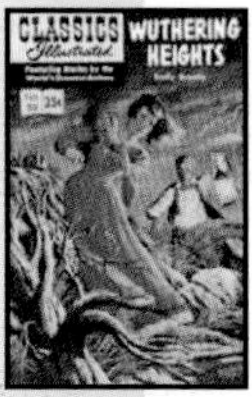
CLASSICS Illustrated
WUTHERING HEIGHTS
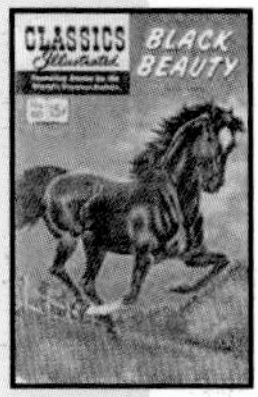
CLASSICS Illustrated
BLACK BEAUTY
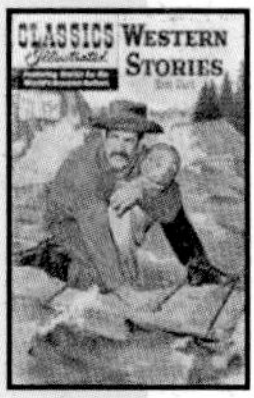
CLASSICS Illustrated
WESTERN STORIES
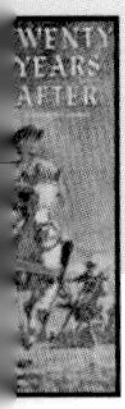
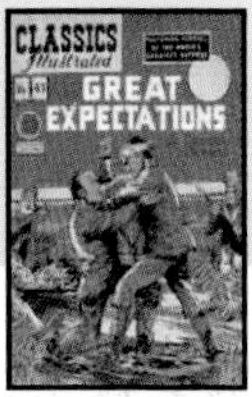
CLASSICS Illustrated
GREAT EXPECTATIONS
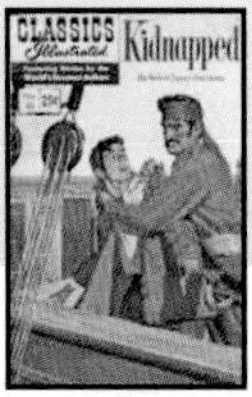
CLASSICS Illustrated
Kidnapped
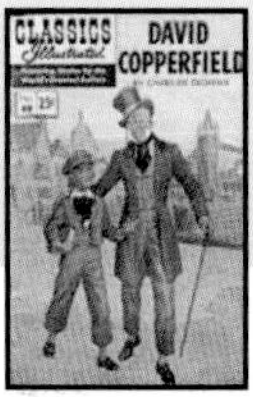
CLASSICS Illustrated
DAVID COPPERFIELD
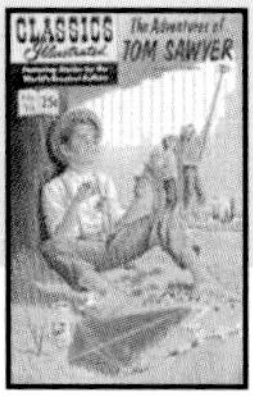
CLASSICS Illustrated
The Adventures of TOM SAWYER
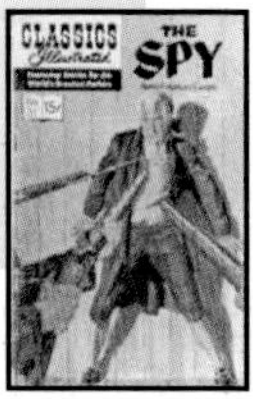
CLASSICS Illustrated
THE SPY

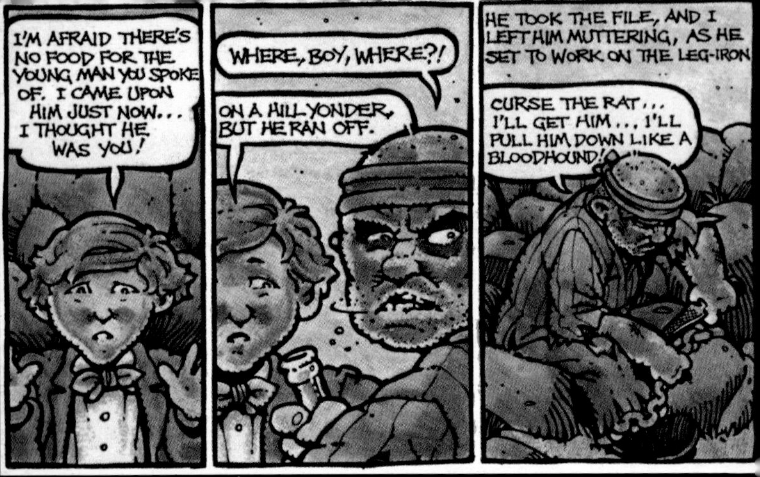
I'M AFRAID THERE'S NO FOOD FOR THE YOUNG MAN YOU SPOKE OF. I CAME UPON HIM JUST NOW... I THOUGHT HE WAS YOU!
WHERE, BOY, WHERE?!
ON A HILL YONDER, BUT HE RAN OFF.
HE TOOK THE FILE, AND I LEFT HIM MUTTERING, AS HE SET TO WORK ON THE LEG-IRON
CURSE THE RAT... I'LL GET HIM... I'LL PULL HIM DOWN LIKE A BLOODHOUND!

CLASSICS ILLUSTRATED was re-launched in 1990 in graphic novel/book form by the Berkley Publishing Group and First Publishing, Inc. featuring all-new adaptations by such top graphic novelists as Rick Geary, Bill Sienkiewicz, Kyle Baker, Gahan Wilson, and others. "First had the right idea, they just came out about 15 years too soon. Now bookstores are ready for graphic novels such as these," Jim explains. Many of these excellent adaptations have been acquired by Papercutz and will make up the new series of CLASSICS ILLUSTRATED titles.

The first volume of the new CLASSICS ILLUSTRATED series presents graphic novelist Rick Geary's adaptation of "Great Expectations" by Charles Dickens, the bittersweet tale of one boy's adolescence, and of the choices he makes to shape his destiny. Into an engrossing mystery, Dickens weaves a heartfelt inquiry into morals and virtues-as the orphan Pip, the convict Magwitch, the beautiful Estella, the bitter Miss Havisham, the goodhearted Biddy, the kind Joe and other memorable characters entwine in a battle of human nature. Rick Geary's delightful illustrations capture the newfound awe and frustrations of young Pip as he comes of age, and begins to understand the opportunities that life presents.

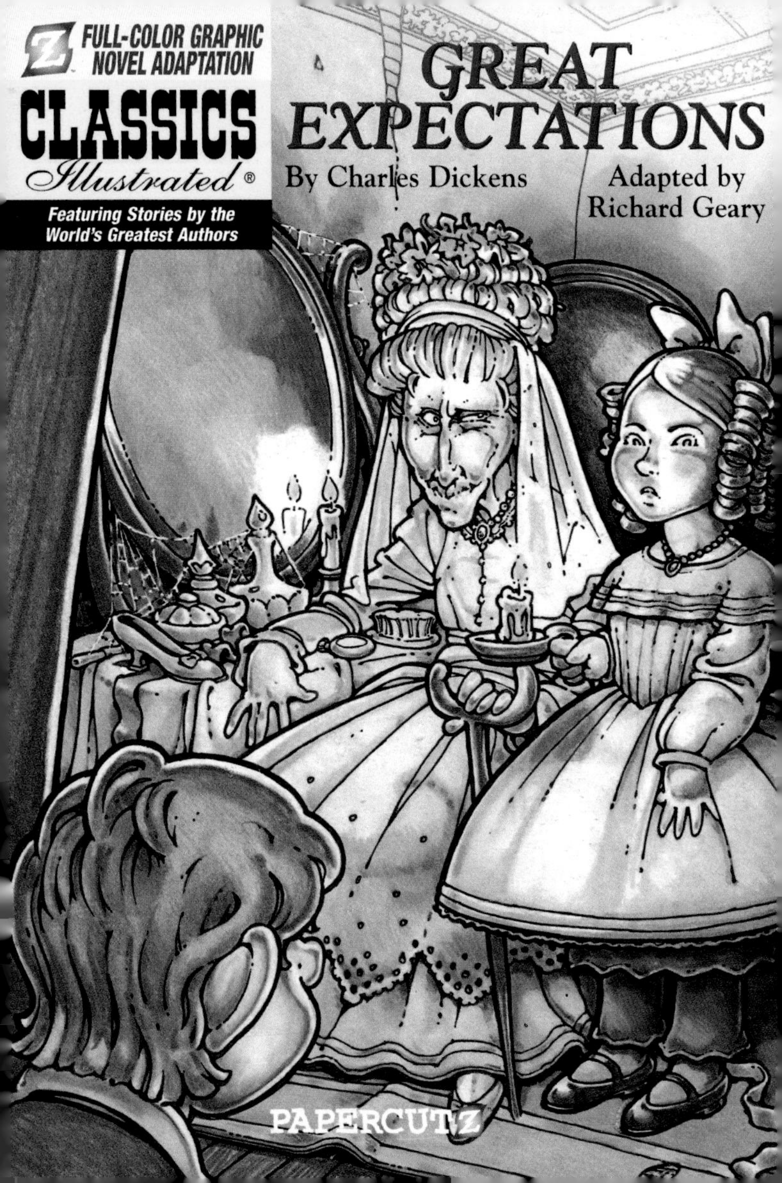
Z
FULL-COLOR GRAPHIC NOVEL ADAPTATION
CLASSICS Illustrated®
Featuring Stories by the World's Greatest Authors
GREAT EXPECTATIONS
By Charles Dickens
Adapted by Richard Geary
PAPERCUTZ

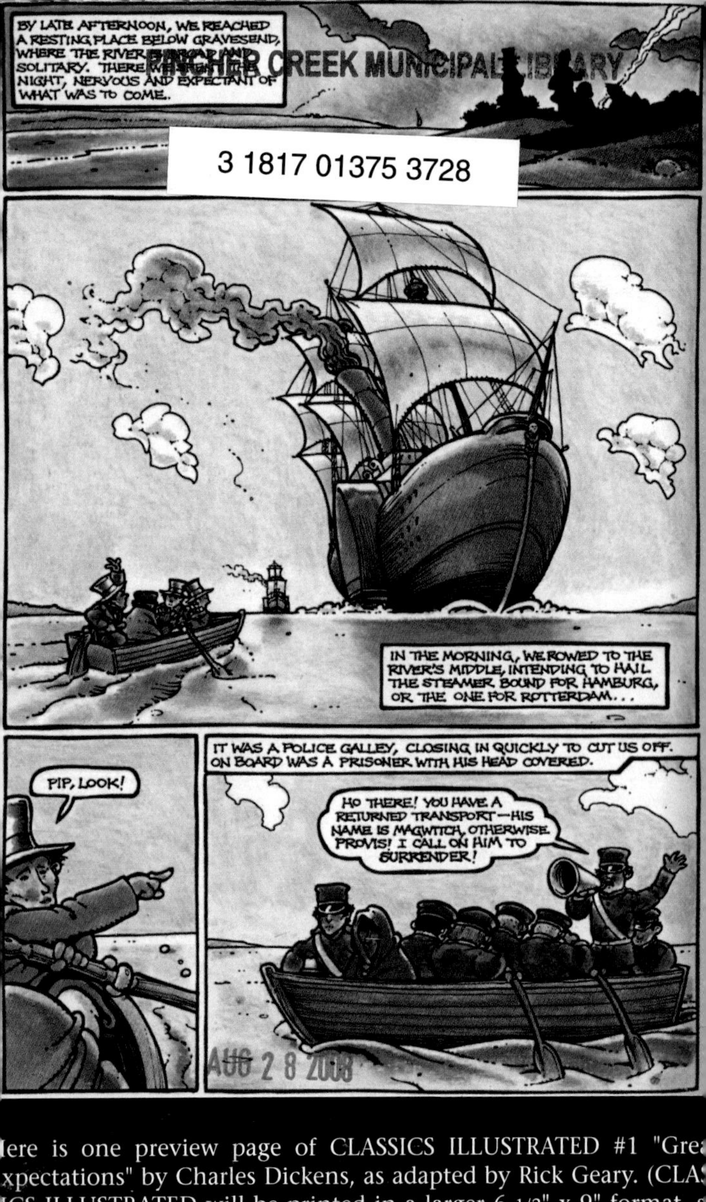
BY LATE AFTERNOON, WE REACHED A RESTING PLACE BELOW GRAVESEND, WHERE THE RIVER ... SOLITARY. THERE ... NIGHT, NERVOUS AND EXPECTANT OF WHAT WAS TO COME.
IN THE MORNING, WE ROWED TO THE RIVER'S MIDDLE, INTENDING TO HAIL THE STEAMER BOUND FOR HAMBURG, OR THE ONE FOR ROTTERDAM...
PIP, LOOK!
IT WAS A POLICE GALLEY, CLOSING IN QUICKLY TO CUT US OFF. ON BOARD WAS A PRISONER WITH HIS HEAD COVERED.
HO THERE! YOU HAVE A RETURNED TRANSPORT—HIS NAME IS MAGWITCH, OTHERWISE PROVIS! I CALL ON HIM TO SURRENDER!

lere is one preview page of CLASSICS ILLUSTRATED #1 "Grea xpectations" by Charles Dickens, as adapted by Rick Geary. (CLAS ICS ILLUSTRATED will be printed in a larger 6 1/2" x 9" format, s ne art will be bigger than what you see here.)